What Kings Ate
and
Wizards Drank

a fantasy lover's food guide

What Kings Ate
and
Wizards Drank

a fantasy lover's food guide

Krista D. Ball

TYCHE BOOKS LTD.

What Kings Ate and Wizards Drank:
A Fantasy Lover's Food Guide

Published by Tyche Books Ltd.
www.TycheBooks.com

Copyright © 2012 by Krista D. Ball

Print ISBN: 978-0-9878248-9-9
Ebook ISBN: 978-0-9878248-8-2

Cover Art and Cover Design by Lucia Starkey
Interior Art by Stephan Lorenz
Editorial by M. L. D. Curelas
Production by Tina Moreau

Contents

Dedication

*To my teachers and professors who instilled in me a lifelong
love of history*

Acknowledgements

A work of this scope is not possible without the help and support of large groups of people. First, a thank you to Tina Moreau of Tyche Books for requesting this project. Second, Margaret Curelas for putting up with my erratic writing behaviour and not once calling me up in the middle of the night screaming, "I know you are only half done and there's only a month left. What are you doing on Facebook??" If our roles were reversed, I would not have exercised such restraint.

A big thank you to Charles Perry and his publisher, Prospect Books, for allowing me to use a number of their translations. Another big thank you goes out to Anniina Jokinen, who runs www.luminarium.org, giving scholars and laypeople alike free access to endless historical information. I'd like to thank EPL's Lois Hole Library who, at one point, had an entire cart dedicated to my interlibrary loans. I also want to thank all of the artists who had to draw pudding bags and pateras, and had to ask me what on earth those things were, just so that I could even begin to convey my artistic needs to my editors.

My writing groups (S&R and Writers Cubed) put up with lots of questions, brainstorming, and beta reading. A special thanks must go out to Debora Geary, Phoenix Sullivan, Gillian Grey, Rebecca M. Senese, G. Clarke, and Sara Reine, who put up with my 1 a.m. sobbing emails mid-book when I was convinced that I should burn the entire manuscript and become a nun. These women deserve medals for what I put them through.

As usual, my poor stepkids need mentioning. Michael and Jacob always get yelled at a lot in the days immediately before and after the hand-in date. As soon as I find where I hid your iPods, I promise I'll give them back.

Finally, this book would not have been possible without Peter's unwavering support. If she were alive today, Jane Austen would have turned you into a hero.

"The pleasures of this world are divided into six classes. They are food, drink, clothing, sex, scent, and sound. The most eminent and perfect of these is food; for food is the foundation of the body and the material of life.[1]*"*
Muhammad b. al-Hasan b. Muhammad b. al-Karim, the scribe of Baghdad, 13th century

Introduction

It was early 2011 and I was neck-deep in writing the second book of my epic fantasy series when Tina Moreau called me up. The literary scene in Alberta is pretty small and tight, and we'd gotten to know each other around the fandom conventions in Edmonton and Calgary over the years. We'd also worked together in publishing before, so a call from her wasn't that out of the ordinary.

The conversation, however, went differently than our usual ones. She, along with Margaret Curelas, had finally taken the plunge and set up their publishing house, Tyche Books. Great, I said. Is there anything I can help with?

Famous last words. You'd think I'd have learned my lesson by now!

Tina was waiting for that question and "casually" mentioned that I should write a proposal for a fantasy writer's guide about food. Oh my. I'd been threatening to write something along those lines for quite a while, but never got up the courage. Who would want a book by little ol' me? I am an amateur. I don't have twenty years' experience and three Ph.D.s and a wing of a library named after me. I only have a bachelor's degree in history. I only read period recipe books and recreate the meals. What do I know? The doubt ferrets waged a heavy war. I ran my ideas by some writer friends of mine, who threatened to tie me to a chair if I did not submit a proposal. So, I wrote out an outline and the rest is history.

Water and basic foods are necessary to our survival. We don't need elaborate cakes, cookies, and meat pies to live. Yet, every culture throughout history has developed different local tastes and preferences that eventually developed into regional and cultural identities. Ask a dozen people about their family's traditional winter Solstice meal and you'll get a dozen different answers. Extend the question to any period in history, and the range becomes even broader and more exotic.

Food is much more than just mere survival; it is an extension of who we are.

It is this history and culture surrounding food that has always fascinated me. Bread riots, starving soldiers, Corn Laws: all of this tells us so much about what it means to be human. Whip a man and he'll continue to obey your orders. Stop feeding him and he'll desert to the enemy. Don't pay the peasants and they'll grumble; tax their grain and they'll storm the castle.

Food is power.

My educational background taught me that point on an intellectual level. Yet, I never quite grasped the humanity involved in the why of those events. Why did peasants revolt over the price of bread, when they were being strung up for poaching a grouse? Why on earth would a halfpenny increase in grain cause peasants to storm the gates? I could not wrap my early-twenties brain around those ideas.

It took working with Edmonton's homeless population many years later for me to understand the power of food. I ran The Mustard Seed—Edmonton's evening meal program and was interviewed fairly often as part of that role, and the intercity committees that I belonged to. It was at one of these interviews by a local newspaper that it hit me. I was asked what I'd learned from being in the role. I'd not been asked that question before, and it took me a moment to gather my thoughts. What had I learned? Apparently, everything my professors had tried to teach me:

> "Food is power—and it can be used sometimes as a weapon. Foods that are healthy are often more expensive... [Affordable food] is often processed food—potato

chips, French fries—that have no nutritional value. At no point do we, as a society, teach these people, who are the most vulnerable, how to eat healthy. So they just buy what's most affordable. I've learned how much society uses food as a way to divide people by who can afford, and who cannot.[2]"

Food is a basic need and, with basic needs, come power and powerlessness. Day after day, I witnessed a charity mindset that had not changed much in a thousand years. Attitudes and preconceptions regarding the poor often remained stuck in Queen Elizabeth I's time, when table scraps, suspect food, and nutritionally-void foods were given to the poor.

I don't mean to say that these donations were not appreciated; of course they were. Anything given out of the goodness of someone's heart was graciously accepted and received. However, I admit that some days I felt like I'd been transported back to the early Christian church days, where fasting monks dropped their untouched dinner into baskets for distribution to the poor.

I learned how food could be used as a weapon and how society uses food as a means of dividing those who can afford to eat well and those who cannot. I learned how I could bring people together and pull people apart using nothing more than a plate of food. I finally understood why those peasants rioted.

Yet, it's rare to see food riots in fantasy novels! Worlds with distinct caste lines drawn along income lines do not seem to also draw the lines along food. Not enough of our farmer-turned-hero protagonists have the threat of a hanging whenever they kill a deer for an evening supper.

What Kings Ate aims to change all that.

There was a fair bit of confusion in the early days when I announced this book. Many people thought I was writing an historical cookbook. Still others thought I was writing a variation of the popular official and unofficial guides to fantasy books. While writing a historical cookbook or a Cooking with Elves: An Ogre's

Guide would be a blast, that was never the main intent of *What Kings Ate*. At its heart, this is a writer's guide. It just happens to also be a comedy and a historical cookbook. Three for the price of one, if you will.

Whether you are dragging your rag-tag rebellion through enemy territory or wining and dining cutthroat rivals, eventually you will need to feed these people. I hope to present you, the author and creator of your own universe, tools to consider when looking at troop movements, adding conflict, adding drama, and adding realism into your work.

Does that mean only fantasy writers can enjoy this book? Not at all. In fact, I think anyone who loves old recipes and history can find a lot to enjoy in this book.

I will be focusing on historical fantasy and epic fantasy. Fantasy is vast and varied, and a large component of it is set in a quasi-medieval Europe (often Britain) or set in a recognizable historical or alternative historical setting. However, just because I will be focusing on fantasy authors doesn't mean this guide won't be helpful to writers in other genres.

Steampunk, set in the alternative Victorian era of wheels and cogs, invention and steam, has historical components that will challenge many a writer who aims for a very realistic flair. In discussions concerning this book, many writers have admitted to me about being clueless on topics such as how to feed their airship crew in the age of coal, or how ice arrived in downtown London in August. So, sometimes airships and steam trains are going to sneak onto these pages.

Likewise, those who write either historical novels or historical romances might need the occasional starting point or a general overview to help with getting one's troops into a siege position, or for organizing a feast where the hero falls in love with the heroine. Many of the concepts discussed in this book can be used either directly or indirectly to help steer your research and fuel your creativity.

However, I didn't want to forget all of the fantasy readers out there. You are wonderfully loyal and supportive. You own every single Dragonlance and Forgotten Realms book. You love Tolkien and Brooks, Jordan and Sanderson. Perhaps you even Live Action Role Play (LARP) or enjoy a game of Dungeons & Dragons on your weekends. Perhaps you love the works of Jack Whyte and Bernard Cromwell and want to know more about pickled tongue.

Or, maybe you are just the curious sort. You love fiction, and also learning about new things. You're interested in learning how people ate before refrigerators and transport trucks. You'll find lots to enjoy here—and a number of recipes to scare your kids.

This book's entire purpose is to make novels more enjoyable for readers out there, who are tired of reading books where the heroes bake tea biscuits in the forest, or where chocolate-dipped beef jerky protein bars were passed around at the Battle of Hastings (I'm not even making that up).

Readers are my lifeblood. So I've aimed to make this book as fun for you as (I hope) it will be informative for writers.

Why the Focus on Fantasy Writers?

I've had a love affair with fiction for a very long time, but I also love the entire process of writing and publishing. On top of my fiction writing, I've also worked as a slush reader for a micro Canadian publisher, and served as a fiction magazine intern. I've read and critiqued hundreds of new writers for science fiction and fantasy, helping them with their manuscripts. I get a number of emails asking for technical help with historical facts. One of the biggest issues I've seen while doing these tasks is the complete and utter lack of knowledge about the most basic of human needs: food.

I've read stories where armies successfully forage for food in metre-deep snow. Adventuring parties manage to stalk, kill, gut, and stew a deer in less than an hour. Or, the hero pulls out glass jars of tomato paste, ketchups, and sauces, even though he's carrying everything in a backpack. Or, heroines baking leavened bread in elaborate stone ovens while staying in dirt-floor huts.

When I first mentioned that I was writing this book, the response was overwhelming. It actually surprised me how many writers and readers alike were frustrated by these same tales! I was bombarded with hilarious quotes from readers and very frustrated authors who wanted to get things right but couldn't boil an egg without burning it. So, after much brainstorming and thought, I decided that the best thing I could do was to create a basic guide, a getting-started-with-food handbook, if you will.

I address the basics of common food challenges in fantasy. Travelling in foreign lands (with or without your legion) is difficult to manage for many writers, so significant space is devoted to this challenging aspect of getting your heroine from Point A to Point B without dying of starvation or conjuring up a McDonald's.

We will dive into the unique challenges of your world, including the availability of food (there is a reason lamb isn't served at Christmas) and how it might be sold, delivered, and preserved.

No fantasy guide would be complete without a chapter on medicinal beverages and alcoholic "tonics" for our thirsty wizards. Also, I will address the social division of food between the very poor and the royal courts. And finally, I will present some recipes and meal ideas to help your heroine keep her army fed while she invades the North Country.

This book will have a Northern Hemisphere bias, and will feature a Medieval Britain prejudice. The fact remains that a significant amount of the epic fantasy novels are still based on these locations and time periods, so I felt it was important to dedicate priority to them.

However, I also firmly believe that the fantasy genre could use some new life and focus. In supporting that belief, I will also be including examples from different cultures, time periods, and countries. Just because cast iron was used in Britain does not mean cast iron needs to be used in YOUR epic fantasy!

So, shall we dig into some cabbage pottage?

Chapter 1: On the Road Again
Keeping Your Party Well Fed On the Road

"Slit a chicken's throat, and skin it after inflating[1]"

On the whole, modern life is good to us. If I get the munchies on the way home from work, I can stop at one of a dozen fast food drive-thrus, grab a latte, or even hit a vending machine filled with a variety of snacks, some of which might be actual food.

Things are a little different when you are walking (or running) in a pre-refrigeration era, or, if very lucky, travelling on the back of a beast or in a carriage. You will need to carry food with you or have places to stop and stock up. If not, you will probably starve to death long before you can rescue the prince and save the kingdom from doom. And that would be bad.

Do you remember those old video games where your character is carrying two hundred pounds of items in a backpack, including a ladder and fifty feet of rope? Traditional fantasy can sometimes read like those old video games; the heroes have unlimited food and drink conjuring bags.

Hungry? Poof! A dead rabbit appears in your pot, entrails and fur already removed.

Thirsty? Poof! A lake of safe water appears just around the bend.

If your characters are moving across vast distances, sooner or later you will need to address food and water. Running away from rampaging orc hordes takes a lot of calories.

Are your intrepid heroes sauntering down a well-travelled toll road where there is a village every ten kilometres? That's an easy distance to cover, so there will be plenty of opportunity to eat. Or, are your adventurers travelling through a rough trail in a sparsely-populated area? Are they slogging through the forest, hacking a path through the underbrush as they go? Any of these situations will greatly impact your hero's ability to perform the tasks ahead.

While reading this book, consider these questions. How will your hero carry his drinking water? What will your heroine be eating? What is your adventuring party's experience in the terrain they are exploring? Do they have any outdoor experience, as a farmer will have different knowledge from a soldier, and different again from a pampered aristocrat? Are your heroes legally allowed on the land they are occupying? With those questions in our minds, let's hit the trails.

Backpacking through the Wilderness

Walking long distances works up an appetite. I'm a casual backpacker. I don't get to scramble the peaks like I used to, but I try to squeeze in a couple weekend jaunts into the backcountry every year. Ultra-light weight has been the theme of hiking in the last decade. Modern technology allows us to reduce the weight of what we carry. It's about time, too. My joints aren't as young as they used to be.

No matter how much lightweight titanium equipment I own, it sadly still weighs something and that weight adds up, adding stress and demand on a person's body. For a four day hike in Jasper National Park in September, I typically carry:

- Hiking boots and a pair of flip-flops
- Poles
- Pack
- Tent, sleeping bag, self-inflating sleeping pad, pillow

- 1 change of clothing, plus a face cloth, dish towel, extra underwear and socks, a sweater, PJ bottoms
- Rain gear
- Food, stove, fuel, cooking utensils
- Water bladder, water filtration system, emergency water filtration pills
- First Aid kit, compass, map, altimeter, emergency chocolate supply

That comes out to be about 27 pounds when I step on the scale fully decked out. The most I've hiked with was around 50 pounds, but I was carrying a field radio from the Korean War that was the size of a space shuttle. I've seen some people get down to 18 pounds, and others as high as 40 pounds. Put into perspective, a Roman soldier, who missed out on the "ultra-lightweight" rage, marched carrying sixty pounds of gear. Every day. For years.

How does all of that weight and exercise impact the hero's body? The most obvious effect is that with more weight comes a slower pace and the more tired he'll become. It's not easy to carry the gear, protect yourself from the elements, and have enough food to keep your morale and energy high, all the while ensuring you can physically keep up the pace without exhaustion setting in because you're carrying a kitchen sink on your back.

That added weight combined with the exercise greatly impacts one's nutritional needs. This is bad news when we need our hero to be in full strength to arrive at the castle to challenge his evil brother for control of the kingdom.

Over the years, I've had to filter water and share my snacks with people on the trails because they had no concept of what walking in the woods or up a mountain is actually like. These were always marked to semi-marked trails, too, where paths were already worn into the forest. Imagine cutting through brush as many heroes end up doing. They'd drop from exhaustion within days without proper food and water.

Calorie estimates for women usually fall in the 1800-2000 calories a day, with men in the 2300-2500 range. That's for the average person, doing everyday things like working in an office and exercising a couple times a week. 2000 calories looks like this:

- Breakfast: 1 slice toast with margarine, 4 strawberries, ½ cup yogurt
- Lunch: Peanut butter sandwich, 1 cup of mini carrots, 1 kiwi, 1 soy latte
- Dinner: 1 hamburger, 1 cup of steamed broccoli, 1 glass milk
- Snacks: 1 orange, cucumber, ½ grilled cheese sandwich

Should I pause here so that everyone can make the resolution to go on a diet? Okay. I'll wait.

Now that we're back, let's look at the calorie needs of our active heroes. After all, we want rippling abs and not gaunt ribcage.

NATO estimates the average fit male taking part in normal military operations consumes 3600 calories a day. Those engaged in combat operations consume in the range of 4900 calories. That doesn't take into account cold weather or elevation, both of which will add additional calorie needs.

Women generally consume fewer calories than men; an average woman backpacking can expect to need 2500-3000 calories a day for normal hiking, and more if it is in the winter, high elevation, or strenuous hiking, such as running away from an assassination squad for weeks on end.

Travelling food needs to be light, transportable, easy-to-prepare, nutritious, and long-lasting. Many heroes of fantasy rely on foraged and fresh foods alone. We often read about our heroines snacking on bread purchased at the market four days ago (and yet it is still fresh) and picking cupfuls of berries or frying up the fish leisurely caught by her romantic interest.

These heroes would need approximately one kilogram of food a day or about 3000 calories (more if it's a busy day). So, what does that look like? You're looking at 12 slices of whole wheat bread, 5 ounces of cheese, 2 large onions, 6 carrots and about 7 ounces of beef. That's a lot of food.

So let's look at how to make sure your hero's abs of steel stay in mint condition.

There Is a Horde of Orcs Chasing Me. Can We Stop for Some Rabbit Stew?

If time is of the essence, your hero will not have time to field dress a deer, locate water (unless he's following an uncontaminated stream or river), fish, or club a baby seal and make a fur coat. Yet, how many of us have read fantasy books where the heroes have done all this and still had enough time to seduce the assassin travelling with him?

My eighty-three-year old father has been hunting most of his life and he offers this advice to the hero wanting to hunt rabbits while being chased by orcs: go hungry.

I used to make rabbit snares for Dad. I was six or seven, and he showed me how to tie the wire together so that he could set the snares out in the snow. He'd check them a couple days later and bring home the frozen, dead rabbits.

Snaring rabbits and smaller creatures like squirrels and rats is difficult to do if on the run with little time to stop. It's even tougher for a stranger to an area to hunt rabbits because bunny tracks aren't easily visible in the undergrowth and fields to the untrained eye, unlike when there is snow on the ground. Rabbits have "runs", which means they take the same path to move around. It makes snaring rabbits easier in the winter; you just need to look for tracks and set the snares (or traps) in the brush where the footprints are the heaviest.

In the summer months, the net method will be useful for adventuring groups with a pet ferret (authors: this gives you full license to justify that ferret you've been dying to include in your novel. Use this knowledge with care). Cover the rabbit holes with small nets pinned down with wooden pegs. Drop your ferret into one of the holes, who will rush through the rabbit underground and cause quite a stir. The rabbits will run away from the ferrets and jump through their holes, getting tangled in the nets. The hero dispatches the rabbits quickly, usually by breaking their necks with a swift twist.

A musket-carrying heroine might have much more luck bagging a rabbit. Early-era muskets had really bad aim, but the new rifles coming out of the Napoleonic wars were significantly better. With any weapon, however, it's only as good as the person using it. That's not even considering the noise; the assassination squad chasing your group might hear the shots before the stew is fully cooked, and that would be bad.

If there are no ferrets (shame on you) and no gunpowder in your world, can your adventuring party still make rabbit stew in the forest? Perhaps you really want to write a campfire scene where the party members are eating rabbit stew. It might even be *vital* that you include a rabbit stew scene. It is very doable, and will probably be necessary if the group is travelling a long distance in a sparsely-populated area. So let's get out the pots and pans. We have work to do.

First things first: your party will need the essential small rodent and rabbit snaring gear:

- Wire or twine
- A sharp knife
- A club (to kill any animals still alive and caught in the snares and traps) or the guts to snap necks (and gloves to protect the hands)
- Knowledge

While your party is gathering firewood, have your heroine make and set the traps and snares. Set out as many as she can, as it greatly increases the odds of catching something. In the morning while the gruel is being prepared, check the traps. If lucky, your party might have fresh rabbit for breakfast along with their cooked oats.

Have your party skin the rabbit away from the camp; they don't want to attract predators.

Besides, it smells. And is icky.

To cook the poor creature that your heroes have just murdered and gutted, they will need:

- At least thirty minutes of cooking time plus ten to boil the water (more if the water is from a stream and cold, or if there is a lot of water, or not a lot of fuel)
- Flour and fat to make gravy
- A heavy pot so that the meat doesn't burn
- A means of getting the pot out of the fire
- A means of scrubbing the pot (it will be charred and ashy on the outside and messy inside)
- A means of stirring the food so it doesn't stick to the bottom
- Enough firewood to sustain the fire
- Water
- Vegetables, such as carrots, turnips, and onions for taste and nutrition

A handy woodsman will be able to use quickly-carved sticks for a number of these jobs. A well-prepared hero will have a *patera* with him. A *patera* was a cup, cooking pot, and bowl all-in-one used by Roman soldiers. They were about seven inches in diameter and made of bronze. He'd be able to cook and eat his meal all from the same pot. A small pot like a *patera* will reduce fuel needs, water needs, and make clean up a breeze. It's so much easier to lug around than a cauldron, too.

If your heroes prefer, rabbit can be spit roasted. Rabbit is a very lean meat, so can burn easily. Just set up a simple spit and rotate the rabbits often (so that they don't char on one side and be undercooked on the other), and tend the fire. You might find it easier to cook over very hot coals so that you can keep the spit lower to the ground, and not use up more precious fuel.

However you cook it, make sure to crack the bones in half and suck the brown marrow out. It's quite tasty and was really the only part of rabbit I ever liked.

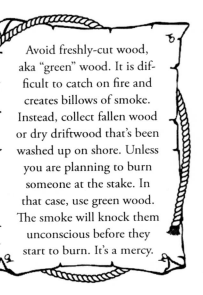

Avoid freshly-cut wood, aka "green" wood. It is difficult to catch on fire and creates billows of smoke. Instead, collect fallen wood or dry driftwood that's been washed up on shore. Unless you are planning to burn someone at the stake. In that case, use green wood. The smoke will knock them unconscious before they start to burn. It's a mercy.

My Hero Is a Carnivore. He Needs Venison Stew!

Ahh, venison stew. The old standby in adventure fantasy and many a historical war novel. Our heroes are in the forest. They successfully stalk a deer and kill her, and just at the fall of twilight, there is hot, bubbling venison stew in their bellies.

It is possible to stalk and kill a large game animal with spears and bows. After all, our ancestors did it for millennia. However, it is important to consider the frustrations of hunting and if your party has the time and tools necessary to bag large prey.

Stalking a large animal is dangerous and difficult, especially if you are relying on arrows as opposed to modern hunting rifles. You'd have to be lucky enough to have camped in an area populated by deer, caribou, moose, and other large game animals. They aren't as plentiful as one might think. These animals also run fast. *Very fast.* A moose can run over 50 kph. If you miss, you're out of luck. Even with today's weapons, it can take avid hunters several days to catch their prey, and that's when they are going back to the same area. It will be very difficult to do in an area that your hero doesn't know anything about.

Solitary game hunting for survival in a strange land would be very difficult for an inexperienced or pampered hunter. A prince might have had experience shooting the arrow at a deer, but did he have experience finding where deer gather? Would he have experience in field dressing the deer—bleeding it properly and gutting it? There's really no point to killing the animal if he has no way to actually eat it.

A Roman-style patera is a perfect cook pot for your team of adventurers

Consider the amount of meat these animals provide. Smaller deer can render upwards of sixty pounds of usable meat, whereas a larger animal, like a moose, can easily yield three hundred pounds or more of meat. The meat would spoil quickly without any means to preserve it and would attract scavengers. Even if you carried it in your pack, the flies would soon be swarming around you and your pack would start to smell. It would be a huge waste of energy, life, and meat for something that will be left to mostly rot.

But, sometimes, a good ol' pot of venison stew is necessary to get the romantic subplot moving along. If your party takes down a deer and makes some stew, they'll need:

- At least 2 hours to cook the meat
- Flour and fat, if you want gravy
- More fat, if you want the meat browned with a little extra flavour
- Water, enough to cook the vegetables and to make gravy
- Enough firewood to keep a fire going for at least two hours
- All the cooking needs listed for rabbit stew
- Any vegetables you want

If your party has enough time and is large, spit-roasting the deer or elk is also an option. Getting the rack set up to accommodate a large animal will be tricky, so have an expert look after that task.

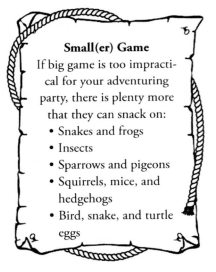

The party will need to take turns looking after the fire and the rotation of the animal every half hour, since it will take most of the day to roast it, but it's a mess-free way to cook a large animal for a group.

Before pulling back your bow string, though, ask if your hero is permitted to hunt. Not all trees and hedges are open for hunting. Today in Canada, hunting and foraging is strictly forbidden in provincial and national parks, except in special circumstances (i.e.

Small(er) Game

If big game is too impractical for your adventuring party, there is plenty more that they can snack on:

- Snakes and frogs
- Insects
- Sparrows and pigeons
- Squirrels, mice, and hedgehogs
- Bird, snake, and turtle eggs

Gros Morne National Park sometimes issues hunting licenses due to an exploding moose population that makes the roads very dangerous). Even picking mushrooms in a National Park can yield a maximum fine of $5000. That rockets to $250,000 fines and five years in prison for poaching a threatened species, such as peregrine falcons. Even taking eggs, and not killing the adults, is seen as poaching.

The concept of forbidden areas to hunt is not new. Hunting wild game in many European regions was forbidden except for the lord of the manor, and pretty much all of the land had such a lord. In some cases, hares and rabbits were considered game (since they were "meat"), but the fines for poaching were significantly less. Killing a deer in a protected woods was breaking the law, and the punishment could range from severe fines up to (and often including) death. If you are writing an historical or a historical fantasy, it is important to investigate what constituted poaching in the time period you are writing in. Were any lands publicly available for hunting, or were they all owned and cut off from hunting?

It is also possible that a forested area could have "common rights", meaning that the area was used by everyone. For example, English farmers had common rights during Norman times. For sixty days in the autumn, farmers turned their pigs out into the forests and fields to fatten up on acorns. Your heroes will need to be extra careful that they don't bag some poor farmer's pig. A local magistrate might see that as "house-breaking" and that charge often comes with a noose around the hero's neck. Tread with extreme caution.

Fishing

Your party decides that rabbit catching is too difficult in the height of summer, and hunting deer sounds too much like work. What's left for them to eat? Human beings have been fishing since we figured out how to make a spear, so why can't your adventurers?

If you are writing a historical novel, ensure that the land rules of the area and time period allow for fishing in rivers, streams,

and ponds. Like game or bird hunting, many countries had laws preventing commoners from fishing on land owned by either the crown or individuals. Some estates might make exceptions and hire locals to fish for them, paying them for their day's work in either coin or fish. Don't assume, however.

If fishing is allowed on the lake that your adventurers are camped by, they won't need much in terms of supplies. A makeshift spear, a handmade fishing rod with tackle, or even a net. If your adventurers are hungry or if you have a number of mouths to feed because you've just sprung a prison of freedom fighters, the trap fishing method used by some Canadian aboriginal groups, including the now-extinct Beothuks (pronounced BEE-oth-ick), might come in handy.

During the annual salmon run, when the salmon entered the rivers to swim upstream to spawn, the Beothuks would gather at a river and build stone weirs and wooden enclosures. Then, they'd wait until nightfall and use torches to attract the fish to the surface, where they would be ready with spears to catch the salmon.

This method would take some time to set up and would not be useful for feeding one or two people. However, if your hero has to feed a large party suddenly, or if they happen upon a nomadic group who has offered to exchange work for food, this is a potential method.

If travelling near the seashore, there will be other forms of sea life available to your party. It's possible to use the spear method as well, though it might mean wading out into cold waters and dying of hypothermia later that evening. And the shoreline doesn't only have fish. Mussels, clams, and sometimes even oysters are foragable from the shoreline or nearby rock faces. They have less mess and fuss than fish, and only take a couple minutes in a pot before ready to eat.

Foraging Berries and Other Delights

Foraging is a common enough trope in Fantasy. Many a book has the hero's party finding enough food to meet their nutritional needs from berries, nuts, and wild plants in an area. Our heroes know everything they can eat in any area and can easily identify it, and that the forest and plains will provide all that they need to maintain their fast pace through the countryside.

The forests are alive with goodies such as:

- Mushrooms
- The holy trinity of strawberries-blueberries-raspberries
- Lesser used berries like blackberries, Saskatoon berries, cloudberries, partridgeberries (lingon-berries), and juniper berries
- Dandelion leaves

That's a lot of food. Plenty to eat, right? Wrong.

This misconception about foraging partially comes from our modern, urban lifestyles. We are used to modern agriculture, where strawberries, raspberries, and blackberries are available all year 'round. Even our farmers' markets often have many different berries and fruits available at the same time because they are brought in from different areas. We don't consider that nomadic people dedicated their entire lives to seeking out food.

I live in Edmonton, which is considered a Zone 3 by gardeners. That means we have a shorter growing season than people in other regions. When the farmers' markets open up in the spring, it's normal to see Alberta greenhouse produce sold alongside British Columbian fruit. In the modern world, we see this as locally in season. In a pre-industrial world, the strawberries and apples would not be available at the same time without the use of hot houses or winter stores (strawberries come into season in the spring or early summer, whereas apples are an autumn fruit).

People who lived off the land in a particular area would have learned the cycle of the seasons and the local wild flora and fauna from their parents or other members of the community. When travelling to a distant land, those same knowledgeable people have no idea what can and cannot be eaten. When Europeans first mapped North America, they routinely took on native guides; people who had grown up in the area. These individuals would guide the cartographers and traders and teach them how to survive. An urban dweller would be hard-pressed to survive as a nomad without assistance.

We have many examples of nomadic people in our prehistory, plus in our written history. Many First Nations and aborigines, Mongolians, and the Bedouin have long histories of nomadic, semi-nomadic, or pastoral nomadic lives.

"Nomadic" covers a wide range of activities. Take the Dorset Palaeoeskimos. They lived along the western coast of Newfoundland and the southern shore of Labrador, engaged in various forms of nomadic and semi-nomadic lifestyles over their two thousand year history in the area. Archeologists have unearthed several structures and evidence to show that the ancient people weren't all nomadic and that they'd built permanent structures for some of the families to live in at least semi-permanently, while others hunted and foraged, continuing the nomadic style.

The people of the Eurasian Steppes practiced Pastoral Nomadism. They travelled in small groups of three to five families, assembling portable villages. They depended upon their personal herds of horses, goats, sheep, yaks, and camels to feed their clans. Any vegetables and fruits would have been foraged, and not grown.

Foraging was a vital skill in pre-industrial societies, and would be a skill that any heroine in fantasy would need to have if she is leading a party into the forests. She would need to know the difference between a baneberry and a chokeberry, and if she was pregnant she'd need to know not to eat hawthorns and burdocks. Likewise, she'd know that dandelions in the spring tasted good with garlic chives and butter, whereas a big snack of Common Camas would give everyone diarrhea (which might be an innocent practical joke that turns dangerous when bandits attack them that night).

However, foraging for one's food nearly exclusively is a much greater challenge when on the move and in a hurry, or lacking knowledge of the area. Take the innocent raspberry; it's commonly pilfered to feed fantasy tropes. While I'm writing this (and, as it happens, a year later as I'm editing this), I'm munching on raspberries from my backyard. My plants run along my fence and are spaced and trimmed, providing easy access to the fruit. Once the fall comes, I'll cut back the old growth so that the new growth will sprout and flourish. Picking berries is easy and fun.

In the wild, foraging for raspberries is nothing like my backyard gardening. The bushes aren't pruned or trimmed back and can easily be five feet tall, with sharp spines to snag and rip your leather gloves and breeches.

I spent many summers picking wild blueberries and raspberries with my parents. Each time I reached my hand in beyond the outer leaves, I risked the wrath of bees, wasps, and hornets. Tiny black flies would bite around my eyes, leaving itchy, bloody scabs. The mosquitoes would constantly land on the small amount of exposed flesh I wasn't able to cover up. And the more I slapped my berry-juiced hand on the back of my neck, the more it attracted the flies to the blood and sugar buffet that was me.

As I worked, the berries would sweat in the heat of sitting in a pail if I couldn't find a cool place to hide them and would quickly turn to a soggy, juicy mess that would only be good for cooking into jam. Tiny, green worms would crawl from the insides of the berries to wiggle around on top. Raspberries just weren't that appetizing by the end of a hot day.

If you choose, as most kids do at least once in their berry-picking careers, to eat more than you pick, be prepared for one of the worst stomach aches of your life and spending the evening in the outhouse. Too many berries are not conducive to travelling.

And that's just berries! Finding edible mushrooms, digging up roots, picking greens, and pulling up moss will be a full-time job for your hero if that's the only source of food at his disposal.

Foraging is best when combined with ready stores of food, hunting, and gathering of things like seafood. It's difficult to rely solely on the forest to provide all your needs.

How Do I Carry These Leftovers, and Other Challenges?

Chances are, your hero will need to carry food with him. Regardless if it is a lunch, a snack, or several days' worth of rations, he will need some method of carting the food around without needing an actual cart. Carts just aren't sexy, nor are they heroic. Trust me. No one wants your hero riding to the rescue...on a cart.

Food could be wrapped in hides, cloth, leaves, or birch bark, depending upon the local materials available. Skin pouches of various sizes could be used to transport grain or dried fruits and olives. Pasties, pastries, and individual pies can be wrapped in cloth or burlap. Fresh fruit can be put into a net to keep them from rolling around and getting bruised in one's pack.

These food packages, along with the treasure maps and falsified citizen documents, could be placed in birch bark containers, hide pouches, cloth tied to a pole, or even a shoulder sling. Leather panniers made for shoulder carrying or for the saddle could also be used. Baskets made of straw, grass, or reeds could be fashioned into various carrying devices, including head baskets. Flax, wool, or animal and human hair can be spun and turned into hand-woven purses and carryalls.

I recommend your hero stay away from wood, glass, and crockery when travelling by foot or beast. These are heavy materials and will burden him down when running from the local militia. Glass and crockery are also breakable; a broken glass jar of pickles is going to make a mess. Besides, glass was expensive to produce before modern methods were developed. There were cheaper, lighter, and sturdier alternatives.

Your heroine has several choices for carrying her water supply. If possible, she should always have some on hand, especially if she is travelling in unfamiliar territory. Better prepared than dehydrated. She could use a gourd, carried in either her pack or inside a net slung over her shoulder. If gourds or coconuts are not available, perhaps she could use the cured bladder of a stag or a sheep. Leather could even be sewed tightly enough to be turned into large pouches that could carry water for both the heroine and her horse. This is especially useful if they will be travelling through a desert. Steampunk heroines might carry wooden, and later metal/wood combination, canteens. Don't forget the obligatory clock on the canteen, of course.

Don't bother transporting stews or the like. The mess inside one's pack will not be worth it. Make sure to scrub clean all cooking utensils to avoid flies and smells, not to mention food poisoning. Even if germs aren't known to your people, chances are they will understand the need for clean pots, even if they don't comprehend the science behind the action.

To determine what your heroine should be carrying, look at how she ended up on the road in the first place. Did she escape in the middle of the night, or has she always been a wanderer? A wandering peddler will have properly-fitted clothing and gear, and plenty of pockets, belts, and extra pouches for his odds and ends. A witness to a heinous crime might have taken flight in the middle of the night and would only have whatever she could grab. A few minutes spent on considering what she will be carrying will help you determine later on what assistance she will need down the road.

Remember to pick materials that are consistent with your world's technology and rules. Culture and personal habits also need to be taken into account. A race of vegan people probably will not carry their water in salt-cured sheep stomachs if they can avoid it. They would use hollowed-out gourds with wax, clay, or cork stoppers. As long as you choose methods that are consistent, your adventurers will manage to make it to the Netherlands in time to stop a heinous war and save princesses from dark wizards.

My Heroine Is Going to Starve to Death, Isn't She?

At this point in the chapter, you must be wondering how the blazes you are going to feed your adventuring party. I've rained on the rabbit and venison parade, and turned the foraging idea into one black cloud of itchy starvation. Even though I've been a bit (a lot?) of a wet blanket, there are still plenty of yummy foods available for your adventurers to eat.

Assuming you want well-fed and ready-for-action heroes (if you're looking to starve them, skip this section), your party will most likely rely heavily on restocking from village to village, purchasing, bartering, trading, and/or stealing portable food. They can have hot meals in town, with portable foods along the path, supplemented by foraging and the occasional rabbit or pheasant (the anti-heroine is not afraid of decapitation in the quest of a full belly).

Today, portable food means granola bars, protein bars, vacuum-packed tuna pouches, shelf-stable cans of turkey, instant soup, and cheddar crackers shaped like fish. Since these items were not available a thousand years ago, is there an easily carried food out there beyond the dull bread and cheese?

Many a traveller and labourer have enjoyed meat-filled pastries, like calzones or Cornish pasties, as a portable food source. These keep well all day, can be eaten cold, and clean hands aren't necessary, since the part of the shell that is touching one's grimy hands can be thrown out. Breads and biscuits with meat cooked into them would be easily purchased in market towns and perhaps even an isolated farmhouse might have a few dozen in the pantry.

Hard cheese and bread are a popular fantasy bring-along, as well as a staple often seen in historical military fiction. Bread and cheese will keep the energy levels up and they hold up to work on the farm or being in the pocket of a tax collector as she makes her rounds. Rural workers especially would have found bread and cheese useful, since there would have been a lot of cheese (including soft cheese, like cottage cheese), and bread.

However, leavened bread crushes easily and molds even faster in the heat. Hard cheeses get rather oily when it's warm and soft cheese spoils quickly in the heat. A poor farmer might be less likely to part with a slice from her hard cheese wheel, since it had taken months to form and cure, and she is planning to sell it at market. Many cheese wheels at market were sold whole and not sliced. When out

Barmakiyya

Clean a hen, pigeon or another small bird. Cut the bird up and put into a pot with salt, pepper, coriander and lavender. Add an onion, soy sauce, and oil. Cook until the sauce is dried. Then, fry the chicken in oil.

Make a dough with leaven [yeast, like a sourdough starter] and oil, using fine flour and semolina [coarse durum wheat used in cous-cous and pasta]. Roll the bread into flatbreads. Put the fried meat on one dough piece and cover with another, sealing the edges. Put into an oven. It is very good on journeys.

begging door-to-door, you might end up with soft cottage cheese or cream that's four days old, as opposed to an orange slice from the cheddar wheel. A traveller might have found the standard bread and cheese sometimes difficult to access, whereas ready-made pies at market might have been more available.

Experiment with moving your heroes beyond the typical meals that we associate with pre-industrial people: bacon, cheese, bread. The Bedouin, for example, ate locusts. The insects were seasoned and cooked in sand pits. Then, the locusts were preserved in salt and ground up. The powdered mixture could be mixed with sour buttermilk, providing a protein-rich beverage for travellers.[2]

If locusts don't tickle your fancy, perhaps smoked sausages would be more the style of your adventurers. Made with ground offal and leftover meat, then stuffed into clean intestines, sausages could be smoked and salted to preserve them for even longer. Cured sausages could be eaten as is, or could be added to a pot of hot water and some vegetables for a quick stew.

Have fun with your food!

Chapter 2: Loving the City Life

Chuse not an house neer an inn.[1]

Perhaps it's fourteen years living in a city that's made me cynical, but modern people just aren't all that friendly. If someone showed up at my door and asked for a meal and a place to stay the night, I'd very carefully explain how to get to the homeless shelter from my house and offer them a bus ticket if I had one. Then I'd close the door and lock the house up like Fort Knox and hope I wasn't murdered in my sleep. And I'd be considered a nice person for having given the bus ticket and not called the police.

People living in Medieval Europe saw things differently.

Many travellers, especially poor ones, relied on the charity of strangers when rations were tight. People in Medieval Europe, for example, saw charity and kindness to strangers as part of their expression of Christianity. Christianity's role in hospitality meant having a sense of communal responsibility not only for immediate family and friends, but also for strangers, the poor, and even enemies.[2] If charity is a strong component to one's religious base, your hero might find many open arms while he travels.

I Ain't a Religious Man

If dining or overnighting with strangers seems either impractical or out of character, there is still the old standby of inns, taverns, and monasteries. Where your characters will spend their nights while in town is dependent upon a number of factors, including the purpose of their journey and depth of their purses.

A heroine on a holy pilgrimage (or, an assassin pretending to be a heroine on a holy pilgrimage) could follow the example of Egeria. Egeria was a wealthy woman who made the long journey from Spain to the Holy Land in 384, and recorded her journey. Monks and monasteries held a strong place in her diaries of the trip. She was a wealthy woman who could have stayed just about anywhere, but chose to stay at religious institutions whenever possible. This was not uncommon. Monasteries excavated in Palestine often have a guest house, designed to provide shelter and food to pilgrims such as Egeria. These monasteries were following the Rule of St. Benedict, who asked that all guests be received like Christ.[3]

Of course, your heroine wants to be careful when choosing a monastery. If she is of a stout constitution, she might find a strict monastery's austere lifestyle rather afflicting to the digestion. Many Early Church monks in the Mediterranean did not eat meat, for it was a luxury and would send the wrong message. Some Buddhist priests also practiced vegetarianism in different degrees of strictness. Other sects of Early Church monks considered eating raw food a virtuous act; minimal prep meant more time for worship. Your meat-loving heroine might not do so well if a rainstorm keeps her there for several days.

Wayfarer's Honey Refresher
Enjoy this beverage at a local inn on your journey to revive your spirits. A combination of honey, ground pepper, and spiced wine is just the thing to perk up any weary traveler.
Be warned, however. There are many a schemer who will make their patrons sick by combining one part spoiled honey with two parts good honey. Don't risk your health for their purses![4]

Inns, hotels, and taverns are very common places to rent rooms, and grab a hot meal, for a few pennies. Larger cities would have many to choose from. Pompeii, for example, had 118 bars and 20 hotels. Like today, standards varied, as did the food and, *cough*, services offered. Often times, where you stayed came down to the age old divider: money.

A rich baron and his wife will not be staying at a bawdy house, where only coffee and sex were served. A poor labourer might be lucky to get put up in the barn at a local monastery, alongside several other smelly, questionable (and often naked) men.

Before the time of police and 911, innkeepers did not accept random reservations online. Travellers had to convince innkeepers of their worthiness. Sure, a purseful of coin could always assist with that, but a person who looked like a gambler or the kind who couldn't handle her ale might find themselves left out in the back alley to fend for themselves.

If arriving via carriage or horseback, you would pay extra for the inn to stable and feed your animals. This could add to your bill quickly. If you could afford the horses, however, the money probably shouldn't bother you too much.

Some towns had bylaws against serving ale or food to non guests[5], so your adventurers might need to spend the night to get fed. Then again, considering the stench of tallow candles, gassy dogs, and unwashed, vomiting drunkards, your party might not be able to keep any food down. That's good for the pocket book, if not the body.

So, how much will all this dizzying hospitality cost? In Ian Mortimer's *Time Traveller's Guide to Medieval England,* he outlines the costs of staying at a common inn:

- ½ to 1 penny for the room
- 1 ½ to 2 1/2 pennies for stew or pottage (more for wine, and more for meat)
- 1 ½ to 3 ½ pennies for a horse's accommodation and meals[6]

After factoring in tips to the well-endowed daughter of the inn-keeper, plus the three tumblers of wine her ~~breasts~~ bright smile extorted out of you and your losses at dice, your hero's purse could easily be 2 shillings lighter. And for what? Well, frankly, shit, piss, and vomit.

The stench of rotting food, especially in the summer months, would fill the air. Garbage would pile up outside and, even if most of it was being composted, the smell of decomposing organic matter would be rather noticeable. Other patrons would smell like horses, sweat, rotten teeth, and cadaverous bad breath if they were using mercury cures to treat their venereal disease. With all of this, the air would be full of the sickly-sweet smell of burning fat from the tallow candles, while tobacco and grass smoke rose from pipes, and the cooking ovens and hearth fires burned the eyes.

Oh, the joy of it all.

If your hero is a priest, cleric, or monk, consider if their religious orders allow them to stay at taverns, where busty wenches, vile liquor, and lots and lots of sin is happening abovestairs. For example, Wulfstan's Canon Laws prohibited a priest from entering a tavern to eat or drink. Your priest will need to adjust his journey to ensure he travels along the path of monasteries, which is partially why Æthelwold's Regularis Concordia urged monasteries to be hospitable.[7]

If you were staying in a Roman-style tavern, your hero might encounter risottos, beans, peas, and lentils. They might even offer some snacks, such as marinated vegetables, cheese, eggs, pig's head, eels, olives, figs, and poultry.

Landlord, the Bill Please
That'll be one HS* for the wine, one for the bread and two for the side dishes.
Fine.
And eight for the girl.
That's fine too.
And two for the hay for your donkey.
That donkey's going to be the ruin of me![8]
*A type of Roman currency

British and European taverns might offer simpler fare, especially the rougher ones or in the off-season. Pottage or gruel, bread, and cheese would be offered, along with the local ale which might not be all that great tasting, but at least won't kill you, unlike the water supply.

In looking at all this, your hero might ask why on earth would anyone pay to stay at an inn? As disgusting as the rougher ones might have been, inns still offered benefits. Sleeping outside in foul weather can get rather miserable, and an old, lumpy straw bed would be better than the muddy forest floor. An inn would also have hot food. Sure, it might not be much more than some dried peas and salt pork, greyish-hued because of the cast iron pot, but it would be hot and readily available.

Another reason for staying in the inn would be safety in numbers. The highways might be littered with roving gangs (one might be led by your hero's love interest), and there is always safety in numbers. A smart anti-heroine would stay at the inn so that she can rob them later down the road.

Fundraising, the Medieval Way

This chapter has been all about the nutritional needs of being a hero or heroine. Heroing is fabulous and noble, true, but sometimes the hero finds his purse empty and nary a rich philanthropist in sight. What's a hero to do to raise quick cash without getting too sidetracked from the main quest of rescuing the princess from the Summer Castle of Ku'Min?

There are several legal and less legal ways your adventurers can outfit themselves. Depending upon where they fall on the good-evil scale, there are plenty of options.

Goody-Two-Shoes

Monasteries and farms are often in need of additional hands during harvest time and a quick pit stop at one of these places might find the hero earning a penny or two a day. When I say penny, I do mean a penny. In the 14th century in Britain, that was pretty much all that a labourer made per day.

A quick-on-her-feet young lass might work as a messenger for a week to help deliver missives and scrolls to politicians, clerks, lords, and priests. If this is an historical piece, she will probably need to cut her hair off in order to make the penny-and-a-half weekly salary her male counterparts were making.

If your adventuring party is travelling through several cities and towns, they might want to invest in picking up small items along the way to sell at the various towns they stop at. A bolt of silk purchased in a manufacturing town or a bag of spices from a spice farmer would net a significant profit once brought to a city, far from the item's source.

Your party might have come across items that work as well as gold or shillings. Salt, pepper, and cocoa beans have all been used as a means of currency, trade, and/or payment at different times.

The Law Is Always Several Shades of Grey

Individuals with military experience—or enough tavern brawls under their belts—can fetch up to a shilling a day for their work. Generally, however, those hiring mercenaries hire them for longer periods of time. However, if your heroine is in the city for a month looking to break her brother out of the underground prison, there's nothing wrong with her working for the city guard while she learns the secret passages of the area.

Or, let's suppose your good-looking hero happens to stumble into a young widow and sends her bolt of fabric tumbling into the mud. He feels horrible about what he's done. Just horrible. He insists on escorting her home to wash it for her. If, after he covers himself in suds and water in a futile attempt to get the mud out of her cloth, maybe she takes pity on him and shares the stew she's had simmering over her hearth. And, oh, if she happens to not resist his charms and spends a few hours tumbling with him, who would blame him? Nor who would blame him if she happened to put together a small satchel of foods and perhaps a penny or two for having washed her laundry? Women are such kind creatures, after all.

That isn't prostitution. That's simply...heroic luck.

Legal Is Such a Strong Word

Theft is probably the easiest way to get quick cash, though it might come with a stiff penalty if caught: such as losing one's head or hand. Breaking into people's homes in many cultures was considered a hanging offense. That's why Mr. Woodhouse was so upset by the chicken coop robbers in Jane Austen's *Emma*. "Pilfering was housebreaking to Mr. Woodhouse's fears," as Austen writes. Housebreaking was such a heinous crime to these people that it was worthy of an execution.

If that's the case in your world, there are ways around it. Have the "hero" use a hook on a fishing rod to squeeze through partially-opened windows to lift a candlestick out to their waiting hands. If caught, the hero was only stealing and would just end up in a prison where he'd be beaten, raped, and starved for a couple of months. Better than a hanging, though.[9]

Young children raised on the streets will be swift with their hands and pick many a pocket for their friends and family. They'll know how to work in pairs to distract merchants in order to "acquire" fruits, vegetables, and ready-made pies.

If theft is beneath your hero, and paid mercenary work isn't up your anti-heroine's skirts, perhaps assassin or smuggler might work better. Sure, it's illegal, but generally isn't going to get her into serious trouble with the law since she'll probably be working by them.

And, finally, if all else fails, there is always sex for hire. Prostitution is a time-honoured means of acquiring money, deeds, and goods. Pay will always vary, and one should never be too afraid to dabble in the more illicit aspects of the trade. When it comes to filling one's purse, never be afraid to experiment with fetishes.

Taxes: Government Fundraising

Governments sometimes need to raise large sums of cash quickly so that they can invade other nations, pay for marriages, and build their navies. Governments (this includes despots, monarchs, and monarchs who are despots) have levied some crazy taxes in the past, and some have caused rumblings, riots, and revolutions.

Some of the most hated taxes in history include:

- Poll Taxes of 1377-1380: They exempted virgins, which resulted in the public examination of females. By a man.[10]
- Tea taxes: There are too many tea taxes to list, though the Tea Act of 1773 is perhaps the most famous, as it led to the "Boston Tea Party" (known as the destruction of the tea during the period).
- Corn Laws of 1815-1846 which controlled the imports of grain into Britain.
- Salt Tax, which caused the Moscow Salt Riot of 1648

Taxes, polls, and levies are quick ways to raise capital. However, just like today, people hate taxes and get very, very angry when their food (and tea, and beer, and gin) are taxed.

Chapter 3: Where's the Nearest Drive-Thru? Markets, Fast Food, and Community Festivals

To choose Butter at Market.
Put a knife into the butter if salt, and smell it
when drawn out; if there is anything rancid or
unpleasant, it is bad...Fresh butter ought to
smell like a nosegay, and be of an equal colour all
through: if sour in smell it has not been sufficiently
washed; if veiny and open, it is probably mixed
with staler or an inferior sort.[1]

I love markets. I find them endlessly fascinating. They are a place where people gather to sell wares, from cat trees to organic tomatoes. Each farmers' market seems to be unique, reflective of what is popular in each local community. Alberta stalls are filled with local farmers and meat producers, all helping the market goers achieve a 100-mile diet. (Do Canadians eat a 100-kilometre diet, I wonder?) Markets in the small towns along the North Atlantic sell fish and seafood, heavy knitted hats (called "toques" in Canada) and sweaters, plus decorated, wooden containers that are used to store garbage at the end of one's driveway (since anything lighter would blow away in the gale winds).

I'd love to see more variety in fantasy's world of markets. I'd love them to be as vibrant as our real markets. The floating markets of Thailand, with their boats filled with fruits and vegetables, will have different sights and smells than the stalls and tables of a typical North American farmers' market. Likewise, trading and buying goods in an oasis village from a camel caravan should feel different than buying fresh produce and dairy at a steam train station. Since markets often play important roles in many fantasy novels—where deals are made and broken, where pickpockets steal purses and prostitutes steal military secrets—use the scents, smells, and sounds of the market to enhance your world.

The Local Market

Eventually, your party of war-weary adventurers will need to restock, visit a brothel, and annoy a local baron. The best place to do that will be at the local market. A good local market should have a mixture of in-season produce and meat, preserves, ready-made foods, plus imported goods such as spices and ice (yes, ice! I'll explain how it got to market a little later in this chapter). Your heroine might also be able to find a local woman selling their special, homemade pills, potions and concoctions for medical emergencies, as well as a wide assortment of brews. For medicinal purposes only, of course.[2]

Upon arrival at the market, your heroine might see (and smell) the local fishmonger. She'll know that fish should smell like the ocean and not "fishy." However, she won't just see trout, salmon, and lobster—the traditional offerings of the frozen markets today. Instead, she'll find all kinds of edible aquatic creatures, including eels, pike, and minnows from local fishermen. Also, those who work the oceans will have stalls selling more specialized catches, such as crabs, oysters, herring, and flounder. A small child might have a stall selling the mussels and clams she collected from the beach near her home.[3]

Your hero might head to the stalls selling produce directly from their small gardens. Onions, cabbages, turnips, peas, and apples would all be found at different times in a Viking-era market.[4] The hot markets of an Athenian-based world would see cabbages, asparagus, radishes, pumpkins, and artichokes.[5] Your party might even find foraged wild nuts for sale by a wiry young lad who needed a little extra money for his family.

Off to the side, several stalls would be selling cured and fresh meats. A butcher would be set up with his weight scales, selling fresh loin cuts and joints, always ensuring that the scales tipped in his favour. Barrels of salt beef, soaking in its bloody salt brine, would be available for purchase by the piece or pound. Salt fish—flat, stiff slabs of cod—would be available for purchase (make sure your hero purchases a fillet that's a little pliable; too stiff and the stuff will be nearly inedible no matter how much soaking he does).

Hens, ducks, and geese will be in crates for those who need live birds, as well as dead birds in wooden boxes or hanging from hooks. Feathers might not be attached; that's another source of income, after all. If your hero is very lucky, perhaps a few pheasants will be for sale with the blessing of a local baron.

Eggs would also be popular at market, especially in towns where many people would live in apartments and townhouses, as opposed to estates and country cottages. A family of ten crowded into a fourth floor attic apartment would not have the ability to raise chickens, and eggs would provide them with a cheap and nutritious source of protein.

Don't be surprised, however, if the eggs are not fresh. Since hens can be quite unpredictable with their egg-laying, especially if the weather is poor, farmer's wives would have preserved excess eggs to sell when there wouldn't be as many eggs and prices would be higher. Your heroine might try haggling for cheaper egg prices during a cold snap, but chances are she won't get much of a discount even though the eggs won't be fresh.

Your heroine will most likely be used to preserved eggs, however, so she won't be afraid of them, unless you are writing a time travel piece. In that case, her reaction to eggs soaking in lime or cooked eggs suspended in vinegar might be rather hilarious (quick tip: the lime might give the eggs a slight chemical taste).

How to Preserve an Egg?
Combine 2 lbs of lime [calcium oxide, not the fruit] with 5 gallons of water. Let the chemicals react for ten days, stirring every morning. Once the chemical process was finished, wipe clean eggs and add to the solution. Eggs could be added at any time and would store for several months.[6]

Your party will be able to pick up baking—perhaps even the market is situated around a communal oven or a privately-owned bakery—and biscuits, tack bread, flat breads, and cakes would be welcomed after eating little more than dough and water mixtures cooked on hot stones.

If steam powers your world, fresh produce and dairy will be all of the rage in the cities and large centres. Consider that for millennia, milk had to be purchased locally since it would spoil so quickly. Being on a cart for four days would churn raw milk into curds and whey, assuming it didn't spoil completely in the heat. With the inability to transport milk safely from the country to the city, dairy would be very expensive within the city walls, since limited space prevented individuals from having herds of animals.

Trains, steamships, and steampunk airships would change that. The Victorian era of steam, with trains and canals, saw a huge explosion in milk availability in cities. Cows could be milked in the morning, and that milk would arrive in the city by nightfall, for people to purchase on their way home from the factories. Farmers, seeing the huge opportunity for profit, would have larger and larger herds, allowing for more and more dairy to be available. Soon, fresh milk straight from the farm could be delivered to the doorstep of families. Perhaps your Victorian hero sets up an anonymous milk delivery for his impoverished love interest. Who needs jewels when she has fresh, from-the-farm milk delivery every day?

With trains and airships come market stalls and makeshift markets opening up on canal docks and train stations. Butter, milk, and cheese would be readily available, as would fresh produce (such as strawberries) that doesn't travel by road as easily as onions, carrots, or cabbage. Those could still be transported by carts, instead of the more expensive rail and ship method.

Hard cheese has always been a money maker for farmers because it didn't spoil easily. Even farmers in the middle of nowhere could make it and ship it to city markets without worrying about it spoiling. Because of that, wheels of cheese would actually be expensive because it would be priced on quality. So your hero might not be able to afford the fancier hard cheeses; they might all be out of his price range. He'll also need to be wary of the bright orange cheeses; some in the Victorian era were dyed with red lead.

The dockside market might also have something your heroine has never seen in July before: ice. Harvesting and storing ice is actually an old process, going back thousands of years in China. Later, the Greeks and Romans developed their own system of storing snow in pits for instant ice. With advancing technology in shipping, ships could harvest frozen northern ponds and bring the chunks of ice to southern ports. Ice would be sold at a premium; it might be well outside your heroine's budget. However, if she is a spoiled duchess, she might not understand that a glass of sherbet might cost her a week's worth of scrubbing pots and pans in a tavern.

Your hero might pick up an iced drink for his love interest, the financial consequences be damned. In a large centre, there might be an iced beverage stall. Saltpeter would be dissolved in water, which would cool glass bottles enough to produce an iced beverage. While all the rage in France in the late 17th century, it might be outside of your world's technology or materials.

Your travellers might find strange foods for sale, and perhaps even items that offend them. A co-worker of mine did some travelling in South America several years ago and was rather startled by the fetal leather accessories for sale at the local markets. She'd never heard of leather made from unborn calves before, and was completely horrified when the vendors tried to get her to touch it!

A writer named Athenaeus was horrified to discover that some peoples, like the Scythians, gave their newborns cow milk instead of employing a wet nurse or purchasing breast milk. He also argued that women who produced too much milk should sell their surplus so that other mothers could purchase it for their infants.[7] Just like today, modern women often have to endure the judgement of others in terms of the decisions they make for themselves and their children; I'm sure your world will have plenty of judgement to throw around, too.

Fabrics, foods, and exotic crafts would arrive from faraway lands by caravan. In a large centre like Rome or Paris, merchants might sell bolts of silk for the highest price, brought in from across the continent.

Also, don't be surprised if the occasional hothouse food is available. Hothouses were very popular in the 19th century. A keen farmer might have their produce available for market a few weeks—even months—earlier than others. The strawberries your hero buys for his love interest in March will be worth the premium prices when he sees her smile. Assuming she doesn't have an allergy, of course.

Sugar, Spice, and All that's Nice

Sugar was an important commodity in Europe, especially England and Northern Europe who didn't have a local source. Sugar was generally imported from Morocco, but Cyprus, Alexandria, Venice, and Genoa also exported sugar. Because of its cost, sugar was treated more like a spice than a key ingredient for centuries in Europe.

Sugar came in cones called "loaves" and was guarded under lock and key. In the 13th and 14th centuries, sugar cost about 2 shillings a pound on average, though sometimes it spiked to 8 shillings a pound.[8]

To put this cost into perspective, here is what 2 shillings[9] could buy instead:

- 24 dozen eggs
- 6 chickens
- 1 pig
- 20lbs cheese

For a poor family, a pound of sugar was well beyond their reach.

Spices were another important import across the world. The Spice Trade brought eastern spices west, entering the culture of the worlds it touched. Cinnamon was highly valued in antiquity and was heavily used by the Egyptians in embalming, as well as used in the anointing oil of Hebrew Priests (Exodus 30:23). When European trade and colonization in the South Pacific, Africa, and the West opened up, new spices entered the markets of ordinary people.

Spice increased in price with each mile of travel due to taxes, tolls, levies, transportation costs, and greed. To pick up a pound of cinnamon or ginger in 13th century London, it could set a person back up to 2 shillings, whereas pepper could go from a few pennies to 4 shillings. Saffron, still expensive today, was in the 12 shillings range.[10]

Spice shops, common in towns, but less so in small villages, could sell premade mixtures. There were various mixtures, but there were two common ones:

- Powdor Fort—a hot mixture of ginger, black pepper, cloves, and mace.
- Powdor Dounce—what we'd called Christmas spice today, a mixture of ginger, cinnamon, nutmeg, cloves, black pepper, and sugar.[11]

These could be purchased in small amounts for those with a little ready money, such as blacksmiths, but not enough to warrant purchasing spices by the pound, such as a rich baron. Poorer folks might save up for special occasions, such as Christmas or Easter, to splurge on some spices.

Not to mention that a recipe can always be changed; if saffron is too expensive, perhaps the recipe might taste just as good with a pinch of freshly-ground ginger and cloves.

Salt

In the modern world, we use salt as a condiment, so it's easy to forget that it's actually a mineral, NaCl (sodium chloride) to be exact. We need it to live. Today, salt is so common that we toss it on our streets during the winter months. This wasn't always the case.

Before it was discovered buried underground in nearly every country around the world, salt was a rare commodity. The Tuaregs of North Africa had caravans 40,000 camels long, trading salt to merchants that spread it throughout Africa, the Middle East, and Europe. Coastal regions could make their own salt from evaporated sea water, thereby reducing the costs. Inland countries were not so lucky.

The earliest record of salt production was in China, about 5000 years ago. Boiling or evaporating seawater is one of the oldest ways of obtaining salt. It remained a useful technique well into the 18th century in France to avoid paying salt taxes, and in India's struggle for independence to avoid the British salt monopoly.[12]

Ancient Egyptians used a type of salt along the Nile called natron in their mummification process. Later, the Romans built the *Via Salaria* (Salt Road) to bring salt to Rome from the coastal trading regions.

Salt was a valuable product that preserved food for the winter months. Oppressive salt taxes could make the lower classes riot, such as the Salt Riots in Moscow in the 17th century.

Daily Bread

No discussion about markets would be complete without a section on bread. Homer called the human race "bread-eating." Before health magazines and fad diets told us carbs were an evil to be stamped out, bread held a vital position in the diets of many cultures. Cyril of Scythopolis (a monk) noted in his journals that any new monastery erected the church first, with the bakery built second.[13] From the slaves building the Great Pyramids to the workers in London's cloth factories, bread has helped sustain human beings for millennia.

Today, bread holds a lower role on the modern table. It's sliced vertically and used as toast, or in a sandwich. Sometimes, the middle is dug out and thrown away so that chili and soup can be poured into the centre. It's often white, rectangular blocks that have been whipped until the bread is a tasteless, fluffy shadow of its former wonder.

I can imagine that the first attempts at turning wheat into an edible, fully-cooked food were probably dubious. Hot stones and ashes would have been the means of cooking the unleavened dough, as ovens wouldn't have been invented. Those very early attempts were probably ashy, chewy, and barely palatable.

The ancestors who settled down into farming, ending their nomadic lives, would have moved to more bread in their diets, so no doubt those individuals would have discovered new shapes, grains, and combinations to help make their daily bread a little more enjoyable. However, if your story is set in ancient or prehistoric times, the bread might not resemble anything we're used to eating today, especially without yeast or baking powder. Even more common unleavened breads like matzah (matzo) would have tasted a bit different, since we're used to modern milling and cooking methods.

For the purpose of this section, I will mostly be dealing with wheat bread. The reason is because the bulk of epic fantasy out there is set in a quasi-European setting, so I felt wheat bread was the best way to address many of the common questions concerning bread.

That doesn't mean bread wasn't handled in different ways; it was. "Bread" varies around the world, so it is very important to research the grains used if you're writing a historical story. For example, the "corn" eaten in the Fertile Crescent back in the 3rd century B.C. was not maize. "Corn" originally referred to cereal grains. When Europeans landed in North America, the maize used by the natives was referred to as Indian Corn. In fact, many recipes well into the 19th century still refer to Indian Corn. So if you try out some old cookbooks that call for corn, confirm if they mean cereal grains or maize.

Daily Grind

The phrase originates from when grain had to be ground for bread. The process required several hours of work by a woman on her knees grinding grain between two rocks. The monotonous, never-ending work that we do every day is still a grind for many of us. Some things never change.

43

Remember to research when wheat was introduced to an area if it was not a native plant. This is perhaps one of the largest errors I've seen in historical fictions, be it historical, romance, or fantasy. There have been plenty parts of the world where wheat did not grow and was not introduced until the arrival of Europeans, including places like the North American prairies.

In the middle ages, "bread" wasn't just one item. Just like today, there were many flour choices, though the social hierarchy we have today is rather reverse:

- White breads (In order of quality: pandemain, wastel, and cocket). The quality was determined by how much the flour was sifted.
- Whole wheat breads, such as cheat (bran removed), Brown Bread (had the husk mixed in). Brown bread was probably used by the wealthy for trenchers (serving plates).
- Other breads made from peas, beans, acorns, and grain chaff mixed in.

Where Does the Phrase Upper Crust Come From?

Bread ovens used to have fires lit inside them to heat the inside. Then the ash was brushed out and the bread was placed inside on the floor of the oven. However, the bottoms would be dirty and ashy, since fully cleaning the oven would have caused it to lose too much heat. So the bread was cut horizontally, not vertically. The rich people got the "upper crust" whereas the bottom pieces could go to the servants or poor.

Bread evolved to be cooked in various forms, be it over hot coals by herdsmen and raiders to clay or stone ovens for those in town.[14] The Egyptians had an array of breads, many being freshly made with yeast, milk, eggs, and honey. The compromise was that these rich, starchy choices didn't travel or keep well, necessitating the need for further options in bread.

Originally, bread was little more than a pancake of ground wheat and water, with perhaps some herbs or meat mixed in. It was heavy and coarse. However, yeast was soon discovered as a means of "raising" bread to make it more attractive. Today, yeast comes in an envelope on the shelf, or sometimes from a sourdough starter. In yeast's early days, it came from several different sources:[15] [16]

- Millet would be kneaded with must (must is freshly-pressed grapes and is the first step in winemaking)
- Wheat bran soaked in must for several days before being kneaded, heated, and mixed with flour. (This bread did not keep well, though it was good. It also was only available in the autumn).
- Mix barley flour and water into a dough. Form into a round shape and make a dent in the middle of the dough, about halfway down. Cut a cross into the top. Fill the dent with water and let it sit for a few days. When the dough splits, it can be used as yeast.[17]
- A dough made from barley and water that was baked in ashes and kept until it fermented. It would be dissolved in water before using.
- Keeping the previous day's dough and mixing it with fresh dough the next day.
- Making a form of sourdough starter by boiling flour and water into a porridge and leaving it to ferment.
- The foam that formed during the alcohol-making process could be combined with flour.

Flour, be it wheat, rye, or barley, would need to be sifted or at least picked through. Most people don't use flour sifters today since the flour is already well-processed. Without modern processing, ground grains would be heavy, coarse, and your hero might bite into a chip of stone that got mixed in the flour. Great teeth he might not have by the end, so make sure to have healers on hand who can do dentistry.

I don't mean to imply that grain mills didn't exist until recently. They did. Jiahu, a Chinese town some 9000 years old, had stone mills to process rice. Though, we can probably assume their mills were not able to process rice flour on the same level as today's machines. Plus, the stone wheel would have chipped and sheared off pebbles into the flour.[18]

Don't Fall for Fake Bread!
A baker might "augment" their bread with chalk, bones, and/or ashes! Don't be a victim. Only buy from reputable sources.

Many people preferred white flour bread in the Middle Ages, just like today. Typically, only richer farmers and the larger landowners ate white bread. Peasants and poor farmers ate a lot more rye and barley bread instead. Maslin was a hybrid bread, where wheat was mixed in with rye to produce a lighter texture. During hard times, the poor added whatever they could to their flour to make bread. Rye flour, legumes, and even ground acorns could all be used to make basic breads during times of famine or poverty.

Flour would need to be kept dry or it would mold. If your world is a damp one and people are living in one-room shacks, it might not be possible to have several months' worth of grain ground at the local mill. If local law prevented personal baking of bread, most poor bread would be made in the ashes and coals of the home fire pit to avoid paying for the master's ovens. The large loaves at the market would have been made in approved bakeries and, thus, more expensive (unless your local Baron has passed a bylaw setting the price of bread in his region) and might be out of the reach of the poorest individuals.

Bread dough could be mixed the evening before so that it would have enough time to rise by the morning. The dough would need to be placed in a warm place in the kitchen or near the hearth, or else the dough wouldn't rise.

Yeast Isn't the Only Leavening Agent
Try some of these:
- Egg
- Mashed banana
- Crushed flaxseeds and water
- Tofu
- Baking Powder
- Powdered egg

The bread ovens would need to be fired up in the mornings. Stone or brick ovens had a fire lit inside of them to heat the stones. Once the stones were heated up, the ashes were swept out and the bread was added to the oven. Metal doors would be set in place around the oven opening and closed with leftover dough or mud. Using dough would serve two purposes: the dough would help seal the edges so that no heat would escape, and secondly it acted like a timer to show when the bread would be done.

In a communal oven, your family would have its own mark on the bread to easily identify it. That's what the children's rhyme Patty Cake is referring to when it talks about pricking and marking the bread:

> Patty Cake, Patty Cake,
> Baker's Man;
> That I will Master,
> As fast as I can;
> Prick it and prick it,
> And mark it with a T,
> And there will be enough for Jacky and me.[19]

The travelling hero would not be able to quickly bake his own bread in an oven, so either have him make his own, sad little pucks in the fire (which, inevitably, he will burn the first time, and undercook the second time), or have him pick up a hearty loaf at the market already baked.

Also, don't forget that baking powder was not readily available until about a century and a half ago. Baking powder is the reason cakes, biscuits, scones, and dumplings puff up. Without it, a biscuit would be nothing more than a sad press of fat and flour. Before baking powder was invented, most cakes were made with yeast; biscuits didn't exist in any recognizable form for us today.

Before commercial baking powder, potash or ash water would have been used. Potash could be purchased, or made at home. Ash water is, well, water with ashes in it. Ashes from hardwoods would have been used (oak, elm, and cherry, not pines or firs). The ash water would have been boiled and left to settle overnight. Some of the liquid would have been removed and boiled the next morning until the liquid was completely evaporated. A greyish residue would be left on the bottom of the pot. That would have been used as baking powder. Yummy.

When I began researching this book, many people asked if I was going to include bannock as an example of a First Nations food that predates Europeans. Bannock is a popular food in Western Canada. It's a flaky biscuit made with flour, sugar, and lard, and often has raisins in it. It resembles a tea biscuit, which is what bannock actually is.

The "history" of bannock is varied. Some sources insist that this bread was made with ground roots and animal fat before the recipe was changed to flour. Others suggest that it came about when the fur traders married native women, their relationships causing a fusion of traditional cooking. Most sources say bannock really became a part of the First Nations menu once they were moved to reserves and given Indian Affairs rations (flour, lard, and sugar... and often little to nothing else).

Regardless if this is a blending of cooking methods with new ingredients or a result of ingenious people making do in a horrific situation, bannock holds a unique place in history. Just like tomato sauce and Italians, bannock became a part of the history of Canadian First Nations food. It's just not part of all of their food history. We sometimes forget that food culture changes, so feel free to show your world's culture evolving and adjusting to outside influences.

If you opt to have a bread-heavy diet for your people, remember to include some of the nutritional challenges with it. Just as a diet heavy in meat and beer can cause gout and drowsy (known as edema today), a bread-heavy diet can cause malnutrition in the young and elderly, as well as pregnant women.

Malnutrition is often thought of as a condition caused by lack of food. Certainly, that is one cause of it, but absorption problems due to one's diet can also cause malnutrition. A diet heavy in whole grains and legumes is a diet heavy in fibre, which can cause absorption issues. Add to that a diet that lacks folic acid, protein, calcium, and Vitamin C, and a pregnant female's health—plus the health of her unborn child—could be compromised, leading to miscarriages, deaths of both child and mother, and medical conditions like spina bifida.[20]

Toutons

If there is any dough left over after rising and forming into the bread pans for baking (a process that could take up to twelve hours with sourdough), the dough can be fried for breakfast. Heat up a pan or heavy pot with a small amount of pork fat. Roll the dough into small balls and press between your hands. Drop into the pan and fry on both sides until puffy and golden brown. Serve hot covered with molasses and butter. This is a perfect substitute for bread and biscuits while in a wagon train or travelling large distances with a cart.

Even though a bread-and-grain heavy diet was linked to many medical problems, it was also the reason that so many people survived as long as they did. Grain prices were often regulated by governments, kings, and sultans; those that did not regulate the prices might instead give out daily portions to the city's very poor. The risk of starving now would have overruled illness later, even if these individuals knew the risks.

Fast Food

I realized I needed this section when I mentioned Victorian fast food. Many people thought I was joking. Fast food, after all, is a modern development. No one ever ate premade food in centuries previous. Right? Wrong.

Human beings are inherently about convenience. It doesn't matter how bad the hamburger drive-thru is for us, many of us still go through it because it's convenient. We're hungry, we're tired, and it's too hot to cook a roast. Why go through all that trouble when I could just pick up a fast food meal on the way home? People have been saying that for centuries—and entrepreneurs have been heeding the call.

Early Roman streets were lined with food kiosks. Most Plebeian apartments didn't have kitchens and cooking facilities, so the population relied heavily on street vendors. Sausages or cooked meats covered in garum (a fish entrails sauce) could be purchased from vendors while going about one's business.[21] Over two thousand years later, Victorian factory workers had access to over three hundred food vendors along their routes to work.

Steampunk heroines would stop at a kiosk for a mug of coffee, tea, or chocolate, drinking it there before handing the cup back (can you imagine how dirty some of those mugs might have been!). The beverage might only cost them a penny, far cheaper than the cost of coal to get their stoves going in the morning, assuming they even possessed a stove in their apartment.

After downing a hot beverage—welcomed on a cold January morning—our heroine could pick up a slice of currant cake for half a penny (if she could afford it, she'd pick up another for later in the day). Or, perhaps she'd want a boiled egg, too, which would cost another penny.[22]

A miner or a fisherman working away from home all day might bring a meat pocket with him to keep him going. These are like the ones recommended in Chapter 1 where a cooked packet of food would keep a hero going throughout the day. Don't buy from a stingy stall; the hero needs to eat! Make sure those pockets are filled with lard, bacon, bone marrow, chopped kidneys, and egg yolks.[23] A kitchen sink is too heavy to include, but everything else is fair game.

If your work is a steampunk, Regency romance, or a world based on those, your hero might stop partway through his day to eat at a chophouse. Today, "chophouse" is just another term for steakhouse or restaurant. They are establishments with several different cuts of meat ready for customers to order. In a historical context, however, a chophouse is a very basic form of steakhouse.

The hero would purchase a steak from the local butcher, cut to order and wrapped in cabbage leaves to keep it fresh. He might stop by the bakery and purchase a couple of biscuits before heading to the chophouse. There, he'd pay a couple of pennies for the meat to be grilled to perfection (or at least to quasi-edible standards). A good chophouse might have some cooked potatoes, ale, cheese, and pickles available to purchase.[24]

There are plenty of options in market towns for your adventurers to find ready-available food, even if it will cost them extra coin. However, if there is a shortage of fuel and the law forbids salvaging for wood, ready-made food might be the best option for them.

Feasting

There aren't a lot of reasons to feast anymore in the modern era. We have large celebrations like wedding receptions or 50th anniversary parties, or perhaps a work Christmas party where the liquor flows and the buffet is intense. However, in the Middle Ages, feasts held a different meaning than what we see today. Many feasts had religious aspects, such as celebrations to a particular saint. They brought together the community in a way that everyday life did not. Two people celebrating their anniversary is not a feast, no matter how much food is consumed.[25]

The Middle Ages had several feast days, providing the rich and the church (who were often the same people) many opportunities to wine and dine their neighbours. When developing your fantasy world, or trying to arrange how to seat your Highland alpha male at the head table, consider the reasons why your people are celebrating.

People celebrate different milestones and events. In many African and North American First People's cultures, the milestone of adulthood was cause for a celebration feast. That was less of a focus in medieval Europe, but the wedding was a celebration that replaced the ascension to adulthood.

People living in the Middle Ages did not work for about 80-100 days a year.[26] This was due to commemoration days, plus Sundays. Then, there were the three major religious feasts—Christmas, Easter, Whitsunday—where many people did not work for an entire week (farmers would have still needed to feed their livestock, of course). Religious holidays could be very strict, where sewing at home would be forbidden and even sex might not be allowed for fear of eternal damnation. No wonder people drank so much.

Private and public banquets would require long-term preparation. When I used to run the soup kitchen at a homeless

> In the fantasy world, religious dates can be made up, which can be both liberating and terrifying. If you're looking for help developing your pantheon, I strongly recommend Julie Ann Dawson's Pantheon Building. It is meant for role-playing dungeon masters, but the concepts are perfect for fantasy and science fiction authors who are developing a religious system in their own worlds.

agency, I didn't actually do my own shopping for major meals like Thanksgiving, where I expected 800+ people for supper. When the time came, I gave my suppliers a week to gather the following (partial) grocery list:

- 600lbs frozen turkey
- 2 cases instant stuffing
- 250lbs potatoes
- 6 cases frozen peas/carrots/corn
- 4 cases frozen broccoli/cauliflower
- 1 case instant gravy mix
- 70 dozen rolls

That meal was a lot of work. I had to arrange volunteers before the meal to help cook all of the turkey, debone, and prep into trays. I arrived eight hours before the meal was served with six other volunteers, and a shift rotation began throughout the evening with upwards of forty helpers to get us through making that meal. I had to be able to tell four hours before the meal was ready if we were falling behind in case we needed to pull in more volunteers. Imagine pulling off a meal like that when the turkeys had to be killed and plucked!

Banquets and celebrations for princes and kings could be excessive, especially if the celebration was open to the entire population of the county. When Alexander III of Scotland married Margaret, Henry III of England's daughter, in 1251, the shopping list was even bigger than mine. Cattle, rabbits, pigs, and wine were purchased months in advance of the marriage feast. Leading up to the feast, 68,500 loaves of bread were made, 10,000 pieces of haddock prepared, and 700 pieces of poultry purchased.[27] Don't forget the extra candles for the kitchen, the corridors leading to the great feast, and for the great feast itself! Now that was a party. (For a tongue-in-cheek feast checklist, see Appendix II.)

Sometimes feasts and banquets were not for any real reason, other than a stately figure showing up for supper. When Queen

Elizabeth I dropped by Lord North's house for a couple days, the poor man ended up entertaining over two thousand people and spent more than £640 feeding them! Amongst the feeding frenzy, nearly 5000 loaves of bread were consumed, 11 cows slaughtered, 2500 eggs eaten, and 2600 pigeons baked and boiled.[28] No one would blame your miserly hero's father for developing a bad case of body odour and bad attitude if it meant guests stayed away!

Even the clergy joined the bandwagon of parties. The Bishop of Salisbury threw a banquet to celebrate his appointment in 1414. His menu? The first course was a "light" offering of chicken, peacock, meatballs, porridge, venison, and a stew of wine, sugar, spices, pork, and chicken. The second course moved to the more exotic crane, heron, and partridges, plus the usual roasted piglets. The third course had a fried meat and little bird theme, with pigeons, quails, larks, fritters, and puff pastries dominating the setting. Finally, the dessert course arrived with spiced wine, wafers, and candied fruits.[29]

Feasts weren't only for the living. Funerals and death rites have often been celebrations of food. Perhaps the afterlife of your world requires a feast for the poor in hopes of the rich lord making it to the afterlife. Or, perhaps the religious beliefs of your world require a rich man to bequest all of his money to the poor and hold a community feast before his death. These death bequests of food and feasts could be used to bolster (or destroy) political relationships,[30] and could land your hero in afterlife limbo as his wife runs off with all of his money instead of performing the proper rites because she is a non-believer.

Feasts, like today, needed to be varied and wide-ranging in the foods offered to ensure that everyone's needs could be met. Social status has less importance today (at least, to some of us), so we often offer a general selection and meet some specific requirements, like vegetarian dishes. However, when cooking for one's betters in a class-based society, it was vitally important to offer food appropriate to those who were fasting, partially-fasting, observing religious holidays, didn't eat specific foods, had eating disorders, had weird food ticks, and so on. Sometimes, it was easier to cook the entire contents of one's kitchen!

Agricultural festivals are still popular in rural communities, where rodeos, community meals, and outdoor sports are held. Harvest festivals like Thanksgiving are still celebrated today, though our modern world turns to large family dinners or perhaps volunteering to honour the tradition. If you create a harvest festival for your heroine to find a suitable mate, make sure the celebration is held in a logi-

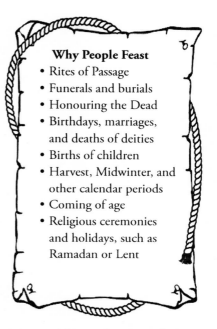

Why People Feast
• Rites of Passage
• Funerals and burials
• Honouring the Dead
• Birthdays, marriages, and deaths of deities
• Births of children
• Harvest, Midwinter, and other calendar periods
• Coming of age
• Religious ceremonies and holidays, such as Ramadan or Lent

cal time in the autumn. (Also, if you are writing a time travel piece, ensure your Thanksgiving celebrations are held at the right time! Countries who celebrate Thanksgiving hold it on different days!).

Harvest isn't the only time to celebrate, however. The arrival of spring and the ability to plant is cause for celebration in many quarters. Likewise, the midst of winter is another time to celebrate surviving the cold and diminishing daylight. Whatever your world's reasons for celebrating, make sure they have lots and lots to eat!

Chapter 4: The Marching Stomach
The Logistics of Feeding an Army

An army marches on its stomach.
Napoleon Bonaparte, Frederick the Great
of Prussia, and/or Claudius Galen, a
Roman doctor

War is commonplace in historical and fantasy novels. It's not surprising, considering humanity's long and bloody history. Rare is there a generation in our history where there was not an armed conflict raging somewhere on earth. Many of the rights we take for granted today, including the right to draw breath regardless of belief, culture, gender, or colour, were gained by armed conflicts. Many of the world's modern nations were forged in war. It's not surprising that many books draw on our violent past.

However, writers sometimes find armed conflict difficult to write when required to deal with the everyday logistics. There are so many things to consider in previous eras of technology that are not relevant today. Instead of a long train of hangers-on, today's military brings along contractors and consultants. Instead of siege engines hauled by oxen, today's armed forces have aircraft capable of handling tanks and other vehicles. It can be difficult for modern people to picture the massive scale a military movement actually took in a time where email, telephones, and the combustion engine didn't exist.

I could write an entire book just on troop mobilization strategies for fantasy and historical fiction writers. While tempting, I promise to only limit this chapter to a general overview of food during an armed conflict.

The Human Body

Chapter 1 covered the calorie and nutritional needs for backpackers, military personnel, and everyday people going about their business. I did not mention the amount of water needed, however. For everyday tasks or a person hiking near a stream, they will have enough access to water through their food, water, and beer. But what about a soldier carrying sixty pounds of equipment during an oppressive summer? What are their hydration needs and risks?

I'm going to cheat by using the eight glasses of water benchmark. There is some debate over the actual accuracy of the two liters of water requirement and that it doesn't take into account food-related hydration, but for simplicity's sake I will be using that benchmark throughout this book.

Let's look at what happens to the human body when it becomes dehydrated. The most obvious sign is they become thirsty and fatigued. As a person becomes more dehydrated, they lose weight; that's why you weigh less the morning after partying way too much. A 1% drop in bodyweight due to dehydration causes a 5% drop in performance, and a 4-5% drop in bodyweight causes a 20-30% reduction in performance.[1] But what does that actually look like?

I'm going to use the 30 kilometres a day benchmark. That's a long day of hiking, but the Romans did it and I've done it carrying gear so it's doable (miserable when out of shape, but doable). A 5% drop in performance means mild dehydration would make that last couple of kilometres very difficult, if impossible to finish. Serious dehydration caused by not drinking nearly enough and sweating a lot would cause your troops to only make 20-25 kilometres. If there was a city under siege, your troops would probably be in no shape to help by the time they arrived. That would be a disaster in the making for sure.

Make sure your troops have their own canteens made from materials appropriate to the world. Be it gourds of water, sheep stomachs of milk, or jugs of small beer (low alcohol) carried by the troop donkey, make sure your troops get enough to drink. You want them ready to perform when they arrive.

Military Culture

One of the first things any writer has to decide is the culture of their armed forces. Is this a regular force of professional soldiers or a group of militia pulled from the fields? Is the military a form of punishment for criminals—choose the army or the jails—or is military life a respectable choice for the upper crust of society?

It's normal for militaries to possess a mixture of cultures, too. The social division in the British army was arguably at its height during the Napoleonic Wars. The lower ranks were filled with children who'd been brought up in the army and criminals who joined up to avoid jail. The upper ranks were filled with people who purchased their commissions and held lofty positions of power, while the lower ranks did all of the work.[2]

If there is a clash of cultures in your military, here are some further questions to ponder:

- Will upper ranks be treated differently than lower ranks?
- Will the poor boys pounding the drums as they walk to their deaths receive better rations than the general who can afford a foreign chef to accompany him into war?

Perhaps there is not a social caste system within your world's armed forces. Is everyone treated absolutely equal, so that rank only means an increase in responsibility, and perhaps pay, while all equipment and rations remain the same?

Consider how modern armies often have all ranks eating the same ration packs in the field, whereas the rank structure on ships can have the officers served by waiters and the rank and file serving themselves at a buffet. Or look at the trouble of France's Louis XIV. The officer tables had become so competitive over who offered the best spread that the King himself had to step in and limit the number of courses an officer's table could have to cut costs.

Call to Arms

So, Warlord Magnis has sent out the order: we're marching to war. Isn't that just fabulous. For some, this call to battle will be glorious news. Spartan soldiers, for example, were trained to look forward to war because they were given better food. During peacetime, Spartans were only fed blood soup with vegetables and a bit of meat—and bile. War time meant good eating.[3]

Established farmers might spend their last days organizing their sons or wives on how to look after the land and animals while they are away. Veterans who have been through a few wars might start gorging themselves, hoping to pack on as much weight as possible, since they remember how much weight they lost during the last campaign. Young

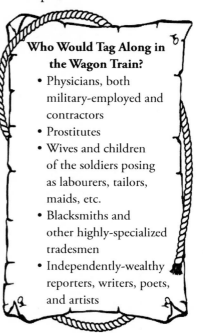

Who Would Tag Along in the Wagon Train?

- Physicians, both military-employed and contractors
- Prostitutes
- Wives and children of the soldiers posing as labourers, tailors, maids, etc.
- Blacksmiths and other highly-specialized tradesmen
- Independently-wealthy reporters, writers, poets, and artists

men might convince their sweethearts to not let them go to war a virgin, and old men might spend the night with their wives and children.

When about to head out, your unattached heroine might go on benders with her friends: booze, men (or women), and food. There will be plenty of time for starvation, celibacy, and prohibition later. Then again, your priest warrior might spend the night before in prayer at the chapel, while his friends are out partying.

Will your hero have his own equipment purchased with his own money, or will it be assigned to him, or will he be forced to purchase it from the military with his "sign up bonus"? If he is bringing his own, make sure he picks up a canteen and a bag for his rations (if he's smart, he's going to fill that thing up with dried fruit, cured olives, cheese, hardtack, and some spices). He should have a small metal, stone, or ceramic pot that can do triple duty as a mug or bowl.

If the military is providing food for its troops, don't expect it to be high-end. Military food has a two thousand year old reputation for being awful. This isn't always the fault of the administrative brass. A moving army needed a lot of food, and food wasn't cheap nor was it in endless supply. It took 18,000 pounds of grain to feed a Roman legion (about 5000 men) for one day. The horses, oxen, and pack animals who carried the equipment needed another 40,000 pounds of food and forage. Every single day.[4] It's hard to give high quality food when there are that many mouths to feed.

Troop rations are often porridge or bread. Roman soldiers combined their cooked grains and breads with local vegetables, wild game, vinegar, and wine. Those ingredients would have been purchased from allies and raided from enemies, so the food supply would have been insecure and varying.

A European infantryman in the 17th century, however, would have been given a diet more appropriate to both the culture and the weather. He would have been given 1 ½-2 pounds of rye/wheat bread, ½ pound of meat (often cured, salted, or smoked, and tasteless), 1 pint of wine, beer, or cider—whatever could be found locally. A century later, blocks of dried vegetables were added.[5]

However, the Athenian hoplites (infantry) brought their own food on short campaigns, plus whatever game or pillage they were able to find. Athenian rowers were trapped inside the ships and unable to forage or fish, so they were provided barley meal, onions, and cheese.[6] Whew, can you imagine how much they farted on that menu? Ick!

Eating on the Path to Freedom (or Violence...or Pillage...or Invasion)

Some fantasy novels set up large caravans of livestock trailing along behind the main body of the army. This could be productive in some circumstances, but most of the time those animals would have just been a hindrance. It was hard enough to feed the oxen, horses, and mules that were working, let alone trying to provide enough fodder for additional chickens, ducks, geese, sheep, cows, and pigs! In most cases, it would have been easier to "acquire" the goods along the path.

The Romans had a fabulous system for keeping military campaign costs low: they stole. Stealing, oh right I'm sorry, *pillaging* the spoils of war is a time-honoured tradition. Today, looting and pillaging are frowned upon. Armed conflict is supposed to be between combatants and have as little direct impact on the civilian population as possible. Crops are not to be burned. Schools are not to be bombed. In the age of modern warfare and Geneva conventions concerning the treatment of prisoners, civilians, and the rules of war, our militaries bring their own supplies or purchase them from the local population. This might not even have occurred to the Romans; if you can steal it, why shouldn't you?

Many times, people did not fight for lofty goals such as freedom of expression or the right to vote. The average man's reason for joining the military was more base: making one's fortune.

Just as Captain Wentworth of Jane Austen's *Persuasion* went to sea to make his fortune, so too have countless men in our history. With booty came money. And with money came power.

But before the pillaging could start, everyone needed to eat first. Moving aside niggling things like respect for civilians and property, feeding one's troops was possible without having brought much in the way of supplies.

However, foraging, pillaging, and stealing were not easy tasks. Guards would be needed to stand sentry while others hunted for rabbits, deer, and fish since foraging might take the group a kilometre or two away from the main camp. Likewise, the supply line where all of the siege weapons, prostitutes, and food are stored will need to be guarded, as the supply carts are a prime way to attack a superior force without much risk. Be very wary of this when laying siege to a well-fortified castle. It's not uncommon for women dressed as prostitutes to slip out of the castle through underground tunnels and caves, and emerge in the rear of the baggage to steal what they can carry...and catch fire to the rest!

If your military has allies in enemy territory, those allied traders will need protection. A caravan of forty camels loaded down with grain, cheese, and oil won't be able to protect itself against a heavily-armed and mobile raiding party.

Likewise, if your army sends out raiding parties to villages and farms, they need to be equipped with the means to bring back their spoils. It's rather pointless to raid a village if they can't carry anything back beyond a few female slaves and some moldy bread and there are plenty of both back at the camp.

Living off of the enemy's land had some downsides. It only worked for smaller armies such as the Greek hoplites or Roman legions. There would be only so much grain stored in any one village, and storehouses could be set afire if attack was imminent. However, as armies grew in Europe and as men were forced, or "pressed", into joining the military, the risk of desertion became too great. Further, criminals could not be trusted to only attack other troops and many were just as happy to rape the daughters of allies as of enemies.

However, the largest challenge to the foraging way of war is winter; it is very difficult to forage frozen farms. Fighting in the wintertime could be disastrous even with supplies, let alone when relying on the local landscape to provide for one's troops plus fodder for the animals.

Also, your enemy might put the call out to their people; after all, you are in their land! When Russia did that during the Napoleonic wars, they received 1000 cattle to eat.[7] Do your troops have that much food on hand?

Last, but not least, good ol' scorched earth policy. If you piss off a nation so severely with your invasion, they might just pack up and move north, burning everything in their wake. Try to avoid this happening. Very bad for morale.

So your commanders might decide, upon reading this section, that foraging and pillaging isn't for them. What's left? Well, perhaps the tribute is more to your taste. The Romans were famous for using this technique, as did the Germans during the Thirty Years War (1618-1648). In fact, it worked so well they used it again in the Franco-Prussian War (1870-1871).[8] The tribute system works by conquering lands and allowing those people to keep their lands, ranks, and daughters, provided that a regular tribute of food and goods is given. A steady supply of grain, olives, cheese, and meat would go a long way to reducing the financial costs of war and that always makes the accountants back in the mother country happy.

The problem with this system, beyond the obvious stealing aspect, is that it's difficult to control marauding soldiers, especially if they are criminals pressed into service, aka forced to join up.

If your hero is leading the army and you want him to be liked by all readers (fantasy romance authors: I'm looking at you), perhaps the Wellington system might work best. Arthur Wellesley, 1st Duke of Wellington, led the British Army against Napoleon through Europe. Wellington put out orders that food was to be purchased, not stolen, from allies such as Spain. Also, troops often received rice, meat, peas, and cheese.[9]

Or, perhaps the Russian version of this might work better in your world. In 1812, a law was passed requiring the provinces to provide military commanders with requested supplies. The commanders would give the farmers and towns receipts, which could be reimbursed by the government.[10]

Perhaps your hero will buy the affections of the local populace by spending money around. Of course, your hero will need to raise taxes at home, but that's hundreds of miles away. No need to worry about the home crowd for now.

Since bread was a common wartime food in many cultures, you will need to decide where the bread will be made. There are a few choices for your troops. They can invade a smallish town that has a bakery, or perhaps several farms with their own ovens installed. Then, the ovens could be taken over and used to bake bread for the troops. Though, four ovens going all day long wouldn't be able to produce enough bread for a legion.

You could do what some European armies began doing in the seventeenth century and bring your own field ovens.[11] Just outsource jobs to local bakers in need of a change of scenery and you'll have bread for everyone.

What's for Supper?

Meals would vary greatly, depending upon the weather, the environment, the local population's hostility, and supplies (and money). Fuel would have to be considered, as it was yet another task that someone would have to look after. Breakfast might be a simple affair of leftover bread and meat from the evening meal, and perhaps some beer or cheese. A smart soldier will keep back a little of the cheese and bread to stuff into his pocket for later when he's out on picket duty.

The evening meal would be more bread, more beer, cooked grains, and on good days some cooked wild boar or deer. Perhaps even some fresh fish. Stews might have had pieces of hardtack (a twice baked biscuit) or *buccellatum* (the Roman equivalent) added to them to add bulk and starch.

Russian wartime troops during the Napoleonic era had it much leaner, with only flour, groats, and meat. Thankfully, the vodka ration helped offset any culinary discontent. [12]

More diplomatic officers would go into town to bolster relations and spread some money around. These officers might return with meat, vinegar, wine, cheese, beer, fresh fruits and vegetables, which would be a welcomed delight to digestive systems tired of grain and more grain, with a side of grain. Also, this trade might allow for vital medicinal ingredients such as opium and strong wines, as well as local plants and mixtures.

If lucky enough to have succeeded at this, perhaps the locals won't demand your hero be strung up from the town bell after he has a clandestine affair with a local maiden. Or, the locals might not poison the water supply. It's just never a good idea to steal from the locals unless your troops can overpower them.

Of course, your heroine should be cautious of the food provided by overly helpful villages, too. John the Cappadocian, a 6th century prefect from the Byzantine Empire, ordered bread to be baked for his soldiers. There was a fuel shortage, so the bread wasn't baked long enough. The bread became moldy and killed five hundred soldiers.[13] While it was an accident for poor John, the locals might be more aware of their decisions.

Troops *inside* a castle or fortification would eat rather differently. A castle's storerooms needed enough medicine, grain, alcohol, and meat to survive an onslaught by one's neighbours. Sieges in books are often exciting events. The mobile force arrives and within days it seems that they have either conquered the castle, or the castle troops have successfully repelled the attack. In reality, sieges could last a lot longer. Sometimes, a superior force manages to capture a fortification in days (i.e. the capture of Yang-chou in China in

1645 took a week and a half), whereas the siege of Leningrad in WW2 lasted from 1941 to 1944. Cities and castles needed to be prepared.

If your story takes place inside the city walls, heavy rationing would be implemented. Nothing would go to waste. Giant banquets, fat lords stuffing themselves, and fair ladies being served eight course meals and eating none would be set aside. There would be no time for whiny princesses; the castle's job will be to protect both the lord and his family, plus the lives of the civilians who fled for safety within those walls.

Lunch might be a meager meal of bread and beer, and perhaps cold meat (chances are, breakfast would not be eaten). Supper would be the same, eating the foods that would spoil the soonest since it could be months before they receive reprieve from the attackers. Eggs would be preserved, dairy turned into hard cheese, and some animals slaughtered if there wasn't enough grain to feed them (hopefully there would be enough salt and/or firewood to cure and smoke the meat).

A city under siege will have their food chain and water cut off as fast as possible. A secret underground well and a well-stocked cellar would stand between starvation and submission and stubborn triumph.

The Naval Tradition

Life aboard ship is very different from marching through enemy territory. Infantry can trade, steal, and conquer for their food supplies. The navy's only hope is pulling into a friendly port or overtaking a ship with better supplies than their own. Even in military cultures where soldiers had to provide their own food, naval soldiers were usually supplied something—no guarantees about it being edible, of course. The meat and fish were always over-salted, and often infested with maggots.

Soldiers often ate hardtack or hardbread, a baked until hard-as-rock flour, water, and salt biscuit. Hardtack was expensive to purchase because it took extra fuel, but was vital for long voyages. Bread would mold after a week and expeditions could last weeks or months. Grains often were infested with mice, rats, and bugs, not to mention would spoil in wet and humid conditions. Fresh fruit and green vegetables would spoil too quickly.

Hardtack would be tossed into a pot with some beans, any

Naval Bean Soup with Salt Pork

Soak 5 gallons of beans and 80 pounds of salt pork in water overnight. Boil the beans with 15 pounds of the salt pork. Remove the pork when it's tender. In a separate pot, cook the rest of the pork until tender. Cut up 6 pounds of stale bread and add to the soup, stirring it in.[14]

grains that hadn't molded, along with some onions, garlic, and salt beef or salted tongue. Fresh bread would not exist on-board, since firewood would be very limited, so foods like hardtack meant sailors could have bread every day.

However, there was a bright side for many people when joining the navy. Meals were always hot, protein-rich, and many ships offered a goodly portion of beer to help wash it all down. True, ancient navies did not provide much in the way of food and provisions for their naval staff, but as time progressed, so too did rations. In the Elizabethan era, for example, a British sailor at sea was allotted:

- 1 gallon beer
- 1 lb bread
- ½ lb cheese
- 4 oz butter
- ½ lb meat

Additionally, there might be dried peas, beans, and oats to go into food.[15] When fresh food found its way into naval diets, it was generally sturdy root vegetables like cabbage, carrots, and turnips, with potatoes coming in later centuries.

This might seem sparse to modern senses, but many of the people who joined the navy's low ranks were from the poor underclass anyway. These people had grown up used to irregular, meager meals. The navy provided regular food, and while it wasn't fancy, it was often better than what was waiting for them back home (or in the prisons if they'd chosen that path).

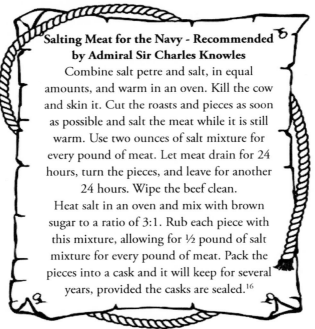

Salting Meat for the Navy - Recommended by Admiral Sir Charles Knowles

Combine salt petre and salt, in equal amounts, and warm in an oven. Kill the cow and skin it. Cut the roasts and pieces as soon as possible and salt the meat while it is still warm. Use two ounces of salt mixture for every pound of meat. Let meat drain for 24 hours, turn the pieces, and leave for another 24 hours. Wipe the beef clean.

Heat salt in an oven and mix with brown sugar to a ratio of 3:1. Rub each piece with this mixture, allowing for ½ pound of salt mixture for every pound of meat. Pack the pieces into a cask and it will keep for several years, provided the casks are sealed.[16]

As well, success for an individual ship meant success for everyone onboard. In such tight quarters, every single person was vital to the success of the ship—right down to the prostitute hiding in the cellars. (You know, the one that wasn't supposed to be down there, but everyone knew she was.) A successful ship would mean fresh supplies when pulling into port, well beyond the standard issue allotment that the homeguard naval administrators allowed.

While an independently wealthy captain would be able to front some luxury goods for his men, such as whiskey and potatoes, a consistently successful captain would always have ready gold and goods on hand at each port. Fresh meat, sugar, rum, citrus, potatoes, and tobacco would flow to the sailors with much rejoicing. After weeks, or months, of eating salted, pickled, and dried food, fresh meat and fruit would have been welcomed. Pulling into port would also allow the seamen an opportunity to purchase their own provisions. They could trade old clothing, booty, and any money on hand for exotic items like oranges, lemons, coconuts, and pineapples.[17]

Luxury items like citrus could be obtained in ports like Port Royal, Jamaica. Citrus, as well as potatoes, tomatoes, and peppers contained Vitamin C, the only weapon against the scourge of the navy: scurvy.

Scurvy was taken very seriously by naval captains, who did not want weakened seamen when faced with pirates, privateers, and marauders, plus the enemy. For the lowest ranks, however, the fear of scurvy at sea varied very little from the threat they faced in European cities before the arrival of cheap potatoes. Life might have been better onboard ship, especially for poor, young boys who would have eventually ended up starving in the streets. However, there was even a limit to how much these individuals would put up with.

Mutiny, Marauding, and Mayhem

Just because soldiers and sailors expect bad food, don't be fooled into thinking you can starve them. The troops still expect edible food and some fairness, especially if the rough ranks are struggling. Sailors who haven't eaten meat in two weeks will not take kindly to a fat commander who is dining on wine and roasted chicken (which should have been kept for its eggs).

An excellent captain would never take more of the beer ration than his men. When the cooper on Captain John Narbrought's vessel found two barrels of beer had leaked, he ordered that everyone drink water that day—himself included. He said that, "for it was ever my order that the meanest boy in the ship should have the same allowance with my self."[18] Add to that a few lucky battles, and that is a captain whose men would defend with their lives.

Captains received the largest portion of any bounty taken from a defeated ship, upwards of 50%. Food stores, ammunition, and the like would, of course, be shared equally, but items like clothing, gold, linens, tobacco, and money would be distributed by rank, with the lower ranks acquiring less and less. When pulling into port, a good captain would spend a portion of his booty on extras for his men: fresh meat, dried fruit, cabbage, rum, additional fuel. Sharing his wealth with his men (and, let's face it, women dressed up like men) would make them work even harder to help earn themselves all more booty, since the Captain would share some of it around again.

If you march your army into a cold climate or sail them into uncharted territory, ensure you have enough beer, women, and meat to keep them from a) starving to death and b) deserting before they starve to death. Once your men start eating the cart oxen, you've lost. Pack up and go home before they end up eating you.

Cannibalism is an ugly, messy word (zombie novels excluded, of course).

Chapter 5: 'tis the Season
The Availability of Food

"Can't you magic up some poptarts? What kind of wizard are you?"
-Frustrated Reader

An interesting thing happened while writing this chapter. I wasn't sure about my original opener, so I sent it to some friends to see if they got the joke. This was what I sent them:

> Readers, confess: How many times have you come across a fantasy novel where the hero has foraged for strawberries, raspberries, and blueberries in early June? How about digging into some delicious lamb stew for the Winter Solstice celebrations?

The response was uniformly confused. Aren't berries available from the late spring to the end of summer? What's wrong with eating lamb in December? Perhaps my joke fell flat but at least I had an additional question answered: this chapter is necessary.

I'm writing this chapter in mid-June in Edmonton, Alberta, which has a significantly shorter growing period than many other cities across Canada, let alone into the US or across the world. I have strawberry plants in south-facing raised beds against my house, and I typically get berries about ten to fourteen days earlier than my neighbours. Mine are mostly ripe right now, and I've been enjoying a couple berries every morning.

Off to the side are my raspberry plants. They won't be ready for another month or so. They'll start to come in around the middle of July and I'll be eating them until the first week of August. When I'm picking my raspberries, the blueberries will also be ripe around that time, provided the squirrels don't get at them.

While I'm eating the raspberries in July, the carrots will only be 3 inches long and very skinny. The tomatoes won't be ready until mid- to late-August, and the potatoes not until September or early October, depending upon the frost. I'll be picking currants and gooseberries around that time and enjoying their tart fruit mixed with the apples from my tree.

I'm sure I'm not alone in having rolled my eyes at fantasy novels and historicals where it's clear the author suffered from the modern urban disconnect. The markets in April are filled with strawberries and new potatoes. Or, the October markets are full of fresh strawberries and apples. Epic fantasy has a bad reputation for doing this, but it's not the only or even worse offender. Historical novels and romance novels (and historical romances) have equal share in the blame, too.

Writing seasons is tough for modern folks living in apartments who never farmed or grew their own food. I grew up living closer to the seasons than most, and I still have a difficult time with the concept. Modern technology, including improvements in greenhouses, transportation, chemicals, and refrigeration, means that we have a nearly-unlimited supply of foods that normally would not be available to use all year around. Going back to the story at the beginning of this chapter, lambs are born in the spring and not at Christmastime.

(Mind you, I'm assuming fetal meat isn't a delicacy in your world. If it is, carry on.)

The technology of lengthening the seasonal availability of plants is not a new concept, though the science of agriculture is relatively new. For the last two centuries, seasons were prolonged by improved methods of irrigation, fertilizer, and hothouse practices, such as covering plants with heat caps. Advancement in seafaring meant that lambs slaughtered in New Zealand's spring could be shipped in ice containers to North America for consumption—even at Christmas. Writing stories set in areas we have never lived (or never visited) adds an extra challenge. It's hard enough to achieve that "like I'm there" approach with a modern piece, let alone when writing a story set in a quasi-Elizabethan London setting! A general idea of when plants and animals come into season is a must if there is a lot of feasting, eating, and everyday living.

There are several ways to get in touch with the natural food and meat production of an area. In my experience, they are always interested in helping authors get the little details right.

- Call your local greenhouse
- Contact your local university or trade school's agricultural department
- Ask food producers at your local farmers' market
- Ask elders and seniors who worked on farms in their youth
- Read gardening books specific to the area you are researching
- Read old cookbooks. Victorian cookbooks are especially helpful, as they give good housekeeping advice, and inadvertently make comments about when specific foods are in season

When creating a world such as a historical romance during the Battle of Hastings, a prehistoric family saga, or a Steampunk adventure, a basic understanding of the availability of food will help bring an extra layer of authenticity to your world. A few minutes of research can save you the frustration later of trying to correct the things your beta readers nitpick apart. Not to mention how readers will pick apart your history!

Britain's Pre-Industrial Agricultural Calendar

Wherever the story is set, take a few moments to consider the agricultural calendar for that area. If you are writing a historical novel, an alternative history, or a Steampunk, you have the benefit of using the actual geographical area that your story is based in.

Since many traditional fantasy stories take place in a quasi-British Isles locale, let's look at the agricultural calendar of Britain. Appendix I gives a generalized look at the traditional British agricultural calendar based on the 19th century work of Henry Stephens, *The Book of the Farm*. This overview is just that: an overview. Stephen's book is several volumes long and covers literally everything necessary for a mid-century Victorian farmer to be prosperous.[1] Chances are, you'll just need a general overview. This section should help you get started with your brainstorming.

As you can see in the Appendix, events like ploughing and planting took a significant amount of time and effort. A fallacy about farming is that horses have been the historical pre-tractor animals. That's incorrect. Large oxen with yokes were used for farming throughout most of humanity's farming history. Horses and harnesses were relative latecomers, with the tractor following shortly after. Regardless of oxen or horses, however, pre-industrialized farming was a tough, physically demanding activity that was absolutely necessary for the survival of both the local population and the urban locations elsewhere in the nation.

Ancient Egyptian Seasons

Akhet: July to October, when the Nile flooded the fields.
Peret: November to February, when crops were planted
Shemu: March to June, when crops were harvested

Looking at the list of tasks throughout the year that are time-sensitive, it's easy to see why farmers were often not allowed to sign up for military duty during major conflicts such as WWI. There was too much to do and a failed harvest could mean a famine.

Harvest time was a small window when the crops had to be brought in before they spoiled, either by rain or frost. All genders and all ages helped at harvest. It's something that Miss Mary Crawford, a city lady in Jane Austen's *Mansfield Park*, couldn't understand. Miss Crawford complained that she was unable to hire a cart to fetch her harp from London. She did not understand that the hay was more important than her harp.

Throughout the year, different activities were either the domain of women or men, but harvest was the domain of everyone. The weather could change at a moment's notice, rain could ruin hay crops, and cereal crops needed cutting. Special planning and staggered planting with neighbours was coordinated so that everyone could work on one field, then move to the next.

As food was harvested and animals slaughtered, people scrambled to preserve as much as they could for the winter months. Once it was all done, people settled in for a cold winter and the cycle began all over again.

The Pantry: Early Refrigerators

Today, we have well-sealed homes, refrigeration, plastic containers, and vacuum-sealed boxes. Ants in the house? We put down sticky traps. Wasps? We purchase decorative hot boxes to kill them. Mosquitos? We buy a blue-light bug zapper. I won't even bring up finding someone's hair in your food at a restaurant. Oh, the horror of it all.

The popular saying, "Cleanliness is next to godliness" is considered rather old-fashioned these days. Many folks assume it's a biblical reference, but it's actually a leftover from the Victorian era about dress and tidiness. However, in the world I described above, an untidy wife could injure or kill her family, especially any young children, if she did not practice cleanliness and strict food safety.

Until the late 19th century, no one knew what caused food-borne illness. They did understand that rotting and spoiled food could make a person sick, but the *why* of that knowledge was not understood. Regardless of the why, people understood that dairy needed to be kept cool on slate or stone shelves, and covered using a cloth with rocks sewn into the corners, or another form of weight, to keep the flies off. They knew that berries could not be eaten when covered in mold. They knew that tables had to be scrubbed with salt before and after preparing meat for preservation.

There are worms on the cherries
And slugs on the roses,
And ants in the sugar
And mice in the pies.
The rubbish of spiders
No mortal supposes,
And ravaging roaches
And damaging flies.
-The Housewife's
Lament[2]

A common question I'm asked is how food was stored without refrigerators and freezers. Today, we're told we cannot leave food out for more than two hours or else it should be thrown in the garbage. We buy insulated bags to ensure that our frozen meat stays frozen while we pick up groceries. It's hard for us to imagine how anyone ate without these modern safety mechanisms. So how did the pantries of the past keep food away from pests and have food ready for the cook?

Imagine your heroine sneaks into the larder to seduce her sweetheart. It's a common enough situation in many books. So what would she see in there?

First, the room would be clean. Floors would have been scrubbed regularly, as well as swept, so that dust didn't accumulate. There might not be a window, or if there is one, it's small and North-facing, so that it lets in a small amount of light without warming up the food. It might have a screen over it, so that fresh air can circulate inside the pantry without bugs and wind. During the winter, the shutters could be closed to keep the cold air out.

If hunting season has begun, she might need to duck and dodge the pigeons and pheasants hanging from the rafters on hooks, feathers still on. In poorer homes, there might a duck or a goose hanging, or one pheasant that was a gift from the local lord.

There would be shelves on the walls filled with food and jars, so she'll need to be extra careful about not bumping up against those. The bottom shelf would be made of stone or slate. Raw meat would be on plates in pots on the cold stones. There might be a drop pan on the floor, however, to catch any blood that might drip from around the edges of a plate.

Above the meat might be another slate or stone shelf with fresh vegetables, especially root vegetables which can be harvested and stored. This, of course, wouldn't be the major storage of vegetables. Rather, just a few for the day's meals. The rest are either above the pantry in a loft, or perhaps above a shed taking over part of the hay loft.

The main shelf would house the leftovers from the previous meal in pots with covers, or perhaps a joint of meat covered with linen. If this isn't an estate home with its own dairy room, milk and soft cheese would be here, covered with a weighted cloth to keep the flies away.

Gammon hams and smoked fish might hang from the ceiling to protect them from the cats, which are roaming around to protect the bags of ground grain and dried peas on the floor. The shelves high above will be filled with crockery jars storing jams, jellies, and the like covered in stretched, dried pig bladders. Wooden boxes would hold dried fruit with paper separating each layer. Bundles of drying flowers and herbs will be hanging from nails on the wall, which will add a lovely scent of rosemary and lavender to the pantry.

Richer pantries would have a spice box or small sugar cupboard under lock and key, a chest of oatmeal, and a trough for various mixing and preparing of meat.[3]

Cooking Common Pantry Foods

Look in any North American kitchen and you'll probably find cheese, milk, ketchup, eggs, jam, soy sauce, and bacon. They are readily available foods. It's nothing to pop down to the local grocery store to pick up these ingredients to add to stews, soups, rice dishes, and desserts. But do you know how much work goes into those foods?

In a standard medieval European household, many of the above ingredients were fairly typical foods. Even if the very poor didn't have all of these at once, they would have had one or two at a time. Because of how common these foods were, it's easy to assume that they were easy to obtain. Let's take a look at how to make three of these common foods and the processes involved in making them: cheese, ketchup, eggs.

Cuttin' the Cheese

I was once told that a book cannot be called epic fantasy unless the hero eats cheese and bread. It's an easy, cheap meal. After all, wasn't cheese everywhere because it was easy to make?

Handmade cheese is a labour-intensive process. So much so that many farms used specialists of the trade (in the same way that thatchers or stone masons were a trade). When the cows had their calves in the spring, the dairy maids, or the farm mistress if she couldn't afford help, would begin the cheese-making process. This young woman was no weakling, having to pound, mold, shape, and do more pounding to make butter and cheese. That's where the ample dairy maid image comes from: a woman needed a lot of strength to do the job.

Cheese would have come in different colours, depending upon the time of the year it was made and the types of grass the cows were eating. Cheese would have ranged from white to orange. Today, we add dye to our cheese so that it's all the same colour. Many people don't recognize cheddar unless it's bright orange. In pre-industrial times, no such uniformity would have existed.

I'm going to cover cheese making in much more detail in Chapter 6, but I do want to cover the basics here. To make cheese, rennet needed to be made first. Rennet is a group of enzymes in a cow's stomach. One of those enzymes causes milk to coagulate, separating milk into the curds and whey, which is why it's used in cheese.

Rennet comes from a young calf, ideally one not yet weaned. As soon as the calf is killed, the stomach is removed. After removing any curd, the stomach needs to be scoured with salt inside and out. It should be left to drain after that for a couple of hours. The stomach gets sewn up with two handfuls of salt inside, or stretched and salted, and left to dry in a cool, dark place. It could also be left to soak in a basin of water.

It could take up to eight days of pressing the cheese curds before a round was formed. Once these large wheels of cheese were cured and hardened, a process that could take months, some would be sold at market. The price would be much higher than if purchasing soft cheese or a poorly-made cheese, so the hero might be shocked to discover that he can't afford a well-known (what we'd call an "award winning" cheese today) wedge of cheese after all. In the 13th century, a pound of good cheese could run up to half a day's wages for a poor labourer. Of course, this assumed the merchants would even be willing to cut one of their large rounds into smaller pieces without raising the prices!

Ketchup Makes Everything Taste Better

That's right; ketchup has indeed existed for centuries, though the tomato-based condiment we call ketchup is only a couple centuries old, first appearing in an American cookbook. Mushroom ketchup, walnut ketchup, plus condiments like fish sauce were popular salty sauces and could be served on hot meat or used to flavour leftovers. Mushroom ketchup, in particular, is incredibly salty and tasty, similar to an earthy soy sauce.

I attempted my own version, basing it off a recipe from Jane Austen's era. It took three attempts, since the fermenting mushrooms on the kitchen counter scared several members of my household, who promptly tossed the black, slimy button mushrooms into the garbage. This is rather frustrating when you are on Day 10 of the fermentation. It was even more frustrating when the cats sprayed the later batches thinking urine could improve the smell. I personally didn't think 'shrooms smelled all that bad, but I'm just a human. What do I know?

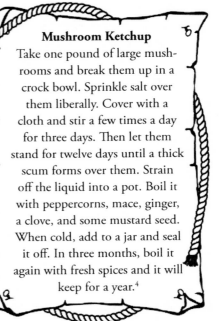

Mushroom Ketchup

Take one pound of large mushrooms and break them up in a crock bowl. Sprinkle salt over them liberally. Cover with a cloth and stir a few times a day for three days. Then let them stand for twelve days until a thick scum forms over them. Strain off the liquid into a pot. Boil it with peppercorns, mace, ginger, a clove, and some mustard seed. When cold, add to a jar and seal it off. In three months, boil it again with fresh spices and it will keep for a year.[4]

When I was finally done, mine tasted nearly identical to soy sauce. I was pretty disappointed that so much work went into creating one tablespoon of a pungent form of soy sauce. Now, I'd purchased my mushrooms from the grocery store; they cost me money. If I was in an area where there were an abundance of wild mushrooms, I could easily see the use in such a condiment. But I know one thing: I'd never give that precious liquid away to strangers who stop by my house begging for handouts!

There are even more complicated dishes in cookbooks like al-Baghdadi's *The Book of Dishes (1226)* where it takes forty days of work to produce a condiment sauce that resembles a soy/fish sauce hybrid.[5]

Eggs

Today, we purchase eggs by the size. Extra-large, large, and medium are common sizes. They are all from chickens, and all in uniform colour and size. Farm eggs, especially in the Middle Ages, would not have resembled our eggs' uniformity to such an exacting degree.

Eggs would be all different sizes and colours. Some would be brown, others white, and some would be speckled. The duck and goose eggs might get mixed up with the chicken eggs on occasion, though it is easy to tell the difference because of the size. A kind family might give your adventurers a basket of eggs for their journey covered with a piece of cloth. Inside, your party finds large duck and goose eggs, various sizes of chicken eggs, and maybe even a few speckled blue-grey quail eggs, tiny against the others.

Hens also do not lay eggs at a regular rate. During warm months, well-fed chickens lay lots of eggs. It's difficult to say how many eggs medieval and ancient birds laid, but free-range chickens today can lay 300+ eggs a year each. However, they lay less when winter sets in. Without a proper feed that encourages them to keep producing, the eggs can dwindle down to nearly nothing in bad weather. Keeping poultry safe in a coop or a fenced yard also can help keep the predators at bay, so that you don't wake up to find your hens dead[6].

And remember to preserve your eggs during bumper laying!

Trade: Online Selling the Medieval Way

I have been instructed by numerous individuals to begin this section with the following public service announcement.

Clears throat

Taps microphone

Attention writers of the world:
Potatoes, sweet potatoes, tomatoes, and corn did not exist in Europe
during Roman times. Nor the Dark Ages. Nor for a good portion of
the Middle Ages, either.

We tend to associate specific foods with certain groups of people. The Irish, potatoes. Italians, tomatoes. Canada's western first peoples, bannock. In actual fact, all of those foods came much later in each of those peoples' histories. Sure, today they are integral to their gastronomic heritage. It's just that these foods are a part of their later food histories.

Take the potato. This rather humble vegetable, so reviled by current dieting trends, originated in the Andes of South America and has at least eight thousand years of history in that area. The Incas first began cultivating potatoes six thousand years ago. Potatoes didn't arrive in Europe until after the conquistadors returned to the Spanish court with their spoils of war. By the close of the 16th century, however, potatoes were being cultivated in Britain, with Scotland and Ireland following suit shortly after.

I find it difficult to picture many European traditional meals with potatoes excluded. It's even a challenge thinking about stew without starchy potatoes added into the mix. Yet, that was the reality for thousands of years. If your world is set in a fantastical ancient Russian fantasy, your heroine will not be cooking the hero potatoes with his venison stew.

Sorry, folks.

But but but! I know what you're thinking. Corn was totally available in Europe. Primary European sources call for corn in recipes. That must mean they had corn! The first time I came across a 14th century document referencing corn, I got confused, too. After all, corn originated in Mesoamerica. The Aztecs even had a corn god (Centeotl)![7] It wasn't until a professor explained my definition of corn was wrong that it finally all made sense.

North Americans refer to corn as the yellow or white kernel cob that's great with butter and salt. Its official name is actually maize, and its unofficial, out-of-use name is Indian Corn. "Corn" is actually a catch-all term used to describe cereal crops, such as the common grains of wheat, barley, rye, and oats. Those aren't the only cereal crops in the world, however. Barley, teff, durum, and emmer are other grains that are less known, but were still important to humanity's diet for thousands of years.

Let's say you want your heroine to eat grits and potatoes for breakfast. It might even be vital to the story that she eats grits and potatoes. You look around at your geography and begrudgingly accept that it's not possible for those to grow there. You don't want to risk being attacked by fervent fans for having potatoes in your fantasy based on a quasi-German medieval world. What do you do?

Trade!

The economic success of a country today means participating in the global economy. Trade is vital to bring balance to the abundance and deficiencies of nations. This hasn't really ever changed, only that we are able to trade significantly more product and with more nations these days because of modern transport.

Cheat sheet!
Ancient Egyptians, Greeks, and Romans didn't know about "potatoes, tomatoes, red peppers, brown beans, avocadoes, pineapple, papaya, cassava, paprika, maize, vanilla, cocoa, peanuts, kangaroo meat, kiwis, and turkeys." [8]

Trade is taken for granted. On a national scale, we trade all sorts of products, from oil to coal, from steel to medical isotopes, from strawberries to avocados. Trade isn't just a lofty ideal that governments and corporations have the monopoly over. I only need to turn on my computer to purchase building blocks from China, New York, and Nova Scotia to help me complete my to-scale model of The Tower of London. I can head over to various craft sites and find homemade goodies and delights that I can't access locally. It's all so easy and I can shop in my PJs, something that I'd be censored for if I did that at the local farmers' market.

The easiest way to develop a trade route for your fantasy novel is to research historical ones. Trade has been around a long time and there is plenty of recorded history about it. From the thriving sea trade connecting India, Egypt, and the coast of East Africa, to the horrific journey of African slaves to the New World, trade has been a key component to humanity's development.[9]

Spice Trade and Silk Road

One of the most famous trade routes is the spice trade across India, the Middle East, and across North Africa. Countries like Britain and Ireland did not have the climate necessary to evolve the exotic spice plants many of us take for granted today. Our standard Christmas spices—cinnamon, nutmeg, cardamom, ginger, cloves, pepper—are imported from all around the world, many from the Fertile Crescent area, India, or North Africa.

When you look at period cookbooks from France and Britain, it appears that spices were common in the Middle Ages. Recipe after recipe contain references to saffron, pepper, and ginger. Does that mean books like *Forme of Curry* (Forms of Cookery, circa ~1390) should be taken as proof that spices were cheap and readily available?

Not exactly. It's important to understand the context of these cookery books. These early British and French cookbooks were written for a different age. These were for chefs who already knew the basic recipes and needed reminders and notes for feasts, banquets, weddings, and coronation parties. Rare would be the person eating saffron and ginger in every dish outside of the very top of society.

The spice trade created wealthy merchant guilds and rich empires, plus brought a taste of the exotic to isolated lands. It also changed the balance of power throughout the world. Taxes and tariffs, as well as the excessive number of middlemen in between the source of the spice and the dinner plate, prompted monarchs at the tail end of the Asian trade routes to fund the famous explorers to seek out new trade routes. The motto Gold, God, and Glory emerged and plunged the world into a frenzied scramble to find nutmeg, pepper, and cloves.

The spice trade didn't just bring spice, however. It brought sugar, silk, India muslin, and wine. Egypt was shipping its wares in the third millennium B.C. Tombs have been excavated in Egypt containing wines that did not originate from there. Scorpion I's tomb (3150 B.C.) is filled with imported wine, leaving behind residues hinting at the trade locations: savory, balm, senna, coriander, germander, mint, sage, thyme. Later, around the first millennium B.C., the Phoenicians (from modern day Lebanon) also developed an extensive wine industry.

Even though these civilizations lacked the great ships of later centuries, they still managed to connect the Fertile Crescent with North Africa, Italy, and India, and beyond to even Indonesia!

Cinnamon, along with pepper, ginger, and cardamom, continued in its popularity into the Roman era, and well into the Middle Ages. Taxes, tariffs, and tolls had been frequently added to spices to elevate them to the highest ranks of society.

Cinnamon's travels were especially long. It grew in Indonesia, was transported to Madagascar, and shipped to Somalia, which was known as Cinnamon Land. The spice than moved up to the Red Sea, overland to the Nile, and then shipped across the Mediterranean[10]. You can see why spices were only for the very rich for most of humanity's history!

Woman using a winnowing tray to separate wheat grains from the chaff. She'd put her dried wheat in the tray and then toss it. The heavy grains would remain in the tray, while the lighter chaff would blow away.

Wheat Trade into China

In present-day Xinjiang, China, skeletons were discovered in the Tarim Basin. Dubbed the Tarim mummies, they date back to 1900 BC - 200 AD. This major discovery has provided a number of clues to trade and language in the area, and has generated debate that the site is early evidence of cultural, language, and trade exchanges between Indo-European and Chinese.

The debate of what the site proves is well outside the scope of this book. I do want to mention one of the important archeological findings: the Beauty of Loulan.

The mummy is the oldest found in the basin so far (nearly 4000 years old). Importantly, she carried wheat and a winnowing tray in her burial spot. Evidence shows that wheat did not exist in the Tarim Basin during this period—why would she have those items then?

To some scholars, this suggests Southern Siberian traders came south to Tarim Basin, through the Altair and Tien Shan mountains by horseback to trade wheat and tools.[11]

In this tale lies many fabulous story ideas—either historical or fantastical—waiting to be written. A woman bringing her magical seeds with her to a new land. A girl sold to a rival warlord to buy peace and introduces wheat to an area. Whatever the reason, it is tidbits of food history like this that can make your fiction explode with life.

New World Goodies

The Americas gave Europe new and exciting foods. While the conquistadors were in search of gold and glory when they landed in the New World, they nonetheless encountered a new array of foods and cuisines that still influence us today. How the women of the Middle Ages survived without chocolate and vanilla we might never know, but future generations were at least saved from this depressing situation. Thankfully, sugar wasn't exclusive to the

Americas. Europe, North Africa, and the Near East might not have survived otherwise.

With exploration and trade, turkey, potatoes, hot peppers, and peanuts were all to be introduced to thousands of diets over the course of centuries of exploration and colonization.

Fish, Rum, Molasses

Visitors to Newfoundland often comment on the food evolution of the isolated island. Way out in the North Atlantic, it lacks the rich soil for large-scale agriculture (not to mention it has a small mountain range going through it) and is assaulted by an unrelenting coastal wind. Even the Vikings who landed a thousand years ago didn't stay.

So, with its inhospitable climate, rough terrain, and isolation, how did Jamaican Rum and molasses become staples of this place? The answer is quite simple: trade. Newfoundland became part of the Triangle Trade: sugar/rum from the Caribbean to Europe, goods from Europe to Africa, slaves from Africa to the Caribbean.

After the arrival of John Cabot in 1497, there was a mad scramble to set up summer outposts to take advantage of the rich cod stocks of the Grand Banks. There, opportunistic fishermen from the mother countries came to make their fortunes in the New-Found-Land that had fish so abundant you could dip your hand into the water and catch one, or so the legend says.

With the ports and plantations expanding in the West Indies, a steady supply of cheap food was needed to feed the slaves. The waters from New England to Newfoundland had an abundance of fish, especially cod, which was salt cured for long storage.

Once the trading ships arrived in the Caribbean to sell their salt fish, they took on molasses and rum as cargo, along with sugar, tobacco, and other foods unique to the area. Newfoundland didn't have a natural source of sugar (neither did most of the northeastern coast of Canada), but sugar was fetching too high of a price to sell to fishermen in a remote outpost. That precious material needed to go to Europe. However, molasses was a sweet byproduct of the sugar process. It was sweet and stored well.

And, well, rum. Do I really need to explain why this is a great thing to have?

So, the fish for molasses and rum trade began, a history that exists to this day, influencing the island's cuisine and culture.

Come to the Dark Side: We Have Bad Stuff

Trade also has a darker side. Human beings have regularly been transported in our history. The Romans and Spartans are well-known to have had slave populations that accounted for a fifth to a third of their populations. The development of the Americas was reliant on the slave ships coming across the Atlantic from Africa. Even today, the trafficking of humans (especially young girls) is alive and well in our world with 2.4 million people being exploited at any given time.[12]

Disease travels with trade, as well as invasion. Individuals from crowded, unsanitary urban centres would have a high immunity to many infectious diseases than those in small communities far away. Jared Diamond, in *Guns, Germs, and Steel*, argues the Andes, Mesoamerica, and the US southeast had urban centres, but they lacked high-volume trade routes and were more isolated from infectious disease outbreaks than their European counterparts.

> **Gruesome Infectious Diseases**
>
> Smallpox, measles, influenza, plague, tuberculosis, typhus, cholera, malaria

Trade has always been an important aspect of human development. Bartering, selling, buying, trading of favours for goods. Whatever the form, the action of exchanging my goods for yours has deep roots in the development of societies and can bring wondrous conflict, relationships, and potatoes to any epic fantasy world. Don't limit yourself.

Chapter 6: Where's the Refrigerator? Food Storage and Preservation, Pre-refrigeration Days

"All the utensils, shells, and dressers, kept with the strictest regard to cleanliness... There should be shutters to keep out the sun and hot air. Meat hung in a dairy will spoil milk. The utensils of the dairy should all be made of wood: lead, copper, and brass are poisonous, and cast iron gives a disagreeable taste to the productions of dairy.[1]" –Mrs. Radcliffe in *A Modern System of Domestic Cookery* (1823), on the need for cleanliness when making dairy products.

This was a fun chapter to research because food preservation is one of those technological advances that continues to astound and amaze me. Consider this: someone, somewhere, figured out that the contents of a newborn calf's stomach caused dairy to not spoil and could instead turn milk into a new food. Seriously awesome. In fact, many of the storage and preservation techniques I'm going to discuss in this chapter are so old that they predate recorded history.

Food preservation allowed humans to settle into agrarian communities, allowed for population growth, travel, and long-distance expansion, colonization and/or expansion (depending on who you ask).

Modern urban dwellers don't worry about running out of food, so many of us make our jams and jellies for fun. It's to show off to our parents (look what I made, Mom!) or to try something new (and make a complete mess of the kitchen). It's something that is for fun, not a task that's necessary to your survival over winter.

This chapter is different than most of the others. I rely heavily on primary sources (i.e. old cookbooks) to explore various techniques and recipes. Because of this unique focus, this chapter will contain perhaps more details than you will ever want to use in your stories. In fact, please don't use this much detail! Use this information as a way to add small tidbits to your work. It's difficult to write about someone making cheese unless you know how cheese is made. And, even then, it's hard to explain it in any meaningful fashion. Just ask my poor editors!

You might not need to include all of the detail, but you might find it helpful to have this information to picture it in your mind! Success is not in the endless details, but rather the small details.

For the non-writers reading this book, this chapter is dedicated to you. All of the topics covered in this chapter were specifically requested by readers who wanted to know how their favourite historical heroes and heroines would have survived. This one's for you!

Getting Started in the Kitchen

When writing a fantasy, or a historical romance, it's important to consider what your peeps will be eating all year around—assuming that you let them live that long. Don't worry; I won't judge if you kill off your main characters. *I promise.*

As I discussed in Chapter 4, pre-industrialized societies heavily relied on their local seasons and environment to maintain their level of self-sufficiency. Today, a poor harvest of oranges in Florida means I will be paying $8 a bag for a couple of months. Two hundred, two thousand, or ten thousand years ago, a poor harvest could mean utter destitution or even starvation. Keeping a balance between your poor harvests and the effects on your kingdoms (or peasants) is important.

The different climates on earth have allowed for a variety of preservation techniques. Some will not work in your fantasy world and others may seem backward to your people. Food preservation is a technology that would have spread with the development of trade networks, so your merchants can have plenty of opportunities to scoff or marvel at the pickled herring, chickens in jars, and potted shrimps (cooked shrimp covered with a salted butter seal and stored on the shelf for a couple of months).

Europeans, especially northern peoples, learned to pickle, salt, and smoke their meat. With the humidity in places like Ireland, salted and pickled meat would not be affected as it would be hung inside in a pantry or larder. However, the system of drying fish on rooftops, as many communities in the Middle East did, would not work so well in Ireland. A trader bringing that "knowledge" to Ireland would be scoffed at indeed!

Food preservation often could bring a community together. Harvesting the grain was not doable by one farmer and his family; they often brought in outside labourers and any help they could spare. Even today, neighbours and relatives often help each other during harvest. Farmers would need to speak to their neighbours and organize staggered planting so that everyone could help cut the fields and bring in the grain and hay, making it the perfect place for a low-country romance.

If your world has sufficient technology to create ovens (or have stoves and ranges, such as in Regency and Steampunk sagas), fruit can be dried even in the wettest of countries. Bread ovens took a bit to get going, but they stayed warm for quite a while. Since fuel was precious, it would have been a waste to let a cooling bread oven sit empty. The oven might be too cool for baking bread, but it would be the perfect environment for drying apple slices, pears, and plums.

In societies where wood stoves were used, apples could be sliced and hung on strings over the stove, the warmest and driest part of the house. Mushrooms, likewise, can be threaded with a needle and twine, and hung over the hearth or stove. (You won't want to do this in a Steampunk story or any urban-based story with coal. Coal stoves eventually coat everything in black soot that tastes really foul. Follow the advice of Mrs. Beeton (a Victorian cookery guru) and put the drying goodies in the wooden cupboards near the stove, where spices and salt were stored. Still warm, but less soot.)

These small details can be twisted and massaged into making a lovely setting. The masculine alpha hero has just scooped up the young, spirited heroine, who fell and hurt her ankle, and has carried her through the torrential rain to her widowed mother's home. Along the way, he considers that this redhead vixen is an offering from the gods of love and hastens his way across the fields. He enters the hovel and sees mushrooms strung up across the hearth, drying. Strings of apples dangle on nails in the wall. The mother is covered in flour.

And the hero realizes these people are way too rustic for his refined tastes, dumps the injured girl on the nearest piece of furniture and high tails it out of there![2]

Making Food Last

There used to be video of a living history group floating around, where the group was trying to replicate a medieval fish recipe using salt cod. Now, salt cod can get as dry as sand on the outside, though you can still bend the fillet. It's not meant to be eaten without some serious forethought and prep, though these poor souls didn't realize it.

They took the fish out of its plastic wrapper, broke it into pieces, and dropped the fish into a pot of boiling water over a fire. There was just enough water to cover the fish, though apparently they'd added more. An hour later (which was represented by about 15 seconds of fast action video), the fish was falling apart and they had to use slotted spoons to get the pieces out of the water. Confident it was cooked, one of the men put a forkful of the fish in his mouth and promptly spit it out, kicking and swearing. Tears streamed down his cheeks.

I pointed and laughed. Salt fish really shouldn't be eaten straight; it needs to be soaked first. Salt burns!

Different parts of the world have developed their own early strategies for preserving meat and plants. Thousands of years ago, people discovered meat hung over a smoking fire would keep through the summer heat and add a lovely taste to it. We've never looked back.

Tribes around the lower Nile dried fish and poultry; the hot desert sun was perfect for laying fish out on the roofs of houses to dry. Cooler, damper regions would need more work to dry meat to remove the moisture. Beating, squeezing, and weighting down with stones were all used to press out juices. Salt was also used to assist with drying of meat and fish.

The first peoples of North America used various methods of drying and smoking fish, depending upon their natural environments. Some would have used stacked stones and birch bark to make a smoke chimney. Others used a rack system, where fish was cut open and laid flat (this worked for meat, too) and attached to the rack. Then it could be dried or smoked, depending upon the area and the rain!

Salt cured meats and vegetables were staples in many European countries before refrigeration. Salt has two very handy properties. First, it is anti-bacterial, meaning it slows or kills the growth of bacteria on the food. By stopping (or even slowing) the growth rate of bacteria, raw meat that would, at best, last four days in the larder could now last three months. Also, if your heroine lives in a country where it gets cold enough to keep food frozen all winter, that salted food can then last until spring!

Meat could be frozen in some parts of the world. Canada can get pretty cold in certain areas. The Beothuks made their own version of freezer bins to store meat. They used birch bark and spruce bark containers to store chunks of meat that had been cut off the bone after the frost had arrived. A few meat quarters were wrapped and stored in one of their storehouses. Seal bladders and stomachs would store rendered oils. With the temperatures staying well below freezing, everything stored in those houses would remain safe to eat for months. Anytime there was a shortage of game during the winter, they only had to head back to one of their storehouses for supplies.[3]

Pemmican is perhaps one of the best-known preserved food stuffs in North America. It's often in the form of beef, bison, or elk jerky, often with BBQ sauce or peppercorns. This is a modernized version of the traditional recipes, which were as varied as the many groups who made the winter staple. Every region had a different pemmican recipe, all based on the raw materials and climate of the area. However, there are some similarities between many of the traditional recipes, so I'll share my personal favourite.

JT was a great man who I'd met when I worked at The Mustard Seed. He'd done so many things in his life, including running across most of Canada and into the US (seriously) and was once a semi-professional boxer. Before his death, he shared many stories and traditions with me, treating me almost like an apprentice of information. He passed away before he'd finished many of the stories, sadly.

He did share a traditional pemmican recipe with me, which I was able to adapt before he died. He even got to taste it and laughed about it being the worst texture of pemmican he'd ever eaten. At least he liked how it tasted.

Take local, free-range, organic meat (I used bison). Cut into thin strips and dry it. I used a dehydrator, which I think was why the texture was so…industrial. However, it was the middle of an Albertan winter; it was the best I could do. Once the meat is dry, pound it down into a powder. JT said the women would do this kneeling over a large stone on top of a buckskin, and then using a handheld stone, grind the meat into a fine powder. I used a food processor. I'm a wuss. See the part about humans being lazy.

Then came the fun part. Once I had my dehydrated meat crumbles, I mixed it with the same quantity of fat. Like meat, there are varying degrees of fats, with bone marrow being on the top. Since I grew up eating boiled bone marrow (and absolutely love it to this day), I decided to use that. I boiled up several beef bones and scooped out the marrow once it was cool enough to handle. I threw in some dried cranberries and blueberries, and mixed it all up.

I formed it into a brick. Once cooled, the solid brick can be sliced or left as is. I wrapped it in plastic wrap because I'm a heathen, but your adventuring party would mostly likely have it wrapped in rawhide and sealed with tallow to keep the air out. It could be wrapped in another couple layers of hide or cloth and buried in strategic areas, if you have a nomadic group who visits the same locations.

Now, how to cook this brick of fatty goodness? I made soup from it by breaking off a corner and pouring hot water over it into a mug. After a few minutes, I had an instant rich soup filled with plump berries, fat, and meat. It was incredibly satisfying and filling just even eating it straight. Adding it to a pot of stew would have made the meal even more exciting. It definitely is a necessary staple for winter travel, and historically it was sought after by traders. No wonder. This could save a person from starvation and improve morale when the temperatures dip to -40C.

Pickling and Preserving Eggs

Chickens have gone through a lot of change in the last several centuries. A nice-sized collection of eighteen of today's chickens will give you anywhere between ten and twenty eggs a day. Chickens went through a fair bit of breeding and tinkering during the Victorian era, not even to mention the engineering that goes

95

into today's poultry concerns. They also had cruder means of keeping the chickens warm in the winter months, so without specialized feed, poultry produced fewer eggs during the cold months.

Henry Stephens in *The Book of the Farm* introduced recipes for special feed, based on the era's science. It's probable there wasn't a huge scientific knowledge about the nutritional needs of chickens in the 8th century.

For the sake of this work, I'm going to use the guideline of eighteen medieval chickens producing three to six eggs a day.[4] Six eggs a day, even for only the summer months and dropping to three for the rest, is still a lot of eggs for a small family. Even with cakes of the day using eggs by the pound, one could only eat so many eggs, especially since so many other foods were readily available.

Some eggs would be sold, either at market or shipped away if trains or airships were invented. Others would be preserved in a lime solution. Still others would be pickled in brine for either sale in the winter months or for the family's consumption. Pickled eggs would be difficult to carry if backpacking, but might be a nice change of pace if stopping over in a town for a few days.

Pigs Have More Than Bacon

Many a bard's tale has the heroine pulling her slices of bacon out of her pack, along with crusty bread. She fries up the bacon on some hot rocks in a fire and lattices them across chunks of bread. This isn't all that inaccurate, actually. We picture bacon slices as narrow marbled slips of meat with lots of artificial smoke favour. Perhaps that isn't what your heroine was cooking up, but it's close. She might have been cooking up smoked tenderloin, smoked or salted pork belly, or rinded bacon (where the skin is left on when they cut into the belly to make the slices). She'd cut her bacon by hand from a chunk, as opposed to having individual slices already wrapped and vacuum sealed. Also, her bacon would probably be wrapped in waxed paper (if very lucky) or cloth and/or cabbage leaves (more likely) and stored in her pack.

Have you ever read a fantasy story where the heroine carries her rashers of bacon in the summer months in her backpack? This isn't too out of the ordinary, but there wouldn't be as much bacon in the summer months as there would be in the autumn or winter. Pigs are usually slaughtered in the autumn. Spring piglets wouldn't have fattened up enough to make killing them worthwhile, though the occasional suckling pig would be killed if there were too many to feed, a shortage of meat, or if an animal was being a complete pain and was sent to the slaughter by an annoyed farmer.

The lack of fodder is another reason for the autumn slaughter as well. With winter about to set in, farmers had to be choosey about what animals they could keep over the winter months, especially in

Religious Considerations

Does your world have religious considerations that prevent parts of an animal to be eaten? Or, does your society have taboos against eating specific animals—or even eating animals at all? Add extra challenges and cultural flair by adding food-related taboos to your fiction.

places where snow fell and green plants died off. They would keep their best breeders for the winter and butcher the rest.

The autumn and winter, and even early spring if a person was lucky, would be when you'd eat bacon. In the summer months, it might be cheaper for your heroine to be noshing down on lamb, beef, and chicken, not to mention fresh produce such as berries, vegetables, and nuts.

A smoked piece of bacon is going to be more expensive than a salt cured piece soaking in brine, but worth it. Can you imagine the mess in the bottom of your heroine's backpack with the drip-drip-drip of salt brine leaking out? Ick.

Of course, bacon isn't the only thing a pig can be turned into. In fact, the entire pig can be eaten. A large celebration, such as a prehistoric summer solstice celebration at Stonehenge, might roast whole pigs for communal feasting. Since it would be for communal eating, the bones and carcass might be discarded, buried, or burned, depending upon tradition and religious beliefs. Whereas a coronation celebration might roast several pigs over open-pit hearths for the aristocracy and religious figures. After the guests have passed out, servants might carefully cut up the carcass to be distributed as alms to the poor who have been lined up outside the palace gates for two days waiting for the leftovers.

A country farmer, however, would probably not roast a whole pig. A pig has a surprising amount of meat on it and has many uses beyond bacon and roasts. A Berkshire pig, for example, can produce about one hundred pounds of useable meat, not counting organs, bones, and fat. To give you an idea of how much meat that is, I get a Berkshire every November from a local

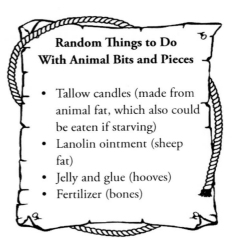

Random Things to Do With Animal Bits and Pieces

- Tallow candles (made from animal fat, which also could be eaten if starving)
- Lanolin ointment (sheep fat)
- Jelly and glue (hooves)
- Fertilizer (bones)

farm called Irving Farm Fresh. The meat fills up one of my freezers completely and I don't bring home the head, feet, skin, blood, or internal organs!

Bones would be sold at market to poorer individuals for their pottage and soup pots to add some fat and flavour. While the marrow in pigs' bones is not as tasty as beef marrow, it is quite filling and hearty, and would add some needed fat to a thin soup.

The organs and intestines would be eaten, sold, or used right away. Sheep and pig intestines were fabulous storage devices. Once washed, scrubbed with salt, and dried, "forcemeat" (sausage filling) could be stuffed inside it. The filling could be made with whatever was in the larder, such as cold fowl or veal, ham, bacon, beef-suet, bread crumbs, and eggs.[5] These could be boiled or baked, and would make good cold leftovers.

To make sausages that could be eaten cold, lean and fatty pork would be combined with salt, pepper, allspice, and in later years, saltpetre (the stuff used in gunpowder). The meat would be rubbed with this and let to sit over a pan (the liquid would drip out). After six days, the pork would be cut up and mixed with shallots and garlic. All of this would be stuffed into clean oxen intestines. The ends would be tied up, quick twists throughout would make links, and then the entire sausage would be wrapped in cloth, and hung up to smoke. The sausage could be eaten raw, or boiled and eaten hot.[6]

The muscle of the pig would be cut into different cuts of roasts to be prepared for long-term storage. Smoking and salting are the most common methods we think of when we think of pork, which is where we get our smoked hams and bacon. The belly can also be turned into salt pork, which could be fried and the rendered grease be used as pan oil (you can do this with bacon, too). Salt pork can be added to pots of soup or pottage, as well. The benefit of salt pork is that no additional cleaning, rinsing, or soaking is needed, since its salt would only add to the flavour of dishes, as opposed to making more work for the cook.

When houses moved to having chimneys, pork roasts could be smoked in the family's chimney, out of the way and utilizing the firewood already in the firepit or stove to heat the house and cook the meals. In places where firewood was short (including urban areas), chimney smoking would be a money and time saver. However, if your urban areas are using coal, do not put the meat up the chimney! Coal smoke does not add flavour. At all.

> **Huh? Houses Didn't Always Have Chimneys?**
>
> Not at all. The communal longhouse that existed in many cultures is because of the lack of chimneys. Even after chimneys were invented, they were incredibly expensive and common people carried on using the open fire hearth inside a circle of stones or bricks for years after.

Anyone with some space can make a smoker out of an old wooden barrel. Drill holes in the barrel so that wooden skewers can be added, where the meat will hang (make sure the meat doesn't touch each other!). Prop the barrel up on some flat rocks and against a stone or brick wall. Make a tiny fire in front of the barrel with twigs. Once it gets going, cover it with wood shavings and sawdust. It will smolder, perfect for smoking.[7]

Check on it every half hour to make sure it's smoking and not on fire. If the wife is smoking a large joint of ham, she might make the adventurers take turns checking on the barrel throughout the night, since it'll take upwards of forty hours to smoke a large joint!

The fat from a pig would be boiled into lard and stored in bladders since pig fat tended to spoil faster than sheep fat. It's a messy, big job that leaves the house smelling like a cross between burnt pork roast and French fries. For the sake of this book, I decided to try my hand at lard making, to share the experience and trials of a medieval woman toiling in her kitchen. My kitchen has several cats, a dog, and electricity, but the concept is the same.

With my last pig purchase, I asked for the fat from around the kidneys. It's supposed to be the best for making flaky pie crusts. They gave me a few pounds of fat and I was set.

I chopped the fat into small cubes, which gave me carpal tunnel syndrome by the time I was done. I should have worn gloves because I couldn't get the greasy feeling off my hands, not to mention that I kept touching my face and ended up with a nasty acne outbreak a week later. Romance heroines beware: keep your hands away from your face!

I heated the oven to 250F and put the fat cubes in a big roasting pan with a little water and let it bake for a couple of hours. The smell was…distinctive. I had a larger appreciation of why wax candles were so sought after; I can't imagine living with that stench all of the time.

Once the lard cooled a bit, I poured it into a funnel lined with cheesecloth to sieve out the small bits of fat and flesh that didn't render. Of course, I bumped the edge of it and coated myself, the floor, the stove, the fridge, and the dog in about two litres of cooling pig fat.

The dog was very, very happy about this situation and spent the day happily licking her paws. The cats were equally amused, as the dog's back end provided a communal lardpop to lick as they walked by.

Me? I was far less amused.

Backyard Goodies

Your heroine's teeth are one of her most important assets, and Vitamin C (along with twine, salt, and twigs for dental care) will help keep her shiny bright. If there are no potatoes and citrus in your fantasy world, how on earth will she get enough Vitamin C to stave off scurvy?

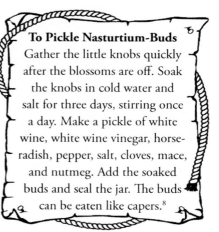

To Pickle Nasturtium-Buds
Gather the little knobs quickly after the blossoms are off. Soak the knobs in cold water and salt for three days, stirring once a day. Make a pickle of white wine, white wine vinegar, horseradish, pepper, salt, cloves, mace, and nutmeg. Add the soaked buds and seal the jar. The buds can be eaten like capers.[8]

Fruit preserves offer a buffer against scurvy in countries where winter is long and too cold for fruit to grow. If your heroine stops at a country house during harvest time, she will probably see servants (or the mistress of the house) working furiously to get the autumn bounty preserved. The heroine might even purchase a crock or two of goodies to take along with her, if she is travelling in a carriage.

As I explained earlier, apples could be dried in cooling ovens or slices strung on string and hung to dry out in warm, dry parts of the home. Cherries could be covered in brandy (a basic form of compote) and covered with a washed, stretched pig's bladder. The pig's bladder would dry and shrink, tightening around the jar's lid and creating an airtight seal. The alcohol would act as its own preservative to keep bacteria at bay.

Dried cherries would be a wonderful score for your heroine to pick up at market or to steal from a kitchen, as they would be lighter than fresh to carry on horseback or in her pack. She'd be able to find them in the pantry in a box with white paper or fabric separating the layers. She could scoop those up and stuff into a sack before making her escape.

Gooseberries could be scalded and cooked with sugar, then mixed with cold water and corked in bottle to make a basic form of fruit syrup. On a cold January night, your starving heroine will be very thankful for the gooseberry syrup that the mistress of the house pulls out of her pantry to go with the mutton stew and bread.

We had a damson tree when I was growing up and they made excellent pies. Imagine my excitement when I found a recipe for damson winter pie preserves in an 1808 cookbook by Maria Eliza Rundell. Mrs. Rundell recommends cooking up the fruit and making a pie filling, then adding to a crock jar, pouring a half inch of mutton fat on top to make an airtight seal. She says to remember to add a forked stick in the fat, or else you will have a difficult time getting the suet out. Then again, this could be another task your party of adventurers could take on; trying to get the pie fillings out of crock jars that have three month old frozen fat sealed around the mouth!

Rose hips also have a high Vitamin C count, plus can be used in many homemade medicines. Wilting roses were left to nature's devices and rose hips formed. Today, we often don't have rose hips on our bushes because we prune, pick, and deadhead our plants, or we have obsessive neighbours who do it for us. These would be gathered, juiced, combined with sugar, and boiled to form a fruit preserve.

Vegetables can also be preserved, providing much needed fibre and vitamins. Dried peas are an excellent source of protein during the long winter months, not to mention add that "stick-to-your-ribs" comfort sorely needed when your hero's bones are shaking from the cold. Pick the peas, scald them in boiling water for a minute, and strain them. Dump the peas on cloth and use another to completely dry them. You can make them the "Russian Way" by putting the peas in cooling ovens spread out over the course of a couple of days. Store in paper bags hung in the kitchen or another very dry part of the house.

Fun Facts

- A dried beef tongue takes four hours of slow boiling after soaking. A pickled tongue three hours.
- Ancient Egyptians filled earthen jars with boiled water and stuck them to the roof at night for cool drinks in the morning.
- To sweeten salt meat, boil the meat in milk until half cooked. Drain off the milk and then finish cooking the meat in water.

Even today, pickling is used extensively with vegetables. Onions, cucumbers, beets, and beans are still recognizable foods for modern audiences and have been stored by soaking the vegetables in a salt and vinegar brine for centuries. All that's needed is clean water, vinegar (any wine-producing world would have this ingredient readily available) and salt. Then, glass or crockery jars to store the pickles.

Dairy

Once we figured out that we could squeeze a teat and get a beverage, humans have been playing with milk. Butter, soft cheese, hard cheese, whey powder, chocolate milk—you name it, we've done it.

We don't know who, when, and where it was discovered that combining the stomach of a calf (or goat or sheep or horse) with dairy would produce cheese. Most probably it was discovered in various places. If stomachs were used to transport milk, it wouldn't take long to figure out that something about a calf's stomach caused the milk to turn into a different food all together. From there, it would just be trial and error.

Hard cheese is a fairly long process when doing it by hand. First, rennet (remember, the calf stomach?) is stirred into warm milk. After about an hour of this, the milk turns into an almost jelly-like consistency. The top of what was milk resembles a sheet of scrambled eggs and needs to be cut up and separated from the liquid underneath (the whey).

The dairy maid would use her curd cutter (or a knife) to make the curd easier to handle, since she will want as little liquid mixed into the curd as possible. Using her hands, she'd scoop up pieces of curd and let the whey drain from the curd. She'd set aside the curd until it was all scooped up.

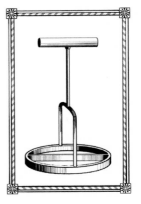

Then, the curd would need to be heated, releasing more of the liquid whey. The whey would be drained off and the process repeat-

This is just one example of a curd cutter.

ed if necessary until as much liquid as possible was extracted.

The curd would be salted (to preserve it) and packed into a cheese mould. Moulds could be as fancy or as basic as you please, but early on they were simple round, wooden moulds with a small hole on the side for any remaining whey to drain out. The moulds would be lined with clean linen and then the curd put inside. A cover would be put on top of the curd. The entire mould would be put into a press where it would be tightened; more whey would be drained out this way. Early cheesemaking would have used a rock on top and the woman would have pressed down on it. Later, a hand-crank press would have been used.

It took about eight days to press all of the whey out of the cheese. The cloth around the curd would need to be changed daily, so the dairy maid had to be very careful not to drop, smash, or ruin the slowly-formed shape of the cheese. After all of the whey had been pressed out, the curd would be wrapped in yet another fresh cloth and left to mature on a shelf. It would be carefully flipped over every few days so that no liquid would rise to the top. Any mold would be scrapped off at that time, too.

When all of the liquid is pressed out, a clean cloth is pulled up around the curd and smoothed around the sides and top. This will eventually become one's cheese round.[9]

European rounds weren't the only way to preserve dairy for long periods. Cheese can be preserved to endure just about any temperature or lifestyle. In the Western Altai Mountains, traditional Mongolian women preserved their yak, sheep, and goat milk by making a winter staple called *kurt*. They boiled fresh milk over dung fires until lightly caramelized. They used this to make cheese, which was then cut and dried on the sides of their yurts.

This process produced a hard strip of dairy, full of fat and protein, that was vital in the winter, though was

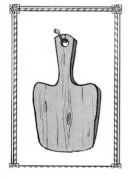

Milk can also be turned into butter. The dairy maid will skim the cream off the top of the milk over several days, then churn it until it resembles wet scrambled eggs. The liquid that comes from this process is called buttermilk. The butter is then put into a swallow pan and paddles (like above) are used to squeeze out the last of the buttermilk.

so hard that it needed to be soaked to be edible. However, because it is so hard, it took up little space compared to trying to carry wheels of cheese from camp to camp.[10]

Keepin' Yer Cool

Food was stored in cellars or pits, on north-facing, shaded, slate-shelved huts, and even underwater. Some people were lucky enough to have springhouses, a tiny hut built over a small spring, where pans and crocks were set up to be in the constant flow of the water.

A springhouse was useful in hot, rural communities, such as the Southern United States, as the water would keep the items inside the hut cool. Milk could be kept chilled by wedging a bucket in the water and suspended in place with rope. Fresh milk could be poured into bottles or jars, and placed inside a bucket filled with water. The bucket would remain cold, keeping the milk chilled, plus uncontaminated from bugs and dirt. The milk could keep for upwards of a week this way, even in the oppressive heat of a Mississippi, USA summer.

Cellars are underground, or partially underground, buildings used to store vegetables, fruits, and other foods that require consistent, cool temperatures. Cellars are most famously known to house wine, but root vegetables, salted meat, and salt were commonly put into cellars. Today, potatoes are still regularly housed in cellars.

Wealthier individuals might have several cellars to store fruit, vegetables and meat, whereas rural or isolated communities might have communal cellars. If a cellar is dug deep enough, it can even keep snow and ice through the winter!

Ice is common to us in the summer months, but it wasn't until the late 18th century that the access to ice year round really picked up. Ice ships would cut large hunks of ice off icebergs and from northern frozen lakes. It didn't start off well, losing two-thirds of the ice to melt. Eventually, ships were insulated better and ice was cut differently so that only 8% of the ice was lost.[11]

I'm always surprised that ice doesn't feature more strongly in Steampunk and Victorian Romance stories, because the ice trade really picked up in the 1860s. In the United States, insulated railway cars were developed by 1867 so that ice could be transported all across the country. Soon, food was placed on those blocks of ice and transported. Then, cars were further insulated to create "ice box" cars, so that food could be transported that would have normally rotted or spoiled.

Bacteria, Germs, and Other Fun Things

Literature and movies have led us to believe that people in the past were filthy dirty. For the most part, they were right. The Tudors definitely had some hygiene challenges, though some of it has been exaggerated through our Victorian sense of hygiene, daily scrubbing, and the modern need to coat one's body in as many artificial scents as legally possible. However, urban centres did smell, especially the larger ones in the summer time. City dwellers would have smelled like horse shit, rotting teeth, body odour, and were covered in dirt, soot, smoke, and grime. Too many people were packed into too small of a space without air conditioning or proper ventilation.

In urban situations, many of the poor did not have proper cooking facilities, or they were shared with several other families. Many times, such as in London during the industrial revolution, poor factory workers relied heavily on "fast food" vendors and kiosks, as opposed to home cooked meals, grabbing a cup of tea (drinking it at the station, since takeout mugs weren't invented yet), and picking up a pasty or individual pie to eat along the way.

Urban centres with small kitchens might have ten individuals crammed into a one or two room apartment. If very lucky, there would be a hearth with a chimney to whisk the smoke from inside and help cut down on some of the smoke stench.

In the farm kitchens, however, things were a little different. Poor farmers still had fresh air, open fields, and the luxury of foraging in the forest. While poaching laws existed in many countries in Europe, there were rarely laws on foraging for berries, fruits, and plants. There were more animals, more private vegetable gardens, and more need for food preservation.

And, therefore, more need for cleanliness.

Let's say your heroine is hiding from her tyrannical father, the Duke of Esto'Flora, and posing as a dairy maid apprentice (by the way, she'd probably have to pay for the privilege of that role). She would need an obsessive attention to cleanliness, or else her actions would (at best) spoil the milk and (at worst) kill everyone. (Then again, if your heroine is an assassin, well, perhaps the dairy is the perfect place for her after all.)

Today, we all know about germs. We learn about them from an early age. "Wash your hands because there are germs on them." We coat our children in anti-bacterial soaps, sprays, and gels to kill anything remotely resembling a germ. However, two centuries ago, people did not know that germs caused them to get sick. They did understand, however, that a lack of cleanliness could taint food, which would spoil it, which was inedible, and could make people sick.

Admittedly, many didn't care or thought it was poppycock, and had no problem wiping their bums with their hands and then prepping your food at the local tavern. Make sure your heroine practices food safety whenever she can. It would prove embarrassing getting stomach cramps while trying to rescue the captive prince in the dungeon.

A good housewife would have scoured her tables with salt and water before prepping a side of pork to be cured. She would have scoured the inside of the calf stomach when making cheese. The pig's bladder would have been scrubbed and washed before it was cut and used to seal jars of jam. Cloths used for covering jars would need laundering, and the larder drip pan scrubbed.

So when your hero stops at a farm house and encounters a widow with several children in tow, perhaps he could offer to lend a hand scrubbing, chopping, or heavy lifting for her in exchange for food and lodgings for the night. While coin is always good, when you consider how much work she'd have to do just to feed her family, a strong pair of hands might help far more than the two copper pieces he was about to toss her way.

Of course, if your hero is a jerk, well, he might eat all of her food and leave a mess behind.

Why Heroines Have Swords and Not Spatulas

Whew! This has been a whirlwind chapter of information, where I'm sure some of you are wondering how you are going to incorporate details without needing to write hundreds of pages on description alone.

Unless you are planning to write a scene where the hero is chatting up the local dairy maid as she pounds cream into butter, there probably will never be any need to use the extensive detail in this chapter. That doesn't mean, however, that reading this was wasted time.

One of the best ways to make fiction authentic is using tidbits of details; hints and nuggets that add to the atmosphere without adding bulk. When your heroine travels north in the spring, she's going to complain how the strawberries aren't ripe, even though they would have been back home. The hero, at the end of a long winter, buys the last pound of dried peas from a monastery and the sidekick bemoans spring's late arrival.

Take this information, massage it, and let peaks show through. Readers will appreciate both the nuggets and that you didn't stop the action to describe food porn.

Chapter 7: Golden Palettes and Starving Bellies
The Worlds of the Rich and the Poor

Pease porridge hot, pease porridge cold,
Pease porridge in the pot, nine days old;
Some like it hot, some like it cold,
Some like it in the pot, nine days old

Poverty is a reality today as much as it always has been. Today, nearly a billion people are going hungry. In the modern world, hunger is not caused by insufficient food, but the lack of access to it.[1] Conversations about hunger evoke a lot of emotions: anger at society, anger at the hungry, anger at the government, racism, classism, a call-to-arms, and apathy. We are socially bred to care for the poor, to help the needy, and to show compassion to the less fortunate, yet we still struggle. If people in a modern society struggle with the concept of hunger and food insecurity, it doesn't take much imagination to look at how a strict class structure could evolve in societies that believed the rich were predestined to be so by a deity.

I've found that new writers often gravitate to the very rich, be it in historical, romance, or fantasy. I don't have any concrete evidence to say why exactly that is. Some theories surround the notion that being wealthy is a part of the fantasy (not many people daydream about being poor and going hungry), whereas people like me put it to simple logistics: it's easier to write rich people.

This chapter is a big one, since I will attempt to cover the social structure of food across many cultures and time periods. The scope is huge, unwieldy, and contradictory; how one group of people lived does not mean other groups lived that way. Just because one era did it a certain way does not mean it was the same a decade later. Societies are fluid. So when reading through this chapter, it is important to not focus on the specifics. When creating a world— even one based on 1425 Italy—think about the why. Don't just have your rich give food to the poor. Ask yourself *why* they give to the poor. Even if you never answer that question in your fiction, your world will be more realistic for having asked it of yourself.

Class Barriers

The word "privilege" has been popping up lately in conversations about poverty, gender, race, and class. Simplified, the theory states that those who have been born wealthy, male, and white (it's used in a western-centric context) have less barriers than others without those three "privileges."

I bring up this theory because it shows how far we've actually come. We speak of privilege in terms of the negative. In discussions of equality, we search for ways to level the playing field between the rich and the poor, the predominant ethnic group and the minority races, the predominant religion and the minority beliefs.

Most of us recognize that there are barriers, but also that it is possible to succeed against them. There are groups and programs to help people break the cycle of poverty and cultural and class glass ceilings. Modern folks realize that it's tough and many won't succeed, but some will.

It would be incorrect to apply that modern thinking to a historical setting, or any fantastical setting with a clearly-defined aristocracy where a tiny group holds all of the land and wealth.

Perhaps the single most important reason for the extreme class inequality in the Middle Ages is land ownership. Or, rather, the lack of it. It's difficult to understand how renting property can impact people so significantly, since the majority of western adults have rented a property at least once in their lives.

However, without property in a pre-industrial society, land affects people in three very distinct ways: fuel, meat, and income.

Fuel

If people do not own their own land that means someone else owns it. That seems rather basic, I know, but if the local land owner is a jerk and owns 95% of the land for as far as a person can see, he can make life very difficult. One of those ways he can do this is with fuel.

If you are creating a world based on a quasi-European structure (or if you are writing a historical or a historical hybrid) and if you will be presenting the story from a poor point-of-view (aka the poor farmer trope), you will have to address fuel.

Wood is often the choice fuel in preindustrial worlds, especially in the countryside. Wood comes from trees. And trees come from land.

Landowners generally did not allow anyone beyond their own household to cut trees, though kind landowners (or, law) allowed the poor to collect fallen wood. This would allow the poor to have small fires, though most of their cooking would be on a very basic scale, since they would not have the fuel necessary to make elaborate meals.

Using preheated stones for cooking does go back thousands of years. This method cuts down on the amount of fuel needed, since the rocks would continue to hold the heat like an oven. This would still not produce the level of heat necessary for grand feasts and balls (neither would be happening in a one-room hut, but that's beside the point).

A very generous landowner might set aside a portion of his land for wood coppicing. Some trees, such as willow and oak, can be

112

Save fuel. Cook puddings, vegetables, and meat together in a cauldron.

cut and new trunks will grow from around the stump. This ensures that the tree doesn't die and there will always be a supply of wood. The landowner might hire a couple of men to look after the section of forest, cutting trees as needed, or perhaps just ensuring that no one takes more than their fair share. A sensible landowner would, however, charge for this. The peasants need to be kept in their place.

There is another use for fuel that has mostly escaped us today: light. Today, we flip a switch to light our houses. Many of us leave the lights on without even thinking about it. We go on vacation and leave the light on over the door. With the cost of oil, wax and/or tallow, lamps and candles would need to be used as little as possible in poorer homes, which meant earlier suppers.

On the flip side, grand balls that continued into the wee hours of the night with thousands of wax candles burning were status symbols. The ability to keep people warm while they flirted (fireplace/stove/hearth) and able to see each other (candles/oils/lamps) at 2 am was not something the poor could manage.

Also, the destitute in the midst of a severe famine might find themselves eating their tallow-dipped candles. If your heroine has resorted to snacking down on the candles, she's probably not going to be burning them at night and will just go to bed early.

Meat

If a landowner doesn't allow anyone on his property to cut trees, it doesn't come as a surprise that killing creatures would then be poaching. Meat was a rich man's food; peasant need not apply.

Any area surrounded by woodland would have deer, wild boar, hares, and rabbits, plus other smaller creatures. However, those animals would be on the lord's land (or the King's), and would be off-limits for the everyday peasant.

Poaching big game could result in the loss of your hands (if lucky) or the loss of one's head (if not), so ensure your heroine is careful with her bow. Some lands didn't even allow fishing, so be careful that the hero isn't caught with his pole dangling, so to speak. Even the hunting of squirrels was considered poaching in many lands, though the punishment was often less severe and was just a fine.

Rules can always be exceptioned, of course. Perhaps the countryside is overrun with rabbits; the local lord might even hold a bounty for killing them, thereby allowing young people to not only hunt food for their families but also earn a penny or two to buy a loaf of bread. Likewise, perhaps the law could be adjusted to allow waterfowl to be hunted by children with either bows or slings.

Landowners and royalty might place food rents on their tenants, which would help pay for their endless parties and festivals. A tenant swineherd or perhaps even a serf might be allowed to keep a piglet from his flock, but hand over the rest. He might keep the intestines from the slaughter of his herd but nothing else.[2] With this form of rent, it would be impossible for the poor to get ahead.

The rich could also afford to eat fresh meat. Their cows could be slaughtered and their lambs stuffed and roasted. They could also afford a wide variety, and the richer one was, the more exotic the meat might become. Wealthy Roman tables, for example, featured flamingo, ostrich, and antelope.[3]

Life was far less exciting for the poor. Living animals provided significantly more benefits than dead ones. Once dispatched, a cow needed to be eaten quickly, or else valuable time and expense was needed to preserve the animal. A living cow could produce milk, which could be turned into butter or cheese (or drank straight). Once the cow's milk dried up, she could become pregnant again, thereby producing another source of income to sell and then providing more milk.

Milk wasn't the only liquid a cow could provide. A small cut to the upper leg bled enough to not kill the animal, but provided enough blood to be mixed with oats and turned into blood pudding. Black pudding, as it is sometimes known, would provide protein and iron. Mixed with lard and oats, it would add fat and fibre, making it a hearty meal when there was little more to eat than salt beef.

Lambs turned into sheep (mutton), which could be milked and shorn for many years in season. A lamb only provided enough meat for one meal; a fully grown ewe could provide wool (thereby, income) for years, plus provide several meals at the end of her life.

Poorer families often kept pigs, as opposed to cattle and sheep. Pigs were cheaper to feed, as they ate table scraps and could forage on common lands eating up acorns and other natural goodies.

If your world is set further back in an Anglo-Saxon era or earlier, animals would have been important wealth indicators. Animals would have been raised mostly for personal consumption, as opposed to trade, so gifts of animals would have been very important and elitist. Modern sensibilities joke about selling a daughter for a cow. However, in eras when most people only could afford to have one or two cows

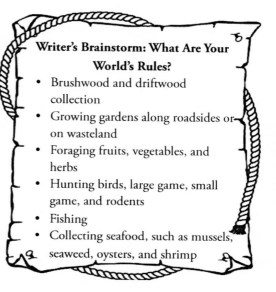

Writer's Brainstorm: What Are Your World's Rules?

- Brushwood and driftwood collection
- Growing gardens along roadsides or on wasteland
- Foraging fruits, vegetables, and herbs
- Hunting birds, large game, small game, and rodents
- Fishing
- Collecting seafood, such as mussels, seaweed, oysters, and shrimp

at a time, offering eight goats and a cow for the opportunity to marry a chieftain's daughter was an honour.[4] Though, I'd hope to get more thrown into the deal than that, if I were a chieftain's daughter!

Income

Specifically, the means to earn a living. Owning land meant money. A landowner didn't work his own land; that was just silly. He'd rent it out to the landless riff-raff. They would farm his land and would pay a portion (or the majority) of the proceeds. They might be allowed to keep a pig and some chickens, earning a little extra money of their own.

A landowner could sell hunting rights on his land for a day or a season. He'd make additional income, but of course the only people able to afford this would be other wealthy people or the upwardly-mobile yeoman and middle classes. A landlord can go fishing whenever he wants (or pay someone to do it for him). A poor tenant can only fish if the landowner provides the permission—allowing him to catch the fish and to sell it at market.

All of this assumes freedom; serfs, indentured servants, and slaves have even more restrictions.

In the West Indies during the sugar rush, African slaves were used on plantations. Sugar, rum, and molasses were too precious to feed to slaves, so salt fish was imported in from Maine, Newfoundland, Iceland, and other fishing nations. Since salt fish was vital to many communities, plus the navies of many countries, the salt fish that eventually made it to the slaves was of the lowest quality.

I had the honour (horror?) of trying low quality salt fish. After

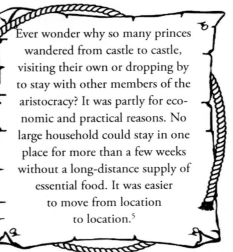

Ever wonder why so many princes wandered from castle to castle, visiting their own or dropping by to stay with other members of the aristocracy? It was partly for economic and practical reasons. No large household could stay in one place for more than a few weeks without a long-distance supply of essential food. It was easier to move from location to location.[5]

soaking all night in two changes of water, salt was all I could taste. Not to mention how fish should flake and how this fish did not. Only someone very hungry with no other food choice would be able to choke that food down.

In ancient Rome, slaves lived off barley bread, by all accounts a chewy, dense, unappealing food.[6] At gatherings, people often brought their own slaves; after all, lifting one's own plate is difficult work. Hosts were not obliged to feed the slaves brought by their visitors, but if you want to show that your heroine is a kind soul, she might insist that slaves be allowed to eat.

Religious orders also need a small caveat. Most people are aware of the grand, lavish monasteries ran by bishops with as much power as politicians. While that was true, there were also plenty of religious orders and individuals who took vows of austerity. Walter Daniel, a 12th century English monk, wrote that a monk's diet should be just a pound of bread and a pint of beans daily. No meat, since meat was a sign of prosperity. Likewise, the Rules of Benedict outlined breakfast as bread with either wine or beer. The main meal should be something simple like beans or pottage, with vegetables and fruit.[7] Of course, choosing poverty is significantly different than being forced into poverty.

Meal Time

These days, we have three distinct meal times: breakfast, lunch, and dinner (depending upon where you live, it might be called breakfast, dinner, and supper). Eating something at each of these meals is important. It has been drilled into us to eat as soon as we rise by doctors, health education programs, and dieting magazines. However, just because we eat by this schedule does not mean, historically, this meal plan was followed.

One of the complaints I have with some historicals lately is that the heroine awakes in bed to a bountiful tray of toast, scrambled eggs, round slices of ham, bacon, sausages, and freshly-baked whole wheat rolls with melting butter. Oh, and tea and chocolate. She nibbles on this, never eating too much, before using her chamber pot, then heads downstairs with the family, where a buffet is laid out with all of the food she was just served upstairs. She eats another meal and it isn't even 8 am yet. She'd put a hobbit to shame!

How people start their day is important not only to their location and culture, but also their status. A rich wife will have different eating habits than the poor girl scrubbing the coal stove in the mansion house.

For example, Roman public life began around dawn, which turned breakfast into the grab-and-go meal modern people most identify with. If eating at home, the busy man might have some bread dipped in alcohol or milk or cheese mixed with honey. He might grab some olives, nuts, or another light food that doesn't require cooking.

Once outside, the streets were lined with fast food kiosks. Pastries filled with cheese, nuts, and dates were readily available, along with other lighter fare. Those Romans didn't have baristas, but at least they had sweet buns and wine in the morning.[8]

By contrast, Europeans for many centuries ate two daily large meals. Dinner was served sometime between 10am and 1pm and it was the largest meal of the day. Supper was served in the afternoon or early evening and was a smaller affair.

In 1542, a physician named Andrew Boorde wrote that labourers should eat three times a day, whereas men of leisure should only need twice daily.[10] That didn't mean people didn't eat between meals. Servants, farmers, and laborers all needed to eat more.

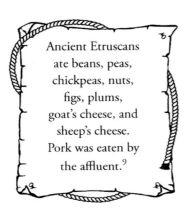

Ancient Etruscans ate beans, peas, chickpeas, nuts, figs, plums, goat's cheese, and sheep's cheese. Pork was eaten by the affluent.[9]

Before the introduction of North American foods into the European diet, Western Europe lived off dried peas, lentils, chickpeas, and beans. The English had their pease pudding, made with dried peas and any scraps of vegetables and meat they had. The Spanish, likewise, had their own pottage called *cocido*, a concoction of boiled chickpeas or beans with salt pork or sausage.

A farmer might have taken a piece of bread and some leftover meat with him into the fields, or a slice of cake. A maidservant might have nibbled on a slice of teabread or some nuts so that she could get the master's dinner ready on time without passing out from hunger herself.

By the 17th century, dinner moved to be around noon or early afternoon, so people began eating a casual meal called breakfast. It might have melted chocolate, bone marrow sausages, bacon, poached eggs, salted herrings, and bread. Even once breakfast evolved as part of some routines in Europe, breakfast was not normally served at the crack of dawn, unless you were a servant girl scrubbing the coal stove and stole a piece of stale bread while elbow-deep in coal soot.

By the 18th century, wealthy Georgians were having soft rolls, breads, jams, marmalade and toast for breakfast. Toast had been invented by this time as a means to getting the rock hard butter on to bread (the butter was put on the bread before toasting). This meal might not be served until 10am in some homes, though gentlemen bound for shooting might make special arrangements with their servants to have a meal ready. Heroes like Mr. Darcy would have eaten cold ham, leftover pheasant, kippers, and preserves before he and Mr. Bingley went shooting; this breakfast would not have disrupted the servants too much in their preparations for dinner and supper.

The poor, be it tenant farmers (people who rented, as opposed to owned farm land), servants, or labourers in the city, did not enjoy the same level of meals as a wealthy gentlemen or even a middle class yeoman. While a gentleman farmer was snacking on kippers and cold ham, his tenant would be eating leftover bread from the previous day's baking washed down with a mug of ale.

In *A Poor Man's House in 1908*, Stephen Reynolds, a gentleman lodging with a fisherman's family, records how his landlords had an irregular income and needed to bring in lodgers to help keep some consistent money coming in. For a time during Reynolds' stay, a family with a young child lived in one of the house's bedrooms and was granted one hour a day to cook a hot meal.

People like Reynolds' housemates would concentrate on filling, cheap food that didn't take much preparation. Even farmers would be selling more of their food than keeping it. They would not be keeping the best for themselves. While a prime rib is nice, it would bring in five times the income that a sheep's head would. The sheep's head could flavour a stew, while the sale of a prime rib could buy a sack of cereal grains and potatoes, which could feed a family for several days with nutritious foods.

Plumb Porridge

Boil a leg of beef in ten gallons of water until tender. Strain out the broth, wipe the pot, and put the broth back in. Thinly slice six small loaves of bread (cut off the top and bottom) and pour some of the broth over into the bread. Let it sit for 15 minutes, then put the bread into the pot and boil for 15 minutes.

Add five pounds each of currants and raisins, and two pounds of prunes, along with three-quarters an ounce of mace, half an ounce of cloves, two nutmegs (all ground together and mixed with cold stock). Stir into the broth and bread.

Remove the pot from the heat and add three pounds of sugar, salt to taste, a quart of sack (sweet white wine imported from Spain), a quart of claret (a type of red wine from Bordeaux), and lemon juice. Serve.[11]

If potatoes were not in the diet, then bread and beer would make up the bulk of the carbohydrates in the diet. Today, we often see carbs as evil. However, when working as hard as these people did, they needed carbs to stay upright. That meant heavy starch diets.

When the gentleman sat down for dinner with his guests, he could have easily had a three course meal. Each course could have several dishes, so this midday meal could easily involve twelve to twenty dishes! A financially prudent baron might ask his house-keeper to ensure that as little food is wasted as possible. A mutton joint on Day 1 can be used in mutton stew on Day 2, mutton pie on Day 3, and mixed with vegetables into individual pasties on Day 4. A kind baron would let his servants eat from the leftovers (and perhaps justify paying them a lower wage). From the leftovers, perhaps a daily or weekly donation to the village's very poor would be made.

Contrast this eating with a ploughman's lunch. Today's restaurants serve elaborate meals of deli meats, eggs, pickles, cheese, lettuce, and so on. A real ploughman's lunch (or dinner or luncheon, again, depending on era and location) will be a much simpler affair. Bread and cheese for sure, with hopefully cold pork or perhaps a small meat pie.

If your hero dines with the local gentleman, supper will probably resemble dinner, especially if there are important guests (which your hero might be). The meal might even feature exotic, imported foods, or perhaps a fine wine to impress guests. There would be several courses of food, some using the leftovers from dinner, but many would have been made fresh by the kitchen staff who had been cooking all day.

At the end of a long day's work, the labourer would return home to a stew or pottage, or perhaps nothing more than coarse, brown bread and cheese, with ale and preserves. Occasionally, there would be meat, but it would rarely

A Well-to-do Roman Supper Menu[12]

- Egg and tuna casserole
- Salad
- Sausages
- Porridge
- Carrots
- Beans and bacon
- Spiced fruit
- Nuts

be a fancy cut for the very poor. A farmer might have a meat roast a couple times a week, but he's more likely to have a mutton roast than lamb kabobs. Also, meat might come in cheaper pieces like organ meat, brains, or a stewed pig's head. Your hero might never find an excellent cut of beef on a spit at any poor farmer's cottage.

Caste-based Eating

Caste-based rules and habits can be informal, unwritten rules of conduct to officially sanctioned rules punishable by law. We have plenty of informal ones in Western society. If a stranger knocks on someone's door asking for food, they are more likely to get the police called on them than invited in for supper. We don't use the good company plates when our teenagers have company over, but we always take them out for our in-laws. We don't generally invite random people off the street into our homes to eat. We don't invite convicts into our homes for a beer and a game of darts. We don't *have* to provide vegetarian options and might even say "oh, there's just a little beef in it," but will also risk censure as being rude and ignorant for having done so.

Now, all of those rules aren't official. There is no hospitality police to ensure that we follow the strictest decorum or maintain our rank and position in society. However, there are plenty examples in history where this was not the case.

Today, there is an expectation that the parent goes hungry if there isn't enough food for everyone. Yet, in many cultures in the past, it was often everyone for themselves, especially amongst the poor. A man earned more money than a woman or a child. If he went without food, it would only contribute to even worse poverty in the long run.

In some countries, there is a culture amongst the poor that has women eating last, behind her husband and children. A stranger or foreigner might rank above the man, or just under the man, but nearly always above the women. You might have a culture that allows the man to eat as much as he wishes, before letting the next in line to eat theirs. Or, perhaps four or five bowls are portioned out, with the husband having his own, the male sons sharing two bowls, the daughters one bowl, and the wives the final one with whatever was left over. Your hero, coming from a nation where women were priestesses and politicians, might offer his bowl to the daughters and wives, greatly offending the husband.

Pass the Pottage

Throughout this book, I've talked a lot about pottage. Sometimes spelled the French "potage", it is nothing more than a thick stew (or a thin soup, depending upon your purse) made of boiled vegetables, grains, and/or legumes and possibly meat and fish. It was a fairly staple food in England from the 9th to 15th centuries, and it even graced the tables of the aristocracy. Different versions using local foods were made across Europe.

A pottage was boiled for several hours to ensure the tough grains were cooked enough to eat. It also allowed for the side benefit that any contamination caused by uncomposted human feces on the fields would be negated.

The meal could be as simple or complicated as you wish. In Chapter 11, I have included my own family's traditional recipe. Today, it's called "Pease Pudding", but it's the same as a thick pottage recipe found in *The Forme of Cury* (1390). In a poor household, there would be so much water that it would resemble a thin broth. Oats could be added to thicken the dried peas and pulses used as the base. A leftover meat joint would add bits of meat, plus fat from the marrow, and overall flavour to improve the pottage. A yeoman household might add rashers of bacon and a salt riblet or two (a salt riblet is a pork rib cured in a salt brine). An affluent household might add a ham bone, along with pepper and salt. A rich house might add sugar, saffron, and currants.

123

It was a food that was eaten by all, but yet again affluence and cash dictated how it would appear on one's table.

Charity: It's Better to Give and Be Seen Than Thought a Miser

Mrs. Rundell in her 1808 cookbook, *A New System of Domestic Cookery*, says:

> *"I promised a few hints, to enable every family to assist the poor of their neighbourhood at a very trivial expense."*

Mrs. Rundell provides her contemporaries (the era of Jane Austen) with many recipes to assist the poor, the sick, and the invalid. My editor had to hold me back from quoting the entire section from her book; it's so fascinating to see the importance of feeding the poor—but also providing a lower quality of food than you are serving your own.

I've successfully managed to sneak in two recipes (whew!) that I think everyone will appreciate. The first is a rice pudding for a "young" family (i.e. a couple in their twenties with five children under the age of seven), or a family all suffering from an illness.

When you (or your servants) are done cooking, the oven will still be quite hot. Have them combine half a pound of rice, four ounces of coarse (cheap) sugar, two quarts of milk, and two ounces of pan drippings (i.e. bacon grease, lard, salt pork drippings). Mix in a pan and place in the cooling oven. By the time the oven has cooled, the meal will be ready with little expense to your family (and no additional use of precious fuel).

The next recipe is a little...cheaper, shall we say. While cooking a pot of salt beef, cut a thick upper crust of bread and put it in the pot when the beef is nearly done. When the beef is cooked, remove the bread. Serve your family the beef, but donate the bread to a poor or sick family. The bread will have soaked up some of the salt, fat, and flavour of the beef.

If you've chosen to write an aristocratic world and are struggling to give your hero a redeeming quality, attention to the poor is always a good one. Perhaps he has given strict instructions to his housekeeper or chef that any water used to boil meat was not to be thrown out, but instead reused to make a vegetable and oatmeal pottage for distribution to the poor. Or, maybe he instructs the servants to set aside a portion of his leftovers to be distributed to the poor every morning.

A good leader might pass laws that favour his purse and the lands of his friends, but he should always take care to look after the poor. No one wants a peasants' revolt; they almost always revolve around food. Your Empress might decree that grain surpluses be stored and not sold to foreign lands, so that there would be free food available to the poor during times of famine (a tradition that started in the 6th century B.C. in China.[13]).

In Rome, food stamps called *tesserae* were handed out. These could be exchanged at the publicly-owned granaries for wheat, which would be turned into porridge. Wheat porridge by itself is very healthy and any additional money could be spent on olives, oil, and meat to add to the porridge to increase the calorie and nutritional content even further.[14]

If your world uses the patron system, like in ancient Rome, patrons might provide daily baskets of food and edible presents. These could be eaten, or sold or exchanged in the street for funds. In exchange your hero will need to ensure he pays respect to his patron and does everything he wants![15]

Monasteries, temples, and churches throughout history and around the world have often been amongst the most generous. From early Christian monks in the Middle East sharing their excess food with the poor to Roman temples giving away the meat from sacrificed animals, religious orders have often charged themselves with looking after the needs of the poor. Early church monasteries were self-sufficient communities that would distribute any extra food or goods to the poor.[16]

The concept of alms to the poor shows up in many religions and cultures. If charity is a major component of your society, baskets can be set on tables for people to donate from their plate to the poor. Or, perhaps your rich do not want to admit the great need amongst the poor and, thus, the servants take care of scraping the plates into the alms baskets after the meal. If charity is linked to eternal life, quite a show could be made at the dinner table at the heroine's household:

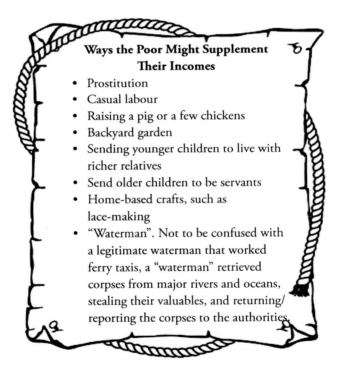

Ways the Poor Might Supplement Their Incomes
- Prostitution
- Casual labour
- Raising a pig or a few chickens
- Backyard garden
- Sending younger children to live with richer relatives
- Send older children to be servants
- Home-based crafts, such as lace-making
- "Waterman". Not to be confused with a legitimate waterman that worked ferry taxis, a "waterman" retrieved corpses from major rivers and oceans, stealing their valuables, and returning/reporting the corpses to the authorities.

- A fasting monk would be served the same amount of food as everyone else, allowing him the opportunity to donate or break his fast. He might give his entire meal over.

- A pregnant woman with sickness might put her fish and meat into the basket, opting to eat the fruit preserves and bread instead.
- A duchess who is disdainful of charity, however wishes to fit in with those around her, might donate the food on her plate that she can't or won't eat, such as fish bones and vegetables in sauce.
- A kindly baron may donate a little of everything on his plate to share his wealth and good fortune.

How would those leftovers be distributed? It's just a basket of leftovers, after all. Again, those are rules your kingdom can set up. Are they based on the Christian principle of charity and hospitality, as it was in the early church days? Or, is it based on political support (keep the poor happy so they don't revolt), or is it simply the rule of a kind Queen that has decreed this? These considerations will ensure that your world has its own flavour.

Let's say your heroine, a young widow with four mouths to feed, comes to the gates of the manor house to beg for scraps. Alms are given out to children and the elderly first. Our widow is given a heaping basket covered with a scrap of cloth. She exchanges an empty basket for the filled one, and hurries back to her home.

Once there, she discovers several pieces of salt beef bones with a little meat still attached, the bones of a ham hock that is yellowish in colour (having spent time in the saffron-laced pottage pot), several cuttings of blackened lower crust,[17] salad greens gone limp from being underneath the cooling meats, and a small fish wrapped in a cloth with a creamy, ginger sauce residue.

Our widow can give the fish to her children to share amongst themselves, while she gets a pot on the boil over her small hearth in the middle of her one-room hovel. The meat, bread, and greens all go into the pot, along with any other items she can add, like oats, wheat, or pulses. The bread will thicken the soup and the meat will add a little fat and flavour to the pot. She might even be able to scrape some meat from the bones, adding extra nutrition.

When travelling, your adventuring party might be helped by people like the widow. So, remind them to drop some coins in her purse before leaving because she'll be taking food from her children's mouths to feed you. It'll make people like your heroes all the more.

That does not mean, however, that everyone follows the rules. Like with any collection of people, there are always the bad mixed in with the good. It won't be out of place for your world to have, oh, the occasional miserly, hateful, prejudiced cleric who cooks up the sacrificial oxen for himself as opposed to sharing it with the poor.

Food Myths

One of the most interesting parts of this book was the myths I came across in talking to people. It seemed to all surround spices and meat. A couple heated discussions broke out between people arguing opposite myths. Both would be incorrect, but both would be arguing commonly-held "knowledge." So let's get the most troublesome one out of the way right now:

Spices were not used to preserve, mask, or recover spoiled meat.

True story. Food scholars have been pulling out their hair trying to kill this myth, but it doesn't seem to want to die. In *Spices: A Global Commodity*, Professor Paul Freedman explains the origins of this myth:

"This compelling but false idea constitutes something of an urban legend...Americans usually assume that in the absence of modern refrigeration meat will spoil almost immediately, but, particularly in the cool climate that dominates much of Europe, this is simply not the case."[18]

Spices just don't do much for preserving meat, and really spoiled meat tastes bad no matter what you sprinkle on it. Salting, smoking, pickling, and air-curing remain the best ways to preserve meat.

Sure, spices are added to cured meats such as Spanish chorizo, but that is more for flavour than preservation.[19]

It's also possible that the myth comes from both our modern tastes not being in line with medieval spice use (i.e. venison and ginger). Today, we understand that food does not require combining to balance one's "humors," but the need to balance foods to promote good health was important in medieval medicine. Also, food augmentation was a serious problem up until the late 19th century when governments around the world began to step in and say, no, you cannot put lead in that cookie. Combining our lack of taste for some of these spice combinations, as well as the known use of spices and augments to make food appear edible (when really it should be in the dumpster) might have added to the myth.

Regardless of where the myth originated from, it exists and scholars have been unable to kill it.

There is also a closely related myth to the spices: spices were cheap.

This myth's origin is easy to pinpoint; it originates from the period cookbooks. *The Forme of Cury* is filled with rich recipes of ginger, pepper, and saffron. Even by today's standards, there were a lot of spices used. These early, surviving cookbooks were meant for aristocratic homes and not the everyday

The Theory of Humors dominated Western Europe during the Middle Ages. The church imposed a ban on autopsies, so physicians had no practical firsthand knowledge of disease and the living body; they didn't even know blood circulated the body until the 18th century. The theory was that humans were made of four elements: fire, air, water, and earth. Sickness was caused by one of these being out of balance, causing anything from a bad mood to death. That's why brains were combined with spices like pepper and ginger, and why vinegar was added to mustard and garlic sauces. This was not to cover up spoiled food, but rather an attempt to keep people well.[20]

labourer. A well-off family in 1424 could spend as much on spices as they did on beef and pork *combined.*[21]

That did not mean no one purchased spices. It just meant that the use of spices in cooking was not as equal as they are today. Before modern transportation and agriculture, spice was a status symbol. When George the Rich, Duke of Bavaria-Landshut married in 1476, the 286 pounds of ginger, 205 pounds of cinnamon, and 85 pounds of nutmeg purchased for his banquets were not to mask bad meat, but rather to show how important and rich he really was.[22]

Another myth was that poor people never eat meat, closely followed by poor people only ever ate meat. This is a really confusing one because it is based in fact…but not quite. The problem wasn't so much of quantity, but rather of access.

Fresh meat was accessible by most affluent people in the Middle Ages. Farms stretched from Ireland to Iraq to India. Poorer people living in cramped cottages often kept a couple chickens and a pig or two. Perhaps even a goat to help control the weeds and provide some meat when she's weaning her kid.

Also, domesticated animals are a lot larger today. Early Medieval livestock was 40 to 60 percent smaller than today's livestock! Today, we breed chickens and turkeys with larger breasts for the white meat; earlier versions did not look the way our chickens do today. These earlier versions would have produced less meat in relation to their size, but still required the same grazing space and food.[23]

Today, we eat a lot of meat, though it doesn't vary much. It's normal for modern folks to eat meat two times a day, and sometimes even three times. We eat the same kinds of meat: sausage, bacon, chicken breast, beef roast, pork chops, cans of tuna. The modern image of "simpler times" (which exists today, not in the past) of roasting joints of meat isn't accurate for most people on a daily basis. Baked hedgehogs, rabbit stew, and boiled salt beef would be more common. Calf's head stew, salted cow tongue, and split pea pottage with bone marrow would have frequented the plates of the lower ranks.

The final myth I want to cover is that everyone in the Middle Ages was obese. This is another confusing one, since there is some truth to it. In many cultures, obesity was seen as a sign of wealth. A person could eat rich foods to their heart's content and not work off those calories. Even in cultures that did not have a formalized culture of obesity, there were still Kings (Henry VIII is a notable example) who were nearly as wide as long when they died.

Yet, the average labourer or farmer was not in any danger of being called "fat." Modern dieters go into shock when they see historical cookbooks. Pounds of butter, dozens of eggs, and liters of cream would make anyone fat, right? Sure, in today's world 4000-5000 daily calories would fatten us up, but in worlds without central heat, air conditioning, internal combustion, and water heaters, those calories would be used up fast.

Boiled Calf's Head

Take a prepared calf's head (hair removed and cleaned, brains taken out). Soak the head and brains in warm water for an hour. Put the head in a pot with enough water to cover it, along with a little salt. Skim off the scum that will rise as the head boils. Boil the brains, chop them, and mix with melted butter, parsley, and salt. Remove the head from the pot, remove the tongue and skin it. Serve the head in the middle of a serving plate, with the tongue and brains around it. Pour melted butter over the head. For an extra treat, add boiled eggs to the chopped brains. Feeds six to seven people, and is in season between March and October.[24]

Of course, even those of leisure would become rotund once their youthful metabolisms slowed down and they'd stopped whoring, hunting, and playing tennis in their "old age" of thirty.

Recycling: Waste Not, Want Not

History books, fiction, and period dramas often focus on the aristocrats. They show people of waste, not people of economy. Movies and books about Georgianna, Duchess of Devonshire, King Henry VIII, Emperor Nero, and Mr. Darcy show the worlds of excess and fashion, where money has no meaning in the face of power, politics, and passion.

Every day people did not have luxuries. They scrapped and toiled to survive. The people who scrubbed Mr. Darcy's floors or who made Georgianna's stockings did not have money to throw away on pianos and gambling. For those on the lower rungs (and those who worked the wealthy kitchens), a lot of recycling and reusing was going on.

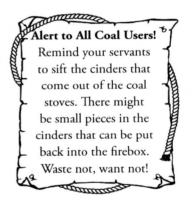

Alert to All Coal Users!
Remind your servants to sift the cinders that come out of the coal stoves. There might be small pieces in the cinders that can be put back into the firebox. Waste not, want not!

The poor had to scratch for whatever means that they could to earn a few pennies and to get food at the cheapest rate possible. Many of these were legitimate jobs. While most only provided enough money to scrape by, occasionally people did make their fortunes.

- Any food leftovers that can no longer be useful to people can go into a swill pail. The leftovers can be boiled up and given to the pigs and chickens. For city folks without animals, this swill (also known as swish or wash) could be sold to the Wash Man for a couple pennies. The Wash Man would then sell the mixture to country pig farmers.

- Rich wash could also be purchased for a small fee. A shop would purchase the leftovers from a large house or gentlemen's club and sell the leftovers. Poor families who could not afford to eat meat on a daily (or even weekly) basis could purchase a mutton bone for their own soup pot (a bone that would have been cooked a couple of times at least, and perhaps even been chewed on by a dog at some point).

- Bones might also be sold to the Bone and Rag man. The bones would be ground into fertilizer

- Used tea and coffee grounds could be used to clean coal-dusty floors. Coal left soot everywhere and the damp, used leaves and grounds would stick to the soot and stop it from kicking around. Everything could be then dumped into the composter to fertilize the crops and/or kitchen garden.

- This household dust could also be sold to the dust man, where it would be sifted for valuables (like in Charles Dickens' Our Mutual Friend), then sold to be turned into bricks.

- Used tea leaves could also be sold to charwomen, who sold them to tea dealers. These dealers used chemicals and dyes and mixed the leaves with fresh ones and sold at the regular price.

- Animal drippings were used as a replacement for butter, and could be sold/given away as such for much cheaper than purchasing butter. My father, who is in his 80s, remembers war rationing in Newfoundland; his parents picked molasses over butter. To replace the butter, they used salt pork drippings. Throughout my childhood, there would often be a pan on the stove of solid salt pork fat that my dad would dip his toast into...before smothering with blackstrap molasses.

If you are writing a poor Steampunk heroine who is on the brink of prostitution, perhaps some of these jobs might help her earn a few pennies to keep her off the streets. She might buy used meat to feed her bastard son. Today, it is difficult to believe that anyone would purchase a trice-boiled bone from anyone to bring home to their family. However, when poverty is absolute, people will do just about anything to survive.

Of course, any cunning, sexually-experienced widow will sell her sheep intestines to women like the infamous former prostitute Mrs. Phillips, who started a successful personalized condom company so that others could continue sinning in her stead. Not all heroines were born to starve.

Chapter 8: The Dark Side of Food Politics, Famine, and Genocide

One for the rook,
One for the crow,
One to let rot,
One to let grow.[1]

There were some heated debates over the inclusion of this chapter; thankfully, all of the arguing was with myself and not my editors. I wanted *What Kings Ate* to be entertaining; a book where readers and writers could all laugh and giggle, gasp and ewww together. Yet, try as I may, I could not get around the dark aspects of food. As a lover (and occasional writer) of dark fiction, I felt that this chapter was necessary for the complete circle of food.

Historically, over 7000 plant species have been used in human diets worldwide. The international community has identified several species that are the most important to the food security of the planet. Some of them are chickpea, coconut, yams, millet, sunflower, barley, lentil, beans, potato, sorghum, and maize.[2]

Now consider that less than 150 plant species are used today in modern agriculture. Even more shocking, there are only 12 plant species that represent the major vegetarian sources we eat in the western world.

Let's put that "12" in perspective.

There are 4000 varieties of potato and 100,000 varieties of rice.[3]

12.

Can you see a problem?

Food security is a huge issue in today's modern world. Even in my own city, food security is a hot topic. Forums and conferences are regularly held to discuss our reliance on imported food, lack of support for local food producers, and the cost of purchasing locally. Through my previous employment of working with Edmonton's inner city, I attended many of these panels, and have spoken about the topic to several newspapers, news networks, governmental panels, and volunteer tour groups. When dealing with topics such as poverty, the economics of compassion, and the realities of the local political, economic, and social attitudes, I quickly became aware that it was so much more complex than dealing with just feeding people.

I look back in time to when the potato famine happened in Ireland and look at how we today would handle such a catastrophic event in our own food network. In our post-modern era, we have dealt with food crises and we want to help. Unfortunately, there are often many barriers in the way, including dictatorships, local violence, terrorists, lack of infrastructure, along with medical, religious, and cultural requirements.

Can you imagine the difficulty of addressing a famine with no internet, no transport trucks, no rail lines, no cargo planes? Add to that mess xenophobia, racism, and a cultural or religious belief that people are born into economic castes or spheres that should never interact, and you have a disaster waiting to happen.

You might ask what this has to do with famine, food security, and crop failure. Crop failure and famines are often acts of the gods, outside of any human's ability to predict (unless you have a crop oracle in your story. In that case, why isn't anyone listening to her? This could have been avoided!). A lack of scientific knowledge in crop rotation, or a "modern" scientific mindset that anything done in the past isn't correct could bring on a famine, too. Likewise, a caste system where poor people need cheap and easy-to-produce food could cause the continuous farming on land that needs crop rotation to survive.

It was difficult to pick a couple of situations to discuss plant diversity and man-made famine brought on by racism and cultural attitudes. There are so many to choose from the world over, and many are still happening today. I opted not to choose modern ones because I did not want my politics to seep into the narratives; I like you too much to put you through that torture! Instead, I've chosen one of the most widely known examples, as well a lesser known example from the days of European colonization.

The Great Famine

The Irish potato famine of the mid-19th century started when a potato blight began spreading across Irish crops. The potato had become a starch staple in Ireland, providing 60% of the nation's food needs. The move to the extreme dependence upon one food was not an overnight decision, but rather the result of a series of laws starting at the beginning of the 19th century.

The move to the heavy dependence on potatoes wasn't an overnight decision. It began in the early 18th century. Ireland's staple diet of cereal crops and dairy products morphed to consisting of mostly potato amongst the very poor. Potatoes were a useful winter staple for the poor, since they are high in starch and vitamin C. Also the potato stores well in the cold. A farmer could grow three times as many potatoes as cereal crop on the same piece of land, and an acre of potatoes could feed a family for the year. It's no surprise that by the dawn of the 19th century, the potato had become the primary food for the poor all year around.

With the potato's spread, a new form of tenant farming system developed in Ireland that lowered living standards and created a cheap workforce. Further, Catholic farmers were unable to own land, causing an even larger gap between the poor and rich than what existed before.

The heavy focus on growing one type of crop, with no crop rotation, and no real variety in the diets of the poor caused the extreme failure of the crops for successive years. Before the arrival of the blight (a potato disease), there had been several crop failures. However, the widespread nature of the blight after 1844 was unlike anything previous.

In 1846, nearly 75% of the potato crop was lost. Losing the crop did not just mean that there was no food that year. It meant that there were no seed potatoes, as many were being eaten to stave off starvation. With less seed potatoes to plant, there were fewer potatoes overall planted the following spring. Rinse, repeat, year after year.

Consequently, one million of the three million Irish people that were solely and completely dependent on potatoes for their livelihoods and for the base of their diet died.

Now, that is a very basic summary of the potato famine. The issue is in fact significantly more complicated than that, because the above does not take into account any of the below:

- Why were these people starving while living next door to a wealthy nation?
- What role did the aristocracy play in causing the economic caste system that created such a reliance on potatoes to begin with?
- What role did racism and classism play?
- Why didn't the government prevent the mass evictions of tenant farmers from their homes?
- Why did the government allow the continued export of Irish grain from the country?

The questions above aren't just directly related to the Potato Famine. A story about a farmer-turned-politician could ask these questions, too, and a deep story about poverty and class could be explored. If you are looking for a complex situation to base your historical novel or perhaps one to base an epic fantasy story on, the Great Famine is perhaps one of the most interesting historical events you can research.

The Beothuk Extinction

The Beothuk people were an aboriginal group living on the island of Newfoundland at the time of the arrival of Europeans in the 15th and 16th centuries.

The Beothuk were a small group that migrated between the coastal and inland regions of the island with the seasons. They relied on seals, fish, and caribou, along with the smaller animals like foxes, rabbits, and martens. As fishermen and trappers arrived and settled in the province, there was a greater push on resources.

Tensions grew between the Beothuk and the Settlers. Violence escalated between both groups, forcing Newfoundland governors in 1769 to issue a proclamation ordering residents to live in peace with the Beothuk. This well-meaning measure went unheeded and violence and encroachment of territory continued.[4]

By the early 1800s, the Beothuk people confined themselves to a small portion of the island. However, the continued expansion of both Europeans and another aboriginal group pushed the Beothuk into cycles of mutual violence. The Beothuk lost access to their

Why Didn't the Beothuk Hunt Moose?

For anyone who has been to Newfoundland, the first thing you notice is the moose. They are everywhere, or as the locals say, "t'e place is lousy with moose." The island has a human population of just over 500,000 people, and a moose population of 100,000 to 150,000! Four moose were introduced to the province in 1904. That's right; the descendants of four moose took over the entire island.

The largest deer-like animal the Beothuk would have had access to would have been the caribou.

food sources and either starved to death, died from smallpox or tuberculosis, or were killed or captured.

Shanawdithit was a captured Beothuk woman who provided us with most of our current knowledge of her people. She died in 1829 and her people were officially considered extinct.

Like with the Great Famine, there are a lot of additional questions to explore when considering the role of too many people and not enough resources on a people:

- What role did the culture of the Europeans and the Beothuk contribute to the rising tensions?
- What role did xenophobia and racism play in decisions of contact on either side?
- Why were the captured Beothuk not turned back to their own people?
- Was this an extinction or a genocide?

As in the potato famine, these questions need not be applied directly to this topic, though these have been explored in many stories and scholarly papers about the Beothuk's demise. Their story is a sad tale of misunderstanding, clashes of culture, colonization, and the strain on resources. However, the lessons learned and the questions posed from this tragedy can be used to fuel new stories, new ideas, and new fantasies.

Gender Politics

This is a tough topic for me. It is very difficult to look at historical agricultural societies without my urban, feminist lens. When I hear phrases like "a woman's place", I bristle and contort. Many fantasy authors, myself included, have worked hard to ensure that our fiction includes equal opportunities for our female characters. I would have rather stuck my fiction in a drawer than turn my beloved Lady Champion Bethany from my Tranquility Series into a domestic servant, scrubbing the floors of the Knight hall.

But—and this is a big but—it is vital that I discuss the reality of the gender roles that have historically existed. Because, they did exist.

Women working "inside the home" is a reality in many cultures, civilizations, and tribes. We can always find exceptions but generally in farming groups women tended the house. We often put the modern glasses on when we hear that phrase. Soccer moms, afternoon tête-à-têtes, and a busy life of grocery shopping, making supper, and cleaning the house all come to mind when we hear "house work" and "house wife." We use the Victorian filter of separate spheres and the 1950s domestic goddess image to cloud those terms, and that would be incorrect.

The traditional role of the average woman was as backbreaking as that of the traditional man in any agricultural setting. The image of the powdered lady in fine silk is only from a select stratum of society. Everyday women worked hard; her job went well beyond breastfeeding children and handy work. If the husband's role was to ensure the animals and grains were ready, the wife's job was to ensure the food lasted them throughout the year with as little waste as possible. The role of the domestic housewife in farming communities cannot be underestimated.

We can also look to semi-pastoral people, such as the Himba, in Namibia. Their traditional divisions of gender roles are different than that of many full farming communities, but still different than what we are used to in the modern world. The Himba women care for the herds, with the small children remaining behind with a couple of women to nurse and care for the little ones. The men confine themselves to intellectual tasks, such as politics. Or the Incas, who ate their morning meal communally, where the women cooked the food at home and brought it to the meal. Spouses ate sitting back-to-back, the husbands first.

It's so easy to look at the traditional farming roles of man versus woman and use a modern eye. However, our information is often skewed. The further back in history we go, the less we know about the average, everyday person. With literacy being something the average worker didn't possess, little has been done to preserve their stories. So, we often think of women in these roles as sitting around, gossiping, and playing with her children. This might have been true for the richest set, but not for the bottom set.

Men worked the fields, moving the large animals and heavy metal ploughs through the dirt in any weather. Even when using horses or oxen, someone had to guide the animals, walking with them, tugging on the reins or ropes, and repositioning the plough each time it became stuck or was knocked off course by a large rock.

Women worked around the homestead. She might be in charge of feeding the pigs when they are stalled near the house (or living cheek-by-jowl in the house). The chickens, geese, turkeys, and ducks would have fallen to her care, putting out the daily feed for them. The vegetable and herb garden outside of the homestead would have been hers to care for, ensuring that fresh vegetables, greens, and herbs would be available year around (depending on where she lived, of course). Foraging for apples, berries, pears, plums, and other local produce would have also fallen to her.

When money was tight, some of these women also hired themselves out as seamstresses and domestic servants. If the local manor was having a party, they might send out the word for needing temporary help. Men and women would apply. Women would be given difficult, dirty jobs and paid less for them. In fact, that is why some of the English Kings employed male chefs, as opposed to female kitchen staff; men cost more. There was a lot of prestige to being able to afford the most expensive help money could buy.

The husband, plus any older boys, would have worked on building the cow sheds, created the hedges around their property (if local customs didn't allow for free wandering of animals or if it was unsafe to do so), and repairing the thatch roofs. They would have washed and sheared the sheep, birthed calves, and slaughtered the pigs.

142

Whereas his wife, and any daughters plus young sons, would have worked cleaning foraged foods, salted butchered pigs, and made dairy. They would have kept the house clean, plus ensured nutritious and hearty meals were on the table each day.

Everyone worked hard for the food on their plates.

Slavery

I've talked about slavery a few times thus far, but I would be remiss if I did not include it here as well. Slavery has existed in various forms throughout history. The most well-known is the use of African slaves in the Southern United States and into Central America and the islands. There are, however, other cases of slavery. Antiquity had plenty of examples of slavery among the Greeks, Romans, Egyptians, India, pre-Columbian Americas, and China.

I did a survey of Twitter followers and asked what a slave was, or to provide an example of a slave. The answer was nearly uniformly the same: the image of a captured African brought to a cotton field, to be whipped and beaten. That answer is not wrong. It just doesn't cover the depth and breadth of slavery.

There are many reasons why a person could end up in slavery:

- Debt: a person in bankruptcy might sell themselves into slavery, or the courts might put them into slavery. Either way, they will be forced to work off their debts.
- War: Capturing the losers of war was a common means of acquiring slaves. We know that the Egyptians and Romans did it, most famously, but there is plenty of evidence to show that it was common throughout antiquity, and perhaps before.
- Serfdom and bondage: A form of modified slavery, but nonetheless slavery in the broad sense of the word. Individually, a serf could not be sold or purchased, but the land on which they lived could be, thereby the new

143

landowner received the serf. Since serfs and bonded individuals could not legally abandon their land, his fate was in the hands of others.

- Orphans and Parentage: Children born in slavery, or left orphaned, often remained slaves. Slave-born and orphan children were stains that many cultures found difficult to overlook. Girls could be sold to temples and brothels (and brothels ran by temples), especially in families with a large number of female mouths and not enough males.

Slavery still exists, even in today's world. There are about 27 million slaves in the world today, more than has ever existed before. Sex slaves, bonded workers, debt slaves, and child soldiers still fight wars, service soldiers, and scrub floors, just as they did two thousand years ago.[5]

When your hero visits the brothels, will he notice young girls with bruises around their wrists where ropes and shackles hold them at night? Or will prostitution be just another job opportunity, where women purchase the right to be apprenticed in the acts of sex?

Or will your hero turn a blind eye to the bruises and scars, just as we do today even though we know our coffee, chocolate, sugar, and fish might have been touched by slaves?

Chapter 9: Beverages, Beer, and Bottled Water

"Wine moderately drank, fortifies the stomach, and other parts of the body, helps digestion, increases the spirits, heats the imagination, helps the memory, gives vigour to the blood, and works by urine.
Wine drank to excess, heats too much, corrupts the liquors of the body, intoxicates, and causes many pernicious diseases; as fevers, apoplexies, palsy, lethargy, and the like.[1]"

It probably says a lot about humans that we have been producing beer and other fermented alcoholic beverages for a very long time. I could cite the medicinal properties of alcohol, along with health benefits, and the importance of beer and wine in urban centres with poor water supplies, and I'd be right.

However, I can't set aside my modern sensibilities, and admit that I think our prehistoric ancestors enjoyed a good blitzing on occasion. If it's good enough for the robins who eat fermenting fruit, it's good enough for us, right?

Alcohol has held a significant place in earth's history, as it is a preservative, an analgesic, a disinfectant, and hey, can really alter a person's mood. It also alters the nutritional composition of the food and can get rid of the hunger pangs.

It would be impossible to list all of the ritual, historical, and cultural beverages that exist or have existed or might have existed. There are volumes out there just on alcohol's history. However, here are a few alcoholic and tea-sipper examples to help quench parched throats in your epic fantasies.

Coffee

I have a confession: I achieved a decade of MMOs (that's geek lingo for hanging out online playing games like EverQuest and Eve Online), a university degree, and several jobs in phone customer support without ever drinking a coffee.

No, I'm not lying. I really did do it.

It wasn't until I discovered the creamy, milky goodness of a non-fat vanilla latte that I realized how incomplete my life had been until that moment. Oh Nirvana, thank you for not forsaking me.

Coffee has fueled many a university degree and has helped many a video gamer achieve level 75 Battle Mage at 4am (it's totally OK if you don't know what I'm talking about... I won't judge).

So despite the glories of coffee, it has a bad reputation amongst the fantasy crowd. I did a quick survey for this section, asking why coffee rarely appears in epic fantasies that are based on quasi-medieval European settings. The reply was fairly consistent: coffee is from the New World (with Columbia, Mexico, and Brazil at the top of the geographical locations) and can't be included in the same way that potatoes can't be included.

So I did another survey. Why don't your Regency romances have coffee? The overwhelming answer? Coffee was a modern beverage. Jane Austen would never have tasted it.

This shocked me, to be completely honest. I don't know what surprised me more, the fact that coffee is a modern drink or that coffee originated in Columbia. Then and there I knew that I had to have a coffee section in this book.

Most of the world's coffee is currently grown in Central and South America, so I completely understand why so many people thought it originated there. But, it did not. Coffee originated in Ethiopia. Legend has it that a young boy tending his goat herd noticed the animals behaving strangely: running around, leaping, and having just a grand ol' time. He saw that they had been eating

146

red berries from a tree, so he tried some, too, and he liked how they made him feel.[2]

Now, I'm not an expert on if there were really dancing goats or not, but I like the story. Coffee "cherries" (as the red berries were called) were chewed, along with the leaves, until the 16th century. Sometimes, they were ground and mixed with animal fat and eaten in that form.

I'll pause while the computer programmers stop reading to go combine coffee beans and bacon grease.

In the 16th century, the berries were roasted, ground, and mixed with water and turned into the coffee beverage we recognize today.

- Muslim monks approved coffee as it kept them alert through their prayers and did not violate the prohibition against fermented beverages (aka alcohol). Coffee began as a special drink that was used in ritual ways in ritual spaces, but it quickly became an international commodity:
- 900s: Coffee appears in writing by the Arab physician Rhazes
- By 1500: Muslim pilgrims spread coffee through the Middle East and North Africa
- 1536: Coffee is exported through Mocha, Yemen. The name sticks.
- 1650-1690: Coffee houses open in England, Germany, Venice, Paris, Vienna
- 1971: Starbucks opens in Seattle[3]

Many early coffeehouses were male institutions, though several in London's Covent Garden area had plenty of female prostitutes hanging out, ready for hire. That did not mean, however, that coffee wasn't drank at home. In fact, the Regency cookery goddess, Maria Eliza Rundell, sets aside space to discuss how to make coffee, plus a section on how to make it for "foreigners, or those who like it extremely strong."[4]

Chocolate

I hesitated to put chocolate into this chapter because it's technically not a drink in the classic sense of the word. However, its historical use has been rooted in the liquid form, so it has found its place here.

Cocoa dates back thousands of years and probably first grew in South America, most likely Peru or Venezuela. It was mixed with vanilla, herbs, flowers, honey, chilies, or maize. It was turned into beverages, a porridge, and a drink with a frothed top. Later Mayan rituals involved chocolate coloured with achiote (a plant used to add red to foods and cosmetics) to symbolize a sacrificial victim's blood. Cacao and ground maize could be mixed together and poured into jars from a standing position to make it froth, and then savory spices and herbs were added.

The Aztecs crushed and roasted the beans, and added various spices, and turned it into a beverage. Cortes recorded that the beverage was bitter, thick like honey, and mixed with chili, annatto (another plant used in dying), and maize, and diluted with boiling water. While Cortez thought the beverage strange, Montezuma II drank fifty glasses a day of it.[5]

Cacao beans were also used as a form of currency. Money actually grew on trees, as Cortes recorded in his journal. There were even counterfeit cacao beans, created by some of the Aztec criminal minds. Drinking a glass of chocolate is akin to us using a $100 bill to snort cocaine or scoop up onion dip to smear on our potato chips!

Once chocolate entrenched itself in European palettes, new combinations were added to the ground cacao. In 1745, it was "in vogue" to drink chocolate as a liquid. Water was most

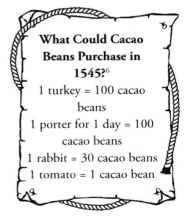

What Could Cacao Beans Purchase in 1545?[6]

1 turkey = 100 cacao beans

1 porter for 1 day = 100 cacao beans

1 rabbit = 30 cacao beans

1 tomato = 1 cacao bean

often used, though some people put cow's milk and egg yolks into it. Others used almond milk.[7] Liquid chocolate was often served with breakfast!

In the interest of scholarly research, I took to drinking liquid chocolate for breakfast. There is a local chocolate boutique in Edmonton called Sweet Lollapalooza (also known as Liquid Nirvana and The Place All of My Money Goes). I picked up a couple containers of his liquid chocolate—little more than chocolate, a bit of sugar, and chili spices—to try this experiment. Each day for a week, I had a small tea cup of hot chocolate for breakfast along with a scone.

Oh my.

I have no idea why we stopped having chocolate for breakfast or whose bright idea it was to tell us it was a bad thing. Like any food, there are always haters who cannot understand the tastes and preferences of other people:

"Some mix several other drugs therewith, which we disapprove of, as ginger and pepper, because they are too hot.[8]"

Those types often take credit for "improving" the taste:

"Chocolate is a dry paste, of a very pleasant taste, and much used by the Americans, who shew'd the way of making it to the Christians soon after the discovering of that country: However, though we are beholding to those people for the invention of it, we have so far improved it by the compositions we use, that the chocolate made in Paris is better than that brought us out of America.[9]"

Chocolate's history is not all happy food goodness, however, as it is tainted with racism, elitism, and slavery. Chocolate has a dark side that can be used in a fantasy novel. Several years ago, I was attending a conference on food security in Alberta and Carol Off, author of *Bitter Chocolate*, gave a talk about her experiences in Côte d'Ivoire. One thing she said stood out to me and has stayed with me. She'd asked one of the children working on the cocoa plantation if they knew what the cocoa beans were for. They did not. These children worked their lives in harsh conditions, many having been kidnapped and forced into labour, many starved and brutalized, and they hadn't even tasted a chocolate bar, the fruit of their lives. There is an unspeakable gulf between the child's hand picking the cocoa beans and the child's hand that stuffs a chocolate into their face and begs for more.[10]

Imagine a world where magic could be harvested, giving people immense power, long life, or perhaps magical abilities. Would anyone care that children far away were being whipped, beaten, and raped? Many people today don't care, and we're only getting a sweet treat from the deal. Imagine if it was the ability to read minds or heal our loved ones? That's a dark fantasy story in the wings.

Be wary of fake cocoa powder. It could be "extended" with brick dust.

Of course, I cannot end this section on a low note. Just as a dark fantasy story could be about child slaves harvesting magical beans, it could also feature socially-minded people fighting against slavery, just like the Victorian aristocrats who boycotted slave-made chocolate and fought the plantations.

For example, one of the original chocolate dynasty families, the Frys, were deeply distressed by the working conditions of the West Africa cacao plantations owned by the Portuguese. The conditions bordered on slavery and the Frys boycotted cacao from those areas until worker conditions improved. So, perhaps your hero takes a stand for worker rights as well.[11]

"Tea"

I use quotes around tea because the word tea is actually fraught with significant issues from a historical point of view. For example, when we hear the word tea there are certain images that come to mind. British aristocrats in powdered wigs and massive satin gowns sipping from tiny cups with their pinkies in the air. Or, a bunch of grannies sitting around with bone china cups gossiping about their

150

husbands. Or, maybe picking up an iced passion fruit herbal tea from the local coffee stop. Or, perhaps a Cree man making a healing tea for his aged mother.

Today, all of those things mean tea to us. However, the term tea is actually considered a very specific product from China. It refers to the green or black/brown tea that we associated with society ladies in lace gloves and expertly pointed up pinkie fingers (which, just so you know, was caused by the tiny size of the cups and not by any weird hand cramping).

How tea was first discovered we're not sure, though some anthropologists believe early humans munched on tea leaves and discovered the glorious effects of caffeine.

Around 1500BC, tea was being consumed in China for medicinal purposes. Tea leaves were combined with seeds, barks, plants, and leaves to create herbal remedies. It is believed that sometime around 1122-256 BC people began to boil tea leaves for their personal enjoyment, as opposed for medicinal reasons.[12]

Eventually, tea went from being a crude, bitter beverage to a cultural rite in China. Pottery, cakes, and social rules sprouted up (just as it would five hundred years later when tea grabbed British aristocratic women by the hemline).

As tea spread through the world, it became a source of power, money, and political strife. Tea broke the American patience, fed up with taxes on tea, wine, coffee, and other items. Whereas, across the ocean, ladies in Britain were learning that with only a tea pot, they could entertain half of London without sending their husbands into the poor house. Tea even caused a building boom in shipping, with British and American shipbuilders racing to build fast ships to trade tea faster for greater profits.

The tea race would make a fascinating steampunk, with airship clippers racing from India to Bermuda to Britain in the quest of tea.

Lesser Known Drinks

I've covered the more popular and well-known drinks. However, this book wouldn't be complete without some weirder ones, like horse alcohol, would it?

Black Drink

A caffeinated tea from the American Southeast, made from the Yaupon Holly plant, and other local plants. It could be used as a form of Ipecac, to induce vomiting. Its use stretches back into prehistory, and was used in ceremonies including ritual vomiting. It was considered a purifier with spiritual roots and typically used by men.

Yerba Mate

Native to South American, Yerba Mate is a caffeine-containing plant that is drank similar to tea or coffee. It was drank by indigenous people and continued in use after European colonization.

Grog

Grog is, quite frankly, whatever you believe it is. There is no one recipe, concoction, or definition for this sailor's drink. The most well-known grog recipe is from the British navy in the 17th century, where rum, water, sugar, and spices were combined together.

Koumiss

A Mongolian drink that comes from mare's milk. The fresh milk would be placed in a hide container and strapped to their horses so that it would be stirred and churned while travelling. It has a low alcohol content allowing it to be used in place of water that could be contaminated.

Get to the Meads, Ales, and Beers Already

Fantasy novels are littered with alcoholics. Hell, even history is! I often wonder if there would have been less war and conflict if everyone drank just a few glasses less a day (of course, the water would probably have killed them earlier, so the constant political upheaval might have balanced out the sobriety).

Alcohol is fairly egalitarian in the western world. We can all pop down to the local liquor store and pick up a case of Alexander Keith's IPA without having to show more than our ID. This is rather Neolithic of us, as many Neolithic sites across China and the Middle East hold houses with pottery shards with alcohol residue still on them. Just regular people with regular beer; no caste system and no priestly purposes for the mind-altering drink.

Today, we see beer as something that is drank freezing cold and use words like "iced", "ice cold", "freezing", and other sub-zero adjectives to describe how the beer should be served. Historically, however, beer was not kept at 4C. For example, the "liquid bread" of the Egyptians, made from rye, water, date juice, and spices, could be served warm.[13] Many other cultures put their "beer by the fire" to warm it up before drinking.

Ancient forms of brewing would have had a large amount of debris floating on the surface of the drink. Instead of straining it, some cultures drank their beer through a straw!

But regardless how you drink it, hot, cold, with a spoon or with a straw, one thing is certain: beer, wine, and spirits are amongst the oldest drinks in the world. Perhaps that says a lot about us as a species. Our ancestors saw some robins drunkenly staggering around after eating berries, so we decide that looked pretty darn awesome and mass produced the staggering.

Mead is served in most fantasy taverns, with metal tankards being slammed down on wooden tables, slopping the beverage all over the floors (for pity's sake—put a lid on that tankard so the flies don't get into it!). From Beowolf to Tolkien, mead features heavily in the literature of the fantastical.

Mead is an old drink made from fermenting water, honey, and yeast together until one gets a simple alcoholic beverage. Archeologist Dr. Patrick McGovern, along with Dogfish Head Brewery, recreated one such old mead, an ancient Chinese beverage from 7000BC, whose original mixture was rice, honey, and hawthorn and/or grapes.[14]

There are endless recipes for mead, beer, ale, rum, cider, and gin, so I couldn't include them all. My one attempt at making honey mead was a complete failure. *Combine sugar and honey and yeast and lemons in a glass jar and it'll be great my ass.* Never in my life have I felt more in line with the Romans, the original Borg from Star Trek, who went around assimilating everything, including beverages. I'm with them; wine is far classier than that scary stuff I made on the kitchen counter.

Lora: An inferior wine that was made from the leftovers of wine production, drank by Roman slaves. The leftover grape pulp was mixed with water and pressed for a second or third time.[15]

But I promised from the early days of this book that I would find a couple of good mead recipes to share. I've hunted and found these two. I've modernized them only slightly and still should be enough for you to a) cause no end of trouble in your own kitchen and b) ensure your hero has enough to drink so that he can run off with the heir to the throne, the crown Prince of Istav.

Strong Mead

Start with bloodwarm water and dissolve honey in it until it's able to handle the weight of an egg without it sinking beyond the breadth of a shilling. Boil the mixture gently for an hour, skimming the scum off the top.

Add ten gallons of water to the honey mixture. In a bag, combine eight blades of mace, three nutmegs, twenty cloves, four sticks of cinnamon, three ginger roots, and a quarter ounce of Jamaica pepper (allspice). Tie sprigs of rosemary together and toss them plus the spices into the honey mixture.

Bring the mixture to a boil and toss out the rosemary. Pour mixture into an earthen pot and let it sit overnight. Strain into a storing vessel. Hang the spice bag inside the cask before stopping it. Let it sit for three months. Taste it. If it tastes all right, pour into bottles. Let them sit for six weeks and then get really drunk.

> The Chinese had a fermented rice or millet beverage called li that was sweet and low-alcoholic.

Small Mead

Take three gallons of hot water and dissolve three quarts of honey and a pound of sugar into it. Boil the mixture for thirty minutes, skimming any scum that rises.

Pour the honey mixture into a tub and add the juice of four lemons, the rinds of two lemons, twenty cloves, two pieces of ginger, and a handful of rosemary. Let the liquid cool until it's blood warm. Make a brown toast and spread it with three spoonfuls of ale-yeast. Add to the liquid. Pour into a cask and let it sit for five days. Then, strain it into bottles. Drink until your mood improves.[16]

If meads are honey based, than beer is cereal and sugar-based. Beer can be made from pretty much anything that has sugar, but is usually made from hops, malted barley and/or malted wheat. Ales are just a style of beer, made from malt.

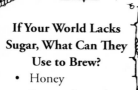

If Your World Lacks Sugar, What Can They Use to Brew?
- Honey
- Sprouted cereal grains
- Fruit and berries

Fantasy novels often talk about "small" beer, the name for a weak beer that's meant more for hydration than inebriation. While the origin of the name is up for debate (there isn't enough paper in this book to cover the debate, so excuse me while I skip over it completely), there is no debate that such differences in alcoholic strengths existed. The mild-altering effects of alcohol have been known since humans first consumed fermented berries. While the chemical process might not have been understood, there has been a long understanding that certain beers and wines quenched your thirst, while others got you dancing on the tables stripping off your chain mail and small clothes.

Ale could be flavoured with more than just berries and fruit. Chickens could also be used.

Cock Ale

Start a regular batch of ale in the traditional way. When the ale is not quite done working, take an old cock and flea him, gut him, and stamp him in a stone mortar until his bones are broken. Take the poor cock and put him in a sack with three pounds of raisins, a few blades of mace, and a few cloves. Add the sack to the ale. In nine days, remove the sack and bottle the ale as usual.[17]

Liquid Bread

Lovers of Joss Whedon will already know the term, of course. It might surprise people that this was an actual fact; liquid bread probably existed in ancient Egypt in some form.

Barley and wheat were turned into a mash and mixed together, and possibly grapes and dates were added, too. This might not have been turned into an alcoholic drink, however. It might have been turned into a hearty gruel in a thin, drinkable form.

Unfiltered beer has a higher nutritional content than leavened bread, with more protein and B vitamins. Workers who built the Great Pyramids received a daily allotment of two or three loaves of bread and about four to five liters of beer a day.

Today exists a popular method of making wheat beer among the Nile peasants and boatmen, called bouza and the process resembles that described 1500 years earlier. Wheat is ground and lightly baked as a leavened bread. The break is broken, diluted with water, and combined with malt. This is heated and processed until it ferments into a beer.

With an alcohol content ranging from 3.8% (day 1 of fermentation) upward to 8.1%, the beer had the consistency of thin gruel and was probably drank through a straw, as it is in many other regions.[18]

Wine

On the front cover of this book, you might have noticed that the "D" in drank has an image of a monk stealing a drink of wine from the monastery cellar. If you read many history books, you probably have seen the image before. It's rather popular. Perhaps it's the image of a Middle Ages monk, the ultimate symbol of self-sacrifice, sneaking down to the cellar to get drunk that appeals to so many people. It's one of my personal favourites from the era: the contradiction between myth and reality.

How did we discover wine? Was it an accident, grapes having been left out to ferment? Did grapes get crushed in a skin or bladder and turn into wine? Did grapes get tossed into a pottery jug and forgotten for a few weeks?

We're not sure about the hows and whys of wine's discovery. Our earliest traces of wine are upwards of 10,000 years old in Iran. We also know that clay jugs were being used for wine storage by about 6000 BC, and that by 4000BC, Persia (modern day Iran) was exporting rose wine.

Grape wine isn't something produced by foraging. New vines don't produce fruit right away, and the picking period is quite short. The grapes would need to be picked quickly and crushed. The crushed fruit would be kept at room temperature until they fermented. [19]

Grapes aren't the only thing that wine can be made from. Berries, fruits, even birch sap, can be turned into wine, though grape wine is the most widely known. Wine is generally much stronger than beer or ale, so it needs to be taken either with water or in lesser quantities to avoid drunkenness.

Wines have been traded since before the Great Pyramids. Various countries became renowned for their wine, including Italy, Spain, and France, each creating their own special variations. Likewise, many monasteries began growing their own vineyards and producing their own varieties of wine. The desire for these specialized wines knew no boundary or enemy territory, either. Even when the French and English were at war (which, in case you didn't know, was often), the wealthy British still longed for their glasses of Bordeaux while at the gambling table. Politics be damned! They needed their wine.

Bartender's Tip: Wine Can Be Served at Different Temperatures
- To serve wine cooled, wrap a wet cloth around the decanter and put it in the wind.[20]
- Mix wine with hot water for a hot beverage known as calda in Ancient Rome.

But, back to our thieving monk on the cover. Now, we all know a glass of wine is good for you. There have been endless studies showing the benefits of a small glass of red wine a day. We knew this back in the 3rd century. "One glass of wine was for good health," wrote Athenaeus, an Egyptian Greek.

Why stop at one? Two glasses is all about the "love and pleasure." The third glass of wine is what knocks you out. If you're at someone else's house, this is when "wise guests go home."

But, some days, you just need a little more. Six glasses of wine can bring on a drunken revel, whereas eight brought on the police, and ten brought on hurling the furniture. More than that and, well, the drunken, wild orgies known as bacchanalia might get started.[21] This is also known as Frosh Week at many a university.

Supped Up Brew

Without the invention or materials to make whiskey and rum, 1-5% beers and 7-15% wines can get rather dull. The hero builds up a tolerance and can slam back ten tankards in a row and not feel any effects beyond a painfully full bladder. The wine is stronger, but the heroine is usually having it with food, so it's hard for her to pound back a jug of it without anyone noticing she's not eaten her meal. So what's a war-weary warrior to do when he needs to forget the world for a while, but doesn't have the stomach for wine at breakfast?

One word: hallucinogens.

One archaeological theory is that some people, such as the Nordic folk, spiked their beers with opium, marijuana, henbane, and deadly nightshade. While there are some hints of evidence, there is no firm evidence for most spiked theories. However, since this is fantasy, you can just make it up as you go along!

Opium and marijuana might have already been used in Turkmenistan in 2000B.C. as a ceremonial beverage.[22] The Egyptians, Greeks, and Romans used opium as a pain remedy. Why not have your assassin anti-hero slip more deadly nightshade into the beer than it normally would have? Perhaps your heroine, dealing with her decision to murder her lover because he'd been possessed by the evil gods, takes up sneaking the hallucinogenic ceremonial mixture in the cups at the temple and the gods get rather upset with her sipping at the offerings to them. If you aim for more realism in your stories, perhaps your "oracle" might be nothing more than a fourteen year old girl fed a steady diet of opium wine.

At this junction, I should point out how to avoid turning your drinks into vinegar. Without access to cork (either from not having it locally available or from not knowing to use it), clay stoppers were used to prevent wine from turning into vinegar. Wine placed on its side with a clay seal would keep the air out, and the wine would keep the clay damp enough that it would not dry out and let air into the wine.[23] For obvious reasons, your fantasy world needs to have invented some form of pottery, at minimum, to enjoy their boozy habit.

It's also vitally important that your hero purchases wines from reputable sources. Wine could be "extended" by adding cheap cider to it. This wasn't just limited to wine, though. Beer could be altered with molasses, as well as potash in the port, and brick dust in the cocoa.[24]

Working Alcohol into Your Story

Alcohol is often taken for granted in fantasy, but can be used in some interesting ways:

- A means to ply hallucinations out of a young woman, either by itself or with drugs to turn her into an Oracle of sorts
- A means of worship and only used by priests and priestess in their rituals
- Something to be banned because it causes uninhibited behavior
- Used as a means of worship or a part of rituals, as well as used everyday
- A gift from the gods, the good or the bad ones
- A common item with no religious or cultural significance at all
- Can everyone drink it? (For example, Romulus decreed that wine was forbidden to anyone but free men over the age of thirty-five, leaving out slaves, women, and youth.[25])
- Is there a cultural hierarchy of alcohol? Is wine considered higher class than mead?

Water and Disease

The history of contaminated water is well known. Any large body of water near a large population—from the Thames to the Ganges to the Mekong to the Great Lakes—will end up undrinkable before too long. Even with today's technology, understanding of microbes, and environmental laws, we still populate our rivers and lakes to the point that many resemble fecal slushies.

Imagine life in a medieval city, like London or Paris, where people didn't understand that chamber pots couldn't be dumped into their drinking supplies. Diseases mutated and bred, causing outbreaks like the Sweating Sickness (England, mostly London) and the Picardy Sweat (France, mostly Paris), creating mysterious illnesses that baffle us even today.

So how did people get access to water if it looked brown and smelled just like what it looked like? Beer. Tea, coffee, milk, beer, and wine all served useful replacements for untreated water. A pot of water boiling for ten minutes would kill most, if not all, of whatever was in the cesspool the water was drawn from. A cup of tea would not make a person sick, unlike a cup of water right out of the Thames. The fermentation of beer and wine would have killed off the microbes living in the water, and milk, well, comes from a cow, goat, or sheep. It's safe, though spoils fast in the heat.

People in the country had an easier time with access to water. With small farming villages scattered throughout a countryside, there would be plenty of rivers, streams, and ponds to provide water, plus any underground wells that got dug. However, fifty thousand people packed into a small stretch of land around a river or lake would be horribly populated.

In Rome, most people drank from wells and collected rain water barrels.[26] Rain barrels could be set along the roads, so that pedestrians could stop and have a drink, and barrels could be set near doorways and awnings, near roof overhangs, and in the garden, so that there would be a personal supply of fresh water for the family's needs.

This method of standing water would attract insects like mosquitos, which can transmit diseases like malaria. Of course, considering the endless list of diseases caused by river water, perhaps the chance of malaria is a small price to pay for catching the sweating sickness and being dead in four hours.

If standing barrels of water isn't to your liking, perhaps bottled water might meet the needs of your high society characters. Anyone who has read a Jane Austen novel or a Regency romance will read about characters "taking the waters" in Bath. This was a late 18th century European trend where the wealthy went to mineral springs to drink and bathe to cure whatever ailed them. Water hospitals cropped up around some of these sites. By the 19th century, sites were exporting water named after their locations around the world.

And what were the names of those sites? Why, some of the biggest names in bottled water today: Evian, San Pellegrino, and Perrier.

Chapter 10: Foods That Heal

"Feed a cold, starve a fever."
–Middle Ages health advice[1]

Herbal medicine has a long and distinguished tradition that spans the length of our existence. Since the moment a human being got a toothache or pulled a muscle, they have been trying to find ways to cure it. Witchdoctors, doctors, quacks, snake oil salesmen, pharmaceutical companies, shamans, pastors, surgeons, healing women, midwives. Whatever they have been called, people have stepped up to find ways to heal people (or convince people they were healing them).

Modern medicine scoffs at childbirth traditions like placing a knife under the bed to scare away the spirits and demons. Pregnancy is a medical condition that must be treated in a sterile environment. Traditional medicine advocates proclaim garlic and urine clean wounds and stop infection, while nurses faint at the notion and demand antibiotics, clean water, and bandages.

One of the challenges with writing medicine in historical books and fantasies is that we are combining our current knowledge (which may or may not be correct) with a stripped-down version of medicine. In doing so, writers often miss the entire reason such procedures ever were considered: bigotry, sexism, religious beliefs, and lack of technology.

Before socialized medicine, which is still not a reality in many parts of the world, people had to pay for doctors and medical advice was expensive. Henry VIII employed surgeons, physicians, and apothecaries because he could afford it; the average peasant could never afford to have the doctor drop by their house (even assuming the individual would lower himself to visit a mere peasant).

Women often took on the role of healer. Some suggest this was because women were associated with midwifery for most of human history, while others believe it is because women are often considered an extension of Mother Earth. Still others believe it was because the woman was already in the kitchen so it wasn't a stretch for her to whip up some poultices and salves. Theories for this are well outside the scope of this book, but the development of such questions is not outside the scope of a fantasy novel.

Medicinal Teas

- Labrador Plant Tea: sore throats and colds. Used to soothe diarrhea and stomach aches.
- Red Cedar Tea: sore throats, coughs, colds. Use to help induce labour.
- Raspberry Tea: Prevent miscarriage and reduce labour pains.
- Dandelion Tea: Help prevent scurvy (when made out of the leaves). Tea made from the roots is a mild laxative.
- Common Snowberry Tea: helps get rid of princes and other targets of note. They are the ghosts of Saskatoon berries and are thus belonging to the spirit world. The living should never eat them. Unless, of course, there is a princeling in your way. In that case, let him drink to his heart's content.

Would women hold the uneducated role of local healer in your fantasy, while men took on the world of science and thus causing gender conflict between the scientific and the common? Would magic take the place of science, making it unnecessary for doctors? Or, would magical healers and science clash against each other?

These are the kinds of questions that you can answer in your own work. I even give you permission to beg, borrow, and steal from this book to develop new ideas and conflicts for your fiction.

However, to get you started, here are some of the more common types of healers and how they used plant medicines.

The Wife Healer

Your heroine has successfully dispatched the purification squad that's been pursuing her for a fortnight. She received a leg wound during the conflict which has been leaking pus for days. No matter how much small beer she drinks, she can't take the edge off the pain and the wound's stench is unbearable.

She can't afford a doctor. Or, maybe she's terrified of her leg being amputated. Or, maybe the doctors are all looking for her because she is a female healer and another healer would be able to identify her. Whatever her motives, she ends up at the doorstep of a poor family. The husband helps carry the heroine to the small bed he shares with his wife.

The woman, going against all conventional medical knowledge because she learned the technique from another woman, cleans the wound to get rid of the smell and painstakingly picks the rocks and pebbles out of it. She splashes it with alcohol and the heroine promptly passes out. The wound might even be kept clean afterward with honey, just as the great physicians used on King Henry V after the Battle of Shrewsbury when he was injured.

Our wife will then order her younger daughters to fetch some rosemary to begin distilling, as well as fabric for a poultice and lots and lots of boiling water. It's going to be a long night of healing.

Many families relied on their wives to deal with the everyday aches and pains of the household. A doctor was very expensive and was only to be summoned in dire circumstances for the very poor (and, sometimes, not even called then). She would rely on the plants in her vegetable garden or items she foraged or prepared herself. She might use some of these remedies:

- Powdered fir and spruce needles mixed with animal fat for open wounds and infections
- Juniper-berry tea stopped bleeding and reducing swelling (as a side note, also stopped you from getting pregnant...or being pregnant)
- Rose hips as a means to prevent scurvy
- Cranberry to treat bladder infections
- Wild onion was used as an antibacterial, anti-viral, anti-fungal treatment
- Willow bark tea to reduce inflammation
- Strawberry leaf tea to treat diarrhea[2]

The healer wife's duty to ensure the health of those in her care was part of her basic activities. Just like today, some people did not trust doctors and only would accept treatment from their wives or other local women.[3]

Not all agreed. People like Gervase Markham, writing in the 17th century, believed that the "art of physic" (health care) was "far beyond the capacity of the most skilful woman." However, he was willing to admit that housewives might learn "some ordinary rules and medicines" from the learned male professors of medicine, thereby both assisting her family in general ways and not casting a bad light on the medicine profession as a whole.[4]

The Midwife and Nurse

The midwife held various positions throughout history and often all at the same time. Even today, some people look on midwives with suspicion, whereas others look at the services of a midwife as a right of health care. In fact, my own province moved to include midwifery as part of the universal health care offered, yet many people comment that they would never use a midwife because that would be backward. Add to that modern paradox with the fear of women involving themselves in medicine and science, and sprinkle with a healthy dose of misogyny and religious fervor and the mid-wife becomes a very suspicious creature.

Midwives did not use popular science and medicine. She did not use electrical devices attached to the temples, nor did she merely stand over a woman and ask how she felt post-birth. She touched, examined and looked. Often, her care was more kind than that of medical science.

The midwife might have dismissed the concept of humors and spontaneous development of infection, and instead focused on try-ing to keep a new mother warm, clean, and safe. A doctor might not physically witness a birth, relying on draperies and coverings so that he never saw the baby emerge from the Queen's womb (and, thus, never noticed the hemorrhaging until it was too late), where-as the midwife would have seen the blood and have applied cold compresses and herbs to slow the bleeding.

It's difficult to say how many midwives existed in the Middle Ages, or how many were practicing. The official records between the 12th and 15th centuries show 1.5% of medical experts in France were women, with 1.2% in Britain and Italy. Yet, midwifery was an all-female activity in the Middle Ages, existed in large numbers, and they were trusted for more than just birthing. Trusted mid-wives, often older women of the community, might be given the responsibility of confirming virginity status in prospective brides or, on a much sadder note, the examination of young girls who had been raped.[5]

So why is there a conflict between the reality and the official records? Mistrust, misogyny, medicine-as-male-domain (which I suppose is covered under misogyny), created significant pressures between the established, educated medical profession of men and the uneducated, apprenticed, unorganized group of women. This conflict could bring alive any scene where a young heroine needs the services of a midwife.

Abortion

I've encountered a lot of interesting reactions to my fiction, and have gotten some fairly oddball comments and complaints. There isn't an author out there who hasn't at some point. Authors often say that you haven't really made it until someone takes the time to blog about how awful your book is. But, there is nothing like getting emails that make your jaw drop. For me, those emails are about abortion.

In one of my epic fantasy novels, a character has an abortion. I've gotten a lot of hateful comments about that. It wasn't because of the politics of abortion; I had been braced for that. It was that abortion is a modern creation and therefore is "anachronistic." It stunned me. It was one of those facts that you just assumed everyone knew. Like, did they think the long list of foods pregnant women couldn't eat was to just irritate them?

So, for those people, I have a very shocking announcement: abortion has been happening for a long, long time and food was in league with it.

I took *Introduction to Anthropology* in my first year of university. I don't remember the professor's name anymore, but I remember when he talked about the role of abortion and birth control in hunter-gatherer groups. Assuming single births, a woman is capable of giving birth to three children every two years. How would any nomadic group function if its women each had three babies to look after?

Nomadic tribes have lower birth rates than agrarian communities because children are a hindrance. (Children in agrarian communities are an asset since they can work the land.) Women could only carry, at maximum, two babies at once, and would need to carry them for the bulk of the first two years.[6]

The Georgians and Victorians brought us the concept of "laying in", where a very pregnant and new mother would be locked up in her room for a month to ensure she did not become sick and die. However, this was a luxury for the leisure class. Working class women in many centuries did not have that luxury, nor did nomadic women. My mother often talks about how she gave birth to her eighth child, and had seven others under the age of nine waiting for their dinner. She gave birth, cleaned herself up, and got to making meals since there was no time to lie around.

The nomadic woman would need to practice birth control in some form to prevent this, either in the form of abstinence for two or three years, plants such as juniper to reduce the likelihood of conception (juniper might also cause a miscarriage before she is even aware she is pregnant), or active abortion once her menses has ceased. Or, perhaps a combination of all three.

Many plants have birth control properties. Many of them also can cause abortions, too. Any midwife worth her salt would know the best combination of plants to end a pregnancy. There might be religious or legal edicts against it, but like on the streets of London during the Regency period, the prostitutes and servants who were used and abused by those glamourous bucks and rakes often need-ed an outlet to protect themselves from pregnancy.

Apothecaries and Shaman-healers

It might seem strange to lump these two together—one is dedi-cated to the science of medica-tion while the other is dedicated to the traditional knowledge of plants—but both are, in many ways, the same type of individ-ual. These are typically men in positions of power. For example, an apothecary has some formal training in medicine and is a respectable member of the com-munity. A shaman is often a spiri-

Electuary of Cloves
Combine clove flowers and a pound of sugar dissolved in rosewater; thicken it until it takes the form of a paste and form into tablets. Take with meals. It has many healthy benefits, including exciting the appetite, gladdens the person, increases the force of coitus, and restrains the temperament.[7]

tual and political leader, guiding the community and looking after all aspects of their health.

An apothecary might create their own special elixirs that will cure all that ails ya. If you are very lucky, the cure won't even kill you! Shamans might have special relationships with spirits or gods that can heal members of the community for a price.

In a fantasy setting, apothecaries can be dealing in healing potions, shamans making deals with two-bit demons, all the while the heroine languishes in agony.

Stocking the Medicine Cabinet

Chances are your modern medicine cabinet looks a lot like mine. Bandages of several shapes and sizes, including a couple of used knee tensor bandages from an old injury. Various types of pain killers in progressive degrees of extra-strength, mega-strength, and a few leftover codeine that you know you were supposed to throw out after your back injury healed but kept for a rainy day. Cough syrup, cold medicines (for day and night), and toothache medicines are tumbled together in a basket for middle-of-the-night maladies.

In eras without modern pharmaceuticals, people did not have the range of powerful and potent pain killers we have now. The potent pain killers they had, like the entire line of opioids, offered fabulous pain relief but brought on nasty side effects like addiction and overdoses. However, there are some specific items that will be growing in and around most cottages and will be available for use in emergencies. This is not an exhaustive list by any means, but rather one to help get you started.

Honey

Honey was often stockpiled in castles. In fact, food supplies ran out before the honey supplies did. Since honey is a food, why weren't they eating it? To prevent infection. Honey has a long history in wound treatment. Tests have shown that honey is acidic and anti-bacterial, so could be used as a barrier against infection.[8]

Poultices and Plasters

Oh plasters, the bane of my existence. I've had a plaster or two put on my chest as a kid. They never worked beyond making me more uncomfortable, but others swear they work. Perhaps these people weren't all that sick to begin with.

Mustard plasters are the most commonly-known type of poultice, though many people use them wrong in their stories (I blame television). The mustard paste doesn't go directly on one's skin because it can cause severe skin irritations. Instead, the mustard is smeared on a cloth and then the cloth is placed on the skin (paste side up), and more cloth put over that to keep all of the heat in.

Patients who use mustard plasters might have a reaction to it and sneeze and cough, which if the person is being treated for a cough, this might be taken as a sign that the poultice is doing its work by pushing the cough out.

Salves

Salves are creams that are put on burns, rashes, and other skin irritations. These might not be made up but the ingredients would be in the pantry. Salves were made from butter, lard, tallow and/or lanolin (a grease from sheep's wool), with a small amount of wax mixed in. Lanolin salves worked wonders on cracked hands and lips.

Strong Spirits

Rum or brandy can offer a significant amount of relief when the heroine is hacking up a lung. Brandy mixed with honey, lemon juice, and (optionally) hot water can help quell the worst coughs, plus help the sick one to fall asleep for some much-needed rest.

The medicinal liquor should be kept away from the regular alcohol supplies, or at least labelled so that everyone knows it is for sickness.

Infused Oils and Waters

Plants had different uses. Some were good for skin infections, aches, and injuries, while others were taken internally for upset stomachs, infertility, and depression.

Infused oils were made by boiling plants and herbs from the garden—or foraged from the roadside. Infused water was made by boiling herbs in water and then put into an alembic, where the water would cool and slowly drip out into a waiting cup.

Pre-made Medicines

Many apothecaries, as well as the healing women before their trade, made potions, pills, and other medicines. These might have been made from honey and herbs, such as sage oil (for joint pain), or more chemical like a rosemary alcohol to help combat influenza.

It's important to have a good understanding of herbs and plants, even when purchasing premade medicines. Take this recipe meant to stop excessive gas:

Take six or eight spoonfuls of Pennyroyal-water, put into it four drops of oil of Cinnamon, so drink it anytime of the day, so you fast two [sic] houres after.[9]

Sounds simple enough, right? Anything to end that awful feeling of bloat and pressure. Of course, pennyroyal is an abortifacient. Pennyroyal oil can, and has, killed many young women over the centuries who have attempted to end pregnancies. Teas and potions containing pennyroyal have been used as birth control. It's also been used to end pregnancies.

Steampunk heroines should also beware of pre-packaged medicines. Opium was regularly used in Victorian medicines, especially cough medicines. It was used because it worked. I've had pneumonia and bronchitis a few times in my life and the cough is so bad that a person risks breaking their ribs. When it gets to that stage, the doctor often prescribes codeine syrup or even codeine pills. The codeine helps control the cough so that the patient can get a few hours of rest. I can see why morphine medications would be thought to be even better, since morphine is so much stronger than codeine.

Unfortunately, morphine addiction was very real in the Victorian era so steampunk heroines need to be especially careful of the medications at the pharmacy. Then again, perhaps an addiction to cough syrup is exactly the kind of heroine you were looking for. If so, carry on.

Chapter 11: The Middle of Nowhere

"In Canada, where the winter is never of a less duration than
five months..."
—William Pybus, *A Manual of Useful Knowledge (1810)*

In 2011, my partner and I went to Newfoundland to visit my
parents. It was his first trip there. He'd grown up in Edmonton,
accustomed to American Big Box stores and being able to find just
about anything within a twenty minute drive. We wanted a power
converter for the sports car our economy car got upgraded into, so
that we could plug our laptops into it while at campsites (if that
isn't a First World problem, I don't know what is). He asked where
the nearest Best Buy was. I told him St. John's, 8 hours away.

Urban dwellers in our modern world are used to having access
to everything they need. It is one of the reasons people continue
to live in cities with its traffic, smog, and congestion. We often see
the country as backwoods, provincial, and hickish. This isn't a new
phenomenon. Throughout history, we have literary examples of
people wanting the city life, especially in cities like New York and
London in the 19th century.

This chapter is about exploring the unique challenges of island
living and arctic climates. So strap on your life preserver, because
you're about to be exiled to the middle of effing nowhere.

Floating in the Water

Britain is a large island with plenty of neighbours, while Iceland is small and isolated. Hawaii is a chain, and the South Pacific is a collection of islands of all sizes. Each one of these examples presented the original inhabitants unique challenges that those living in the Fertile Crescent did not face: the isolation of geography and resources.

It gets even more backwoods when you are talking about a sparsely-populated island in the middle of nowhere. Newfoundland, for all its wonders, is in the direct path of the cold Labrador Current, a massive cold stream that comes down from the Arctic and swims on by the coastline so that the wind is perpetually cold. Whenever the hurricane season hits the tropics, the storms travels up the Gulf Stream and the island is in the path for cold, miserable rain.

Let's say your hero, through no fault of his own, accidentally tries to usurp his brother and, sorta kinda, ended up causing a (minor) civil war.

Oops.

However, monarchs are literal Gods in your fantasy world and can not be executed, so the hero was (unfairly) exiled to No Man's Land, an island in the middle of the Ocean of Tears. It takes three weeks just to sail there, the weather growing colder and colder, the waves getting higher and rougher with each passing day. We won't even talk about the food.

The boat makes land and your hero's heart sinks. For one thing, it's flipping cold in this land of exile. Secondly, it's all rock. Rock and rock and more rock. Oh, look over there. Trees. On top of rock. How can someone survive in a place like this?

When creating an island-based world each island is its own form of ecosystem. For example, I visited an archaeological site called Phillip's Garden in Port aux Choix, Newfoundland in 2011.

It was drizzling that day, and even though it was mid-June, the cold wet seeped into my bones and made me shiver. I stood on the site, holding a child's toy that had been dug that day—a small stone that had been worked and worried until it had a finish that was still glossy even today—and wondered how on earth anyone could have lived there without roads, cars, central heating, and annual trips to Mexico.

People did live in this desolate and harsh region, however. One might even say they thrived. The Dorset Palaeoeskimo lived in the region and built permanent (or at least semi-permanent) structures in the area. They developed tools from the stone around them, and hunted the seals that travelled by their shore every spring.

Harpoons have been made many different ways, depending upon local supplies and technology levels. My favourite place for specific, historical designs is http://elfshotgallery.blogspot.ca. It's a fabulous resource.

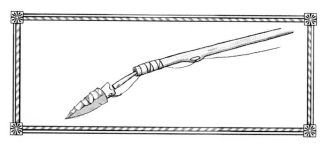

For this general design, the toggling harpoon was made of caribou antler, wood, and leather string (Image 1).

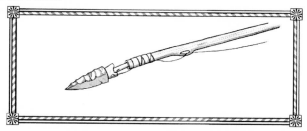

When the harpoon was thrown, the head would detach from the foreshaft (Image 2).

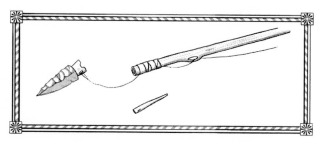

The animal could then be pulled in by the line that was attached to the harpoon head (Image 3)[10.]

The Dorset Palaeoeskimo relied upon the annual harp seal hunt for their survival. The meat was eaten, the oil provided light, and the hides turned into clothing and tarps. But no one can live by seal alone. These ingenious people would have also hunted walruses, fish, birds, and the land mammals of the island. There would have been no landowners refusing to let these people hunt caribou, so the marrow, hide, and antler from these great beasts would have supplemented their diets and tools. Berries and local vegetation would have rounded out their diets.[11]

Your banished princeling will, of course, turn his nose up at any of this "work." However, there are plenty of things his servants will need to know:

- Seaweed would be used as a fertilizer. My mother grew up within spitting distance of the ocean. As a child, she often was sent out to pick up seaweed to put on the family vegetable garden. It could also be dried and burnt. The ash was an excellent mulch.
- Certain types of sea plants, like rock samphire, were basically crisp vegetables that could be eaten raw or blanched.
- Fishing and large sea mammals were not the only sources of meat on islands. Shellfish harvesting would be popular along the shoreline. Fishing and shrimping can be done in some areas with nothing more than a net, a bucket, and a high tolerance for frigid water against one's calves.
- Weighted baskets to full-fledged lobster pots could be set out.
- Whales would occasionally wash up on shores. Just one whale can fill up to 300 wagons, providing meat for salting, blubber for light, and bones for construction.[12]

Resource shortages are the largest issue faced by island dwellers. When winter (or the rainy season) hits, resupply by merchant ships will be either infrequent or non-existent. Small, isolated islands like Iceland would struggle in the winter months without extensive food preparation and storage.

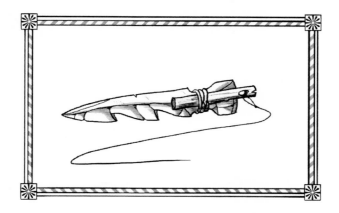

Toggling Harpoon

Shortages of food-related resources such as iron (for pots and utensils), cloth (for preserving), and preserving items like salt would hamper everyday life. Medicines would be limited and it could be months before more arrived. Grains will be limited, if they grow there at all, and once they are gone or spoiled, it could be a long time before more arrived.

Trade between smaller chains of islands can help alleviate the pressures of one island supporting its population, though often a chain of islands have similar resources. The internal trade can help with localized issues, such as spoiled food caches, but cannot introduce other necessary items like cereal crops.

Larger islands next to large land masses fair the best. Japan, Britain, and Ireland have the benefit of being near a very large land mass, allowing for easier access to goods even during bad weather. The risk to cross from France to England is not comparable to the risk to cross from France to Iceland.

If you are setting your world on an isolated island, here are some questions to consider:

- What is the naval technology of the world? A well-developed navy will bring significant goods to the island, as opposed to a technology level of hollowed-out boats.
- Where are the neighbours? Will this be an isolated island in the middle of nowhere, or will there be a chain of neighbours, or is this island a part of a large network of trading nations?
- Will iron exist on this island? This is an important question, as iron means moving away from stone tools. Without the presence of iron, a culture's technology will not move past the Stone Age until iron is introduced from elsewhere. (For more information on this, see Jared Diamond's groundbreaking work, *Guns, Germs, and Steel*.)

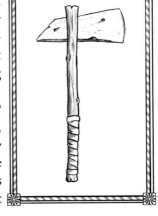

Grab Your Snowsuit, We're Going North

Cold weather sucks.

There, I said it. Edmonton is the coldest place I've ever lived, though it really isn't the coldest city in Canada (I'd argue Winnipeg, Yellowknife, and Whitehorse are all in line for that honour). Nevertheless, it's gotten down to -40C here a few times.

That is not a typo. -40C. That's -40F. That's 233 Kelvin (I don't actually know what that means, but it sounds Star Treky).

At this point, every Canadian reading this book is going to groan and complain that I just perpetuated the frozen tundra myth, while Alaskans are laughing and saying, "Oh yeah? It totally gets colder up here." I'm whining, I know.

So, how the hell do you eat in a frozen wasteland? It's pretty darn tough. If you're writing a scene or a world that has long, cold winters, one of the best ways to do your research is to talk to people who live in climates that resemble your world's weather.

An author writing a steampunk-inspired novel taking place during an Ice Age would do well to research Sir Ernest Shackleton's polar expeditions. Shackleton explored Antarctica and his crew even endured a harrowing experience of being shipwrecked and living on an ice floe. In reading about the crew's survival and subsequent rescue, a detailed picture of whaling stations, supplies, and technology from the Victorian period emerges from the research.

The supply list[13] from one of Shackleton's expeditions is eighteen pages long, but here is an interesting snapshot of how Victorian technology was reflected in the food onboard:

- Special Norwegian tinned food, such as roast reindeer
- 68 cases of milk powder
- 144lb tinned tongue
- 560lbs tinned beef suet
- 450 cans of Heinz baked beans in pork and tomato sauce
- 380lbs of canned marmalade
- 266lbs canned lentils
- 1500lbs self-raising flour

Setting aside the early health issues of canned foods (the cans used lead, leading to poisoning), canned food completely changed the nature of exploration to the furthest, coldest reaches of the planet.

Of course, this won't be of use if lead doesn't exist in your world! If you are writing a Stone Age world, you might find it helpful to look at the traditional hunting and eating practices of the far north peoples that lived in Greenland, Canada, Alaska, and Russia. Without access to horses, they would have used dogs in their place. They would have relied heavily on caribou, seal, fish, migratory birds, plus the occasional whale that would wash up on their shores.

Caribou and seal can be eaten raw, frozen, boiled, or dried and provide vital protein and fat to help the body fuel itself in the extreme cold temperatures. Caribou liver and its stomach contents (all vegetation) would provide people with Vitamin A, while blood would provide an iron source.

Northern people would also fish, which would provide Vitamin C (liver) and even calcium (tiny bones). Migratory birds, such as geese and ducks, would provide eggs and meat.

Except for areas permanently covered in ice, the spring and summer would bring plants. In the far north, the growing season is very short, but would provide several edible plants to help round out your heroine's diet. Mountain Sorrel, Fireweed, currants, cranberries, and blueberries are all edible and would provide a wide assortment of vitamins and minerals. They could be dried and turned into a powder, ensuring that essential vitamins were included in the diet year-round.

Chef's Best Recipes

- Seaweed dipped in animal fat is easy to make, stores well, and gives a healthy boost.
- Seal meat mixed with berries, then frozen to make a quick and tasty "ice cream".
- Dried beluga meat, as well as dried fish, makes a perfect on-the-go snack when travelling or hunting.

Seal and whale blubber were essential to providing omega-3 fatty acids in Northern diets. Plus, their fat could be used as a fuel and light source, vital in a place that is dark for part of the year. The high fat content of these animals will help balance the ultra-low fat content of ground squirrels and hares, which were important smaller, but easier to catch, food sources.[14]

Whatever climate or location you drop your characters into, take the time to research traditional life in those locations. It will feel more authentic—plus will provide additional scrapes and conflicts!

Chapter 12: Recipes to Try

The primary focus of this book has always been a writer's guide. The purpose of this book was to help writers of epic fantasy and historical fiction to find accurate and logical ways to feed their adventurers. Of course, I knew that many of you would pick up this book just for the food. I'd have been remiss if I didn't include a few recipes for you to write about and to cook up at home yourselves.

Throughout the book, I've included primary source recipes for entertainment value; some I've cooked and some I've not. And some I spilled on myself. This section is different because all of these recipes I have cooked myself a few times so I can include the modern instructions.

Some of these recipes are family ones, passed down through the generations. Some are cultural ones, where I've picked just one of a hundred versions. Still others are translations of some of the more common recipes that are often seen at SCA events and medieval feasts.

Try your hand at a couple. It could prove to be an interesting experience.

Fried Cod Tongues

There is a typical reaction to this dish, so let's get it out of the way: *Ewwwwwwwwwwww.* This is followed by: cods have tongues?

Now that is out of the way, let's discuss this interesting dish. To answer the common question, yes, cod fish do in fact have tongues.

They resemble skinned and deboned chicken thighs in size and colour, though they are thinner (about the size of three coins stacked).

Fried cod tongues is a common Newfoundland dish, cooked both at home and in restaurants. You can sometimes even find them served up at the local "chip truck", a battered old delivery van converted into a mobile restaurant where burgers, French fries, and other fatty goodness are served.

Cod tongues are (obviously) the tongue of a cod fish, pan fried. You can also do the same with cod cheeks (yes, cods have cheeks). I prefer tongues as I find cheeks are a little too rubbery for my tastes. Cod tongues are chewy, but have a delicate flavour.

For obvious reasons, this is a dish that only those living in coastal regions are going to have regular access to in a pre-refrigeration society. In fact, even in the modern world, this isn't a common dish beyond the cod fish waters of the North Atlantic. I've rarely seen cod tongues elsewhere, including at specialty seafood shops, since leaving Newfoundland. However, if you can get a few shipped in, cook up a "feed" (lots of food) and enjoy a new food.

1 ½ cups flour
1 teaspoon salt
½ tsp pepper
½ pound salt pork
Cod tongues

- Wash enough fresh cod tongues for your meal (the usual serving is eight tongues per person). Dry them on a cloth or paper towel.
- In a bowl, combine flour, salt, and pepper and mix together. Set aside.
- Cut up salt pork and fry it up until golden brown. Remove the pork cubes for another use (or you can even use them as a topping if you need an extra-hearty meal).

- Coat the tongues in the flour mixture one by one. Fry them in the hot pork fat until golden brown on both sides.
- Place them on a warm plate with a cloth or paper towel to soak up any excess fat. Serve immediately, or place in a warm oven (or, a cooling bread oven) if needed.

A well-organized cook would ensure that the pan drippings from a previous meal needing salt pork (not the actual fat pieces) would be saved so that it would be available as a frying fat later in the week.

Seal Flipper Pie

Now that I have your attention with the cod tongues, I'm going to jump right on in and bring up the seals. I realize that the seal hunt is a contentious issue. However, before the advent of ready-available, imported food, the seal hunt was an important source of food for eons of people living along the North Atlantic on both sides.

Some people like the tender, dark meat, though I confess it always tasted oily to me. However, in a maritime setting that has seals, a food like this would be a distinct part of the local food culture.

Since this recipe requires the use of flour and an oven, it should only be used for a seafaring nation that can bring seals back home or a Northern nation that engages in a lot of trade, or is perhaps along a trade network (which brings the grain to them). This recipe would not be viable for an isolated group without trade and access to iron and grains.

4 seal flippers, cleaned well
Pork fat
2 onions, chopped
1 cup of flour

185

1 teaspoon of salt

1 cup water + more for soaking

- Soak flippers in cold water for thirty minutes. Cut off any excess fat from the flippers. Dip them into flour (save whatever isn't used) and pan fry in pork fat until brown.
- Add the chopped onions. Make a gravy out of the left-over flour. Pour over the fried flippers.
- Cover and bake for 2-3 hours until tender.
- Cover with a pastry and bake at 400F for thirty minutes or until brown and crisp.

Note: This recipe would be made with adult seal flippers and not baby seal ones. Just in case there was some confusion.

Salt Beef Dinner

This goes by several names. Jig's Dinner, Boiled Dinner, Mess, Slop, Naval Supper, Cooked Supper, salt beef pottage, and so on. The further back I go, the more names I uncover. However, they are all variations of a similar meal: salted beef cooked with vegetables.

Cows are big animals. Really, really big. Unless you have a wedding or a big family reunion, it's difficult to butcher a cow and use all that meat before it spoils. Salt curing is one way that beef can be preserved for long periods of time.

I was twenty before I'd had a grilled steak or a beef roast. The only time I ate beef growing up was in this form, unless it was deli "meat", and I use that term lightly. I can imagine many a poor farmer butchering his stock and selling all of the best cuts at the market fresh to those that could afford it. Then, the poorer cuts would be turned into salt beef that could be used to feed his family throughout the autumn and winter months.

- Soak salt beef overnight in cold water. It doesn't need to be put in the fridge unless it's a swelter of a day. In the morning, pour out the water and add fresh water to the pot, enough to fill the pot about half-full when the beef is added.
- Bring to a boil, but watch the pot or else it will boil over and make a horrible mess of frothy salt brine everywhere.
- Reduce heat and boil for 45 minutes to an hour (smaller pieces take less time).
- Prepare your vegetables while the meat is cooking. Cut turnips, peel carrots and potatoes, and core cabbage.
- Add turnips to the pot, cook for fifteen minutes. Then add your carrots, then cabbage, then potatoes, all fifteen minutes apart. Cook until the potatoes are done.
- You can also hang a cloth of presoaked yellow peas in the pot while cooking the meat.

Note: Salt beef redefines "red" meat when it's raw. The meat floats in a bloody-salt brine and is cut into various pieces, though most are palm-sized or a bit smaller. Some will have bone still on it, while others will be just meat and fat. Whatever you do: don't cook your meat in the brine and don't eat it raw. The intestinal distress and salt burns in your mouth will not be worth it.

Soldiers' Couscous (Kuskusû Fityâni)

This is a fabulous Andalusian recipe from the 13th century. With some modifications, it can be adapted to nearly any technology level, too, making it a prime recipe to reproduce. Give it a try and see what you think.

Original:

187

Boil meat with bone-in and any vegetables available. When the meat is cooked, take out the meat and the vegetables and put to one side. Strain the bones and return the pot of broth to the fire.

When it has boiled, add cooked couscous rubbed with fat[15] and leave it for a little on a reduced fire until it soaks up some of the broth.

Put the couscous on a platter and top with the cooked meat.[16]

My adaptation:
1 chicken, cut up
1 onion, quartered
3 carrots, chopped coarsely
3 stalks of celery, chopped coarsely
A handful of fresh herbs, such as rosemary, thyme, and oregano
2 cups couscous

- Boil the chicken and vegetables in a pot of water until the chicken is falling apart, about 1 hour.
- Strain out the meat and vegetables, setting aside 2 cups of the pot broth.
- Mix the couscous and broth together and cover for 5 minutes.
- Put the couscous on a plate, and top with chicken and vegetables. Serve hot.

Fish and Brewis (pronounced "broos")

This is another example of a meal that has a dozen names, but I'm unable to call it anything else but Fish and Brewis. It seems sacrilegious to do otherwise. Salt fish, like salt beef, was an excellent way to preserve a food that would spoil quickly. The North Atlantic used to be teeming with cod fish, to the point that it was used to cheaply feed the slaves of the West Indies in exchange for the tobacco, sugar, molasses, and rum that was being produced.

Freshening Dried Salt Cod

There are a few variations on how to do this, depending on how you like your fish in the end. Some people like their salt cod flaked into pieces. If so, cut it small now. Others like it in chunks. If so, make sure the pieces are cut to your preference.

Wash your fish and soak it in a pot of water overnight. You can keep it on your counter. In the morning, drain the water off. Fill the pot up again and bring to a boil. Cook for twenty to thirty minutes. Add peeled potatoes to the pot and cook until the potatoes are tender. Drain and either serve as is, or mash together.

Remind your guests to watch out for the fine, translucent bones.

Drawn Butter
(to serve on top of your Fish and Brewis)

½ cup butter
2 ½ tablespoons of flour
2 onions, chopped fine
1 ½ cup hot water

Melt the butter in a small saucepan. Add the onion and cook for a few minutes on low heat. Add the flour and blend well. Add the hot water and cook until thickened, stirring constantly. Salt and pepper to taste.

Scrunchions
(to serve on top of your Fish and Brewis)

Cut slices of salt pork into small pieces. Fry it up until golden brown. Keep the fat for another day (it can be used like butter or lard), and drain the pork pieces on a cloth or paper towel. Serve on top of your meal.

Brewis
(to serve with your Fish and Brewis)

Brewis is cooked hard bread, also known as hard tack in other parts of the world. The cakes are oval-shaped and hard as rocks. Split the cakes into pieces, allowing one per person, and cover with water. Soak overnight. Warm the brewis up to a near boil, but don't boil, and serve alongside the fish and potatoes.

Pottages

No tale is complete without a pottage or two, or in this case, three. These are my own recipes adapted from *The Forme of Cury*, *Potage Dyvers*, and *Boke of Kokery*. I served them up for my Yule Dinner guests in 2010 and 2011, to much success.

Cabbage Pottage
1 small head of cabbage, chopped
1 onion, sliced
1 leek, chopped
3L water
Leftover meat (*ideas*: ham bones, salt pork riblets, a cube of salt beef)

- Bring the water to a boil, then add all of the ingredients.
- Simmer for 15 minutes or until the cabbage is cooked.

Note: This is a case of preference, but I prefer this with finely-chopped cabbage. It's easier to serve and eat.

Turnip Pottage
2 turnips, cut into small cubes
1 large onion (or two small ones)
1/8 tsp cardamom

1/8 tsp coriander
Enough water to cover everything

- Add all ingredients to the pot and bring to a boil, simmering for about thirty minutes or until the turnips are cooked.

Note: To make this heartier, add chopped gammon ham or bacon, or a beef soup bone with marrow.

Pease Pottage

I've included a basic pease pottage, or "pudding." I've made this recipe several ways and it's almost like the equivalent of a medieval sandwich: it can be as basic or as fancy as you want it to be, and you can put anything into it. I've found recipes making this with bacon and saffron (which, by the way, is very good when cooked in the fireplace), and I've found very basic recipes where it's simply the peas and some broth.

3 litres of water
1 small bag of dry yellow split peas, picked through and rinsed
1 onion, chopped finely
1 leek, chopped finely
1 carrot*, chopped

- Combine all ingredients in a pot and cook over low heat for two hours or until nice and thick.
- You can also add the ingredients to a cheesecloth and add to a pot of meat so that the meat will flavour the peas. The peas will also flavour the meat broth, too, turning it a little yellow in the process.

*Note: Carrots come from Iran and Afghanistan. As with many introduced foods, they were not immediately prominent in the local diets for years later. Also, carrots came in a variety of colours and medieval

texts reference red and yellow roots. Further, carrots come in various sizes and not just the modern long tap that we're used to. If you are writing a historical piece, double check that carrots were eaten in your story's region. Otherwise, substitute with another root vegetable like parsnips or turnips.

Menu for Pliny the Younger

This is a lovely example of a company menu from the Roman times. Nothing too extreme, but perfect for a special gathering of intellectuals or political hopefuls gathering for spirited conversation.

- Appetizers: Salad, snails, hard-boiled eggs
- Main Meal: Risotto, baked courgettes with sauce, wildflower bulbs in vinegar
- Dessert: Spiced ice wine, fresh seasonal fruits[17]

Meat-filled Pastries

I don't have a fancy name for this dish, since there are dozens of variations of the same recipe: meat cooked inside dough. I love these pastries because they are so portable and use whatever is on hand. They are tasty out of the oven, but also when cold. You can eat them even when your hands are dirty because the piece of crust you're using can just be thrown out. I've cooked these up and taken them on car rides. They are filling and don't make me want to hurl the way that fast food often does.

The filling is to your own taste, so there are no real guidelines:
1 lb meat (suggestions: stewing beef, bacon, gammon ham), chopped finely or minced
1 carrot, chopped finely
1 onion, chopped finely
Salt and pepper to taste

2 tbsp butter, melted
1 tbsp flour

- Combine all ingredients and set aside.

The pastry can be as flaky or as thick as you wish. Again, it's to your own taste. I like to use a traditional pie crust, but puff pastry, pizza dough, bread dough, and a basic flour/lard crust works well, too.

3 cups flour
1 cup lard
1/3 cup butter
1 tsp salt

- Cut the salt, lard and butter into the flour.
- Add enough water to form a stiff ball.
- Roll circles of dough into the size you want the pastries and add filling to one side.
- Fold the dough over and crimp the edges with fingers dipped in water.
- Put a slice or a hole in the top to let steam escape.
- Bake in a 400 degree oven until the crust is golden brown (this will vary depending on how big your pastries are, but generally in the 30-60 minute range).

Pound Cake[18]

In the 16th century, for example, all cakes were made with yeast. However, the Germans and British eventually moved to using eggs to raise their cakes. In Jane Austen's time, cakes were going through that transition, where recipe books like Rundell's *A New System of Domestic Cookery* were giving recipes for both kinds of cakes. By the time Mrs. Beeton put out her books in the Victorian era, most cakes were being made with eggs, and only poor people were using yeast to raise their cakes.

Today, pound cake is a yellow cake, browned on the outside. It's often given terms like "light" and "moist." While this cake is moist, I'm not sure the term "light" can ever be applied to this one.

1 lb butter
1 lb sugar
8 eggs
1 lb flour
1 tsp each nutmeg and cinnamon
½ tsp ground cloves
2 tbsp caraway seeds
6oz wine

- Beat a pound of butter into a cream.
- Separate the yolk and whites from the eggs and beat each in separate bowls.
- Combine all of the dry ingredients.
- Mix the wet and dry ingredients. Your hero's love interest will need to hand-beat this for a full hour, so he better appreciate it when she (or he) gives it to him! (Modern chefs can use a hand mixer for 7-8 minutes.)
- Butter a baking pan and bake it for one hour in a "quick" oven (375 degrees F).

Garbage

Original recipe:
Take fayre garbagys of chykonys, as the hed, the fete, the lyuerys, an the gysowrys; washe hem clene, an caste hem in a fayre potte, an caste ther-to freysshe brothe of Beef or ellys of moton, an let it boyle; an a-lye it wyth brede, an ley on Pepir an Safroun, Maces, Clowys, an a lytil verious an salt, an serue forth in the maner as a Sewe[19].

Today, Western folks tend to be iffy on organ meats and oddball parts like feet. We also don't usually combine bread with our soups and stews. However, the Great Yule Dinner of 2011 was themed Medieval Dining, so I had to give this horrific sounding recipe a try.

First things first: the definition of garbage has changed through the centuries. In the context of the recipe above, it's referring to the more "throw-away" parts of the chicken, such as the organs, feet, etc. (Then again, perhaps the definition of garbage really hasn't changed all that much.)

Since I wanted to modernize the recipe a little, I opted to use some leftover deli chicken, along with chicken liver and kidneys. I wanted my guests to at least recognize some of the food in their stew.

1 deli chicken
2 litres of water
10-15 chicken kidneys and/or livers
4-5 slices of grain bread, stale, and pulled into pieces
Salt and pepper to taste
½ tsp ground ginger
¼ tsp ground mace
¼ tsp whole cloves

- Remove as much meat from the bones as possible. Set aside.
- Boil the bones in the water, along with the spices, for an hour. Remove the bones once the broth is made.
- Meanwhile, chop the cooked chicken and organ meat into small pieces.
- When the broth is done, add the organs first and cook for 15 minutes or until cooked.
- Add the cooked chicken and bread, stirring until well combined.

- Cook for 5 minutes more, or until the chicken is hot and the bread has soaked up the liquid. Serve like a stew.

Pork Fat and Molasses Dip

This is a more modern recipe, perfect for men working in the woods or for Steampunk heroines eating on an airship. When cooled, this can also be eaten as a spread during times of rationing, such as my father ate during WWII rationing.

As with many of these recipes, there is no set amount of ingredients. It's about combining to one's taste.

Salt pork or bacon rashers
1 cup blackstrap molasses
Bread

- Fry the rashers in a high-sided pan. They can be cooked over a fire, on a stove, or over the coal furnace in a thrashing machine or inside a train or airship.
- When the rashers are cooked, take them out of the pan.
- Pour the molasses in with the fat and fry for a couple of minutes.
- Put rashers between bread and dip into the molasses-pork fat mix. Enjoy as your arteries cry out.

Pork Buns

In Chapter 1, I discuss the need for portable foods. Flour buns by themselves are all right, though they lack protein's staying power. They do, however, travel well and handle the elements well, able to handle several days without spoiling. The most logical step to portable food improvement is, of course, adding preserved meat to it!

Biscuits, scones, and buns have gone through a historical transformation from their early days in the ashes to the delicious almond and cranberry scones I make today; scones made from ingredients from around the world. This recipe is another combination recipe, taken from several sources and then mixed in with a traditional pork bun recipe I grew up with.

4 cups flour
1 cup lukewarm water
1/3 lb salt pork or bacon, cut into small pieces
4 tsp baking powder

- Combine baking powder and flour in a mixing bowl. Make a hollow in the flour mixture. Set aside.
- Partially fry the salt pork, but don't cook it completely.
- Cool the pork for 5 minutes. Pour the pork bits and rendered fat into the flour hollow.
- Add the water and mix until just combined. Don't over mix or the buns will be tough.
- Make into preferred shapes (round shapes the size of hockey pucks are good because they can be cut and turned into "sandwich" bread).
- Bake in a 400 degree oven for about 15 minutes, or until golden brown.

Flour note: Any kind of flour can be used for these buns, though water and cooking times might vary. If using a very dense flour, I recommend reducing the heat to 375.

This version assumes the development of baking powder. If your world does not have baking powder, this recipe is still doable. The buns would be leavened by the use of yeast or eggs (most likely, a combination of the two), as opposed to baking powder. The dough would need rising, similar to the process of making sourdough buns.

Krista's Prehistoric Pucks

Choosing the recipes for this book was very tough and was perhaps the hardest to write. I wanted this book to appeal to a wide range of readers and writers, but I also wanted the recipes included to reflect the main themes of this book.

However, I could not have a recipe chapter without testing the biscuit theory. For those unfamiliar with the biscuit theory it is simply that any food-challenge in a novel can be solved by the heroine making biscuits. She will burn the first batch, undercook the second batch, and make perfect flaky biscuits the third time.

Biscuits are made flaky by the presence of fat (lard or butter) and baking powder or yeast to "lift" the dough so that it's light and not puck-like. However, how does one make biscuits without an oven, yeast, or baking powder? What if eggs aren't available? Well, I sought out this answer.

First, I got a roaring fire going in my fireplace. This isn't too out of the ordinary, except that it was 32C outside and in the middle of July. I didn't mean to make a roaring fire, but the firewood was really dry and, well, you know how it goes. Whoosh! Giant fire in the middle of summer. It happens.

I put several rocks in the fireplace so that they would be heated by the fire. I let the fire continue for about an hour, so that the rocks had heated up well and that a good supply of hot coals were present. By then, the fire had died down to only the occasional flicker of flame.

I made a baking tray out of birch bark and put four beef bones in it with a small amount of water. The birch promptly caught on fire. I fished out the bones and tried again, this time soaking the birch bark in water for five minutes. This did the trick and the bones cooked over the hot coals and stones for about 45 minutes. I pulled the bones out and let them cool.

While they were cooling, I kindled the fire again to ensure the rocks were back to full heat, while I got to making the dough.

198

I cheated and used a green split pea and white flour mixture. However, I did have some dried split peas and attempted to make flour by grinding it between two rocks. Hilarious. It took me fifteen minutes to properly grind about two tablespoons of flour so that it resembled the machine-ground flour. (I am very thankful for the era in which I was born). To get it that fine, however, I ended up with several small chips of rock mixed in the flour.

I cooked up some beef bones and scooped out the marrow. Then, I combined the flour and cooled bone marrow, plus mixed in some dried cranberries. I gave it a few kneads and formed it into small buns. I let them sit while the fire died down. The rocks were covered with ashes, so I used a bundle of twigs to brush them off. I put the dough directly on the rocks and let them cook.

It took nearly an hour before they were golden brown, the way I like it. The coals stayed hot throughout (as did the rest of my sweltering home) and the rocks were still hot to the touch. The bread was cooked through and was...interesting.

I blew the ashes off them, and gave up trying to get the dirty ash off the bottom. The bone marrow ended up adding a greasy taste to the "biscuits", almost like I'd put oil on them before baking. They looked like something between a hockey puck and a sad pita bread.

I stuffed some leftover beef into the middle of the pita bread and folded in half. It didn't have an amazing taste, true, but I'll say this for them: they were filling. One small puck the size of my palm with a bit of shredded beef kept me full for hours.

Conclusion
And So It Ends

Here we are; the end. Whew, it's been a fast ride. It's been difficult giving a basic overview of the history of food. Even narrowing it down to the Medieval Britain focus for writers, each one of the sections in this book could be turned into an entire volume on its own. Not only am I sure I have left out material, but many times I had to deliberately leave out material. Sometimes, a writer has to make those choices.

We've covered a lot of history in this book. We've visited the slave huts of ancient Egypt and let you taste the bread that kept them alive. We've packed up our adventuring parties and armies to war, wander, and maraud through the countryside. Our poor heroines have dodged food poisoning, rabbit stew, and morphine cough syrup. Our heroes have baked cakes, led mutinies, and bought cinnamon.

At the beginning of this adventure, I asked you to consider some basic questions:

- How will your hero carry his drinking water?
- What will your heroine be eating?
- What is your adventuring party's experience in the terrain they are exploring?
- Do they have any outdoor experience?
- Are your heroes legally allowed on the land they are occupying?

I hope that I have given you the right tools to either answer those questions, or at least to send you searching elsewhere. If I've done my job well, I've given you hundreds more questions that will make you dive into the books that I list in the bibliography.

However, I must admit I end this book wishing it could have been double or triple the length so that I could have given you more information and more stories. I would have liked to have gone into further detail in the lives of the Beothuk, or explored how a world without iron would develop (based on the works of Jared Diamond). I would have preferred to discuss in detail the Gurkhas, Zulu, Aztecs, and Mayans.

Just because I could not have covered as much as I wanted does not mean you cannot branch out and read about the worlds, people, and cultures that interest you. The benefit of *What Kings Ate*—being a basic guide—is also its downfall in many ways. It's been impossible to concentrate on any one topic to explain fully and completely. It's just been enough to give you a taste. If I've done my job, I haven't answered your questions so much as inspired hundreds more. Perhaps that might become the challenge, as you seek out further information from the base that I've started you on in this book.

If you're unsure where to start, take a look at the bibliography section. Anything here that tickled your interest will be far better explored in those works than I have managed in this one. Some of those books are written by individuals who have dedicated their entire lives to the study of food; I'm sure you will enjoy them as much as I have.

With extra knowledge comes the temptation to show off what you know. One of the challenges of writing fantasy is to develop the world without prattling. The technical writing term is "info dump," but many people don't seem to understand what that means or how to tell vital information from verbal dumpage. So, I prefer to call it "prattling." Information is always vital; prattling never is.

When coming into a specialized subject, such as food and beverages, it is important to know that the majority of the information you learn in this book will never grace the pages of your novel. And that's okay. In fact, that's perfect.

Just as readers will roll their eyes at a writer's lack of understanding concerning the basics of seasonal foods in a quasi-dark age novel, readers will skip paragraphs of culinary details. Moderation is the key.

As with all research, you'll have more than you'll ever need. The goal of research is always to be able to include accurate details without bogging down the reader with detail. In fact, the reader might never even notice your research because they are so engrossed in the story. Never let the details take over the story; let the story dictate what details to use.

Now, I don't know about you, but I'm hungry.

Appendix I
The Agricultural Calendar of Britain

In the initial beta-reading of this book, a number of people asked for a guide of what foods were in season at particular times. This was an impossible feat, since seasonal foods vary not just by country, but by region! It would not be possible to give the entire scope of seasonal foods in this book. In the end, I decided upon Britain's pre-industrial agricultural calendar.

This is a very general guide.[1] Many areas are going to be later or earlier with when certain fruits are in season or out, and a long winter will affect planting and harvesting. However, as a basic starting point, I think it will help you.

September

- Agricultural calendars (as well as school years) start in September because that's when winterwheat, barley, and rapeseed (known today as canola) are sown for harvest the next year.
- Fields would be ploughed this month, and part of that process would involve prepping the ground by removing weeds. Also, the fields will need to be cleared of rocks, as the winter frost brings them to the surface.
- Horses weren't always used for harvesting. Heavy oxen were used for most of farming's history. Even with the

oxen doing most of the heavy work, the man behind the till still needs to steer the animals, help push the plough into the ground, and keep the heavy plough in place and straight. This is a very physical job and the men working the fields will need plenty of food to keep going.

- Women would use this month to plant garlic, onions, and leeks in their kitchen gardens, even if it's merely a tiny strip of land outside of their house. Spinach and lettuce can be planted as well, since they like cooler temperatures. They are fast growing, too, so there would be a harvest of baby greens before the snow comes.
- Assuming laws allowed it, women would take time this month to glean the wild and public areas for fruit. She would also begin making pickles and preserves from any wild foods, as well as produce purchased at market or harvested from her own garden.
- The most commonly eaten foods during this month will be beef, chicken, pork, mutton, beans, carrots, apples, and potatoes.

October

- October is often spent preparing the farm's sheep for mating season. This involves cleaning them, readying fences, and ensuring that there is stable space for the winter.
- Threshing of cereal crops also starts in October. Today, wheat is only a couple feet high, but in previous eras wheat was several feet tall. These tall stalks allowed for both the actual grains, plus long enough stalks to use for thatching roofs.
- Apples will be still in season, and wives will be busy making cider, pickles, and preserves.

- Potatoes, apples, pears, beef, mutton, and pork will make appearances on tables during this month.

November

- Sheep are mating around this time, so ensure that there is a ram for the ladies to enjoy.
- The remainder of wheat, if any, would be harvested. Root vegetables like turnip, cabbage, and onions would also be harvested, and properly stored for the long winter months.
- Menus in November will feature a lot of beef, mutton, pork (basically, any animals that the farmer cannot afford to feed through the winter), plus root vegetables.

December

- Even though there would be no planting or harvesting in December, farm animals will still need to be fed. Any animals that are butchered in this month due to a lack of feed will need to be smoked and salted to avoid spoilage.
- Meals will begin to feature preserves and pickled foods more, with cabbages, carrots, and onions being eaten as well. Apples and pears that have been stored well will still be eaten fresh.
- Goose, pork, or beef will grace many tables until the turkey becomes all the rage into the Victorian era.

January

- This is a month for maintenance and fixing things.
- Meals will feature pickled, salted, and smoked meats almost exclusively. Potatoes, beets, cabbage, carrots, and

onions will still be eaten fresh, assuming that they were stored correctly.

February

- Calving might begin this month, so farmers need to be watchful.
- Dinners will be sparse in choice, with a heavy appearance of dried peas, pork, beef, pickled herring, with any root vegetables and pears still fresh.
- Ducks begin to lay in this month (assuming the weather is warm enough), so extra eggs might be available, too.

March

- Lambing can begin late this month and into the next. Lambing is a 24-hour job; ewes in labour need round-the-clock attention in case of emergencies. Calving can sometimes begin this month, too.
- Lent begins in March. For many people in the late Middle Ages, it was easy to celebrate Lent because there was so little food anyway.
- Eggs and greens will be more available (greens do well in cool temperatures and grow quickly.)
- Salt beef, mutton, and pork will be the main meats, with whatever is left of the root vegetables of the fall (cabbage, carrots, onions, parsnips, potatoes). Dried beans and peas will provide increasing amounts of protein in the diet as winter stores of meat run out.

April

- Lambing and calving continues throughout this month. That adds significant work looking after the young lambs to ensure that they aren't attacked by wild dogs, wolves, and coyotes.

- Potatoes can be planted in April, as well as most vegetable garden produce.
- Early fresh produce also becomes available in this month, such as lettuce, spinach, rhubarb, and radishes.
- With the arrival of calves, so too does butter, cream, and milk. Hard cheese won't be ready yet, though cheese production will begin and any soured milk can be quickly turned into cottage cheese for sandwiches.
- The warming temperatures will encourage the chickens to begin laying more eggs.
- Chicken, lamb, veal, and mutton will be heavily featured on tables this month.

May

- Calving might continue into May, though the lambing should be done. Calves will need to be killed, and their stomachs cleaned and dried so that cheese can be made.
- Cheesemaking and buttermaking takes place in May.
- There will be significantly more fresh food available this month. Strawberries, gooseberries, greens, radishes, and turnip greens (the tops of turnips) will be available. Beans and peas might also be ready.
- There will be more butter and cream, allowing for heavier meals plus rich desserts like cheesecake.
- Eggs, veal, goose, lamb, and beef will grace tables.

June

- Sheep will be sheared this month and the oldest sheep butchered, and cheesemaking will continue into this month.
- Meals will feature fresh mutton, though the mutton will be from old animals so the meals will be more stew-based, then roasted meat. Chicken, veal, and lamb will also feature heavily on tables, as well as herring and rabbit.

- Butter, cream, and eggs will continue to appear on the table, as well as soft cheese. Beans, carrots, peas, and greens will available.

July

- Haymaking will take up a fair amount of time this month.
- Tables will be full of fresh produce, which means wives will be working double time to get food preserved for the winter.
- Beans, carrots, onions, peas, cherries, raspberries, and radishes will be served this month (and also preserved). There will also still be plenty of dairy and eggs.
- Mackerel and herring will be readily available, but beef, mutton, lamb, and rabbit will also be eaten.

August

- August is a busy month as, assuming good weather, the cereal crop will be harvested. Likewise, once the harvest is done, the soil will need to be ploughed for replanting.
- Preserving food will continue into this month. There will still be dairy, and plenty of eggs.
- Beef, lamb, mutton, rabbit, and poultry and game birds will feature on tables.
- With the end of summer, the cycle begins all over again.

Appendix II
Feast Planning 101

Everyone loves a good party, especially one with so much free food and booze that you have to start starving yourself two days before the banquet to be adequately ready for the endless courses of dishes that will be offered.

Feasts crop up a lot in fantasy, romance, and historical stories. All of that dancing, eating, drinking, assassinating, making bastards, heirs, and bastards that will passed off as heirs...who can resist that?

This is a tongue-in-cheek feast planning guide, for both the housekeeper/chef, and the guests, loosely based on Henry IV's coronation feast in 1399.

Guest Behaviour:

1. Can the trenchers be eaten? Trenchers are slate bread that can be used as serving platters in wealthier homes, or used as plates in poor homes. They can also go in the bottom of a plate to soak up all of the sauces. Do they go to the servants to eat or perhaps donated as alms?
2. Will water be provided to clean the hands? A bowl was circulated around in Tudor times where the top rank washed their hands first and it was passed along (seating was by rank). Or, will the bowl be at the door upon entering? Will there be a bowl of water passed around after the meal?

3. Is it acceptable to throw one's bones on the floor for the dogs, or should they be placed in the alms basket on the table? Or, should they be left on the plate for the servants to clear away and deal with (or eat)?

4. Is the pot pie crust edible or is it a means of cooking? Medieval crusts around pies weren't meant to be eaten, but rather a means of cooking the meat or stew in a different manner. Today, we eat the pastry because it's tasty. However, many "pastes," as the dough was called, was just flour and water. That's not all that tasty, especially if covered in ash on the bottom.

5. What utensils will be in use? Some people mistake the Middle Ages England's rejection of a fork as a universal rejection across Europe. This is false, since there are records as far back as Ancient Egyptians using forks.

Chef's Menu:[1]

Anticipated number of mouths to feed: 1000-2000 of varying ranks (lesser ranks can have less food available on their tables).

First Course	Second Course	Third Course
Boar in spiced wine	Venison pie with Ginger Jelly	Cream soup
Spit-roasted beef	Stuffed sucking pig	Fruit preserves in spiced wine
Almond Milk Soup with wine and spices	Roasted pea-cocks	Herons in sauce
Stewed swan	Rabbit in sauce	Pigeon pie
Pheasant pie	Game bird pies with eggs	Pork meatballs in butter
Custard Pie	Beef and venison meatballs in sauce	Apple fritters
Pike in cream sauce		Cheesecake

To Do Three to Six Months Prior to Feast:

- Acquire cows and pigs, plus enough fodder to feed them until the feast.
- Order swans, herons, and peacocks. Ensure adequate housing facilities for them.
- Order 50lbs each of cinnamon, saffron, ginger, pepper, sugar, nutmeg, and mace. Clear a space in the larder for dry items.
- Ensure the Lord of the house and his friends kill enough pheasants for the meal. If not, purchase from other estates who are struggling with cash flow. In a pinch, hire a gamekeeper who can be trusted to do additional shooting.
- Have the dairy prepare enough cheese and butter. Ask housekeeper to hire additional temporary dairy maids, if necessary. Purchase remaining cheese and butter needs.
- Have large barrels ready to preserve eggs.
- Coordinate with local poor to provide special fishing permits for the river. Pay above market rates for fish so that they won't steal and sell it in market. Arrange to have fish smoked.
- Begin stockpiling fuel.

Kitchen Shopping List:[2]

- Basins made of tin, pewter, and glass
- Iron, copper, and brass pots, pans, and kettles
- Platters, sauce dishes, candle-sticks
- Frying pans, pudding bags, towels, and chafing dishes
- Ladles, scummers (to skim the scum off of dishes), drip pans, pot hooks, fire pans, fire forks, trivets, tongs
- Roasting irons

- Mortar and pestles
- Brass kettles, holding from sixteen to twenty gallons each
- Little kettles with bowed or carved handles.
- An iron peel or baking shovel
- Iron ladles
- A grater
- A pepper mill
- Boards
- A salt-box
- A galley bawk to suspend the kettle or pot over the fire
- Spits, square and round, and various sizes

Housekeeper's To Do List:

- Purchase extra candles to burn in the kitchen and dining room, plus enough to light all of the corridors that connect the kitchen with where the feast is located.
- Inspect table linens to ensure that they are clean and not moth eaten. Order more as necessary. If cloths are not used, arrange servants to sand the tables so that The Quality don't get a splinter (unnecessary for the lower rank tables).
- Purchase enough elaborately-decorated salt dishes to place at the head of the important tables. Salt is not needed for the lower ranking tables.
- Have the dairy, hog shed, pig pen, and pantries scrubbed and prepared for additional stores.
- Hire enough male servants in time to be trained on how to carry food from the kitchen to the serving room.
- Hire as many male kitchen staff as can be afforded, such as cooks, undercooks, chefs, and various apprentices and helpers. Hire several young boys from the village to be spit-turners.

In the days leading up to the feast, the mass slaughter will begin. Cows will be dispatched and butchered, so that the meat can be hung and aged. Pigs will be slaughtered likewise and organs and blood will be turned into immediate dishes for the family to eat. Living birds will need to be killed and plucked. Rabbits will need to be caught, skinned, and gutted. Additional fish will need to be caught and prepared. The bread ovens will begin baking thousands of small loaves of bread.

Young boys will be sitting for hours on end, taking turns working all hours of the night, turning the crank on the spit in front of roaring fires. Servants will be scrubbed and dressed in livery outfits and practicing how to run hot dishes from the kitchen to the feast room. Chefs will be shouting and screaming, and apprentice cooks will be shirtless as their sweat runs into the dishes they are preparing.

But none of that will matter. When the new King arrives at the head of his table, all will look upon him and the luxurious feast he has offered them, all that will matter is the richness of his purse.

Endnotes

Deciding the level of annotation for this work was a difficult decision. This is not a scholarly work; it's not meant to be studied, peer-reviewed, and lectured from. It is a very general overview of food for writers. However, my upbringing in the world of history has me used to heavily-annotated works, where a sentence can easily have five endnotes!

Since this is a very general work, it was also impossible to narrow most facts presented to any one book, website, or documentary. I didn't want to turn people off by having streams of reference notes. I've opted to keep this book as general as possible; however, I still include references for anywhere that I've clearly quoted (either directly or paraphrased). Also, if there is only one major source for that information, I've included a reference to the source material. Further, I've occasionally referenced some interesting texts for further reading for specific sections.

Introduction

1. Used with permission, Al-Baghdadi , Muhammad Ibn Al-Hasan (13th century). *The Baghdad Cookery Book.* (Charles Perry, Trans.). Great Britain: Prospect Books (2005). p. 25

2. *Angus, Mike. "Feeding the Homeless." Vue Weekly [Edmonton]. November, 25, 2009. Issue #736*

Chapter 1

1. Al-Baghdadi, Muhammad Ibn Al-Hasan (13th century) and Martinelli, C. (2012). An Anonymous Andalusian Cookbook from the 13th Century. (Charles Perry, Trans.) Retrieved from <http://italophiles.com/andalusian_cookbook.pdf>.

2. Matyszak, Philip (2009). Legionary: The Roman Soldier's (Unofficial) Manual. London, UK: Thames and Hudson. p. 66

3. This list is based on the 2000 calorie meal plans listed on www.choosemyplate.gov, which are based on the USDA Food Guide.

4. RTO Task Group RTG-154 (2010, March). Nutrition Science and Food Standards for Military Operations (TR-HFM-154) in NATO: Science and Technology Organization Collaboration Support Office. < http:/www.cso.nato.int>

5. Curtis, Rick (2005). The Backpacker's Field Manual. New York, NY: Three Rivers Press, p. 67

6. Jotischky, Andrew (2011). Hermit's Cookbook. New York, NY: Continuum Press, p.22

Chapter 2

1. Cockayne, Emily (2007). Hubbub: Filth, Noise, and Stench in England. Great Britain: St. Edmundsbury Press Ltd and Yale University Press, p. 108

2. Isenor, Billy. September 5, 2011. Hospitality. Newman Theological College. M.T.S. Dissertation.

3. Jotischky, p. 29

4. Apicius. (4th or 5th century). Cookery and Dining in Imperial Rome. (Joseph Dommers Vehling, Trans.). Washington: Unknown Publisher (1926), p. 46

5. Mortimer, p. 113

6. ibid, p. 115

7. Lee, Christina. (2007). Feasting the Dead: Food and Drink in Anglo-Saxon Burial Rituals. Woodbridge: Boyell and Brewer., p. 141

8. An engraved stone from Isernia (now located in the Louvre); Faas, Patrick. (2005). Around the Roman Table. Chicago, IL: University of Chicago Press, p. 43, 44

9. Crombie, Neil. (Director and Producer). (2011) At Home with the Georgians [TV]. Episodes 3 (Safe as Houses). UK: BBC Four.

10. Daunton, Martin. (2011, January). 10 Terrible Taxes. BBC History Magazine. p. 58

11. Rundell, M. E. (1808). A New System of Domestic Cookery. London, p. 269

12. Cabre, Montserrat (2008). Women or Healers? Bulletin of the History of Medicine, Volume 82, Number 1, Spring (2008), p. 27

13. Lee, p 27; In reference to Ælfric Bata writing in 987-1002 England, boasting what he'd bring to market.

14. Eggen, Mette. (unknown). The Plants Used in a Viking Garden A.D. 800-1050. Centro Universitario Europeo per I Beni Culturali. [Retrieved] 2012, [from] http://www.univeur.org.

15. Garland, Robert (1998). Daily Life of the Ancient Greeks. Westport, CT: Greenwood Press, p.93

16. Goodman, Ruth, et al. (2011). Edwardian Farm. Pavilion: Great Britain, p.91

17. Faas, p.124

18. Broomfield, Andrea (2007). Food and Cooking in Victorian England. Westpost, CT: Praeger Publishers, p. 9

19. These figures are averages and pulled from various sources and, in many cases, averaged out. However, a great resource for general pricing is: http://www.luminarium.org/medlit/medprice.htm

20. http://www.luminarium.org/medlit/medprice.htm

21. Black, Maggie, et al. (1997) A Taste of History. Great Britain: British Museum Press, p. 108

22. Civitello, Linda (2011). Cuisine and Culture: A History of Food and People. 3rd. Edition. Hoboken, NJ: John Wiley and Sons., p. 9

23. Jotischky, p. 55

24. Martinelli, p.19, Note: The Andalucía, or Al-Andalus, of the 1200s was not today's southern region of Andalucía in Spain. It was the name used for all of the territory controlled in Spain by Arab Muslims, originally from North Africa.

25. Faas, p.189

26. McGovern, Patrick E. (2009). Uncorking the Past. Los Angeles, CA: University of California Press, pg 2

27. Black, p. 48

28. McGovern, p.42-46

29. This is the Mother Goose version, circa 1765. However, there are several other traditional versions that are older than the Mother Goose version.

30. Lee, p. 33

31. Dargie, Richard. (2005). Rich and Poor in Ancient Rome. London, UK: Smart Apple Media, p. 13

32. Broomfield, p 25, 26

33. Hazlitt, W. Carew. (1902). Old Cookery Books and Ancient Cuisine. London, p. 111

34. Bloomfield, p.53

35. Rohr, Christian (2002). Feast and Daily Life in the Middle Ages. Lecture at Novosibirsk State University. Oct 22-25, 2002. Lecture notes: < https://www.sbg.ac.at/ges/people/rohr/nsk11.pdf> p. 2

36. ibid, p. 6

37. ibid, p. 12

38. Mortimer, Ian. (2012). The Timer Traveller's Guide to Elizabethan England. Great Britain: Bodley Head, p. 269

39. Freedman, Paul. "Some Basic Aspects of Medieval Cuisine." Annales Universitatis Apulensis, Series Historica,Vol.11:1 (2007) Ecopy accessed 2011 from < http://istorie.uab.ro/publicatii/colectia_auash/annales_11/4%20paul_freedman.pdf>, p.49

40. Lee, p. 11

Chapter 4

1. Unknown. "An Army Marches on its Stomach (Defence Procurement International)." (2011) Electrothermal. <http://www.electrothermal.com>

2. Perhaps the best example of the mixed culture example is Bernard Cromwell's Sharpe. This highly acclaimed series is well-researched and does an outstanding

job at showing the differences in rank and culture within the British army during the Regency period.

3. Faas, p.14

4. Matyszak, p. 148

5. Cowley, Robert, and Geoffrey Parker (editors). (1996). The Reader's Companion to Military History. New York, NY: Houghton Mifflin Company, p. 161

6. Garland, p.91

7. Lieven, Dominic. (2010). Russia Against Napoleon. New York, NY: Viking Penguin, p. 225

8. Cowley, p.271

9. Lieven, p.25

10. ibid, p. 110

11. Cowley, p.161

12. Lieven, p. 26

13. Koder, Johannes. "Stew and salted meat – opulent normality in the diet of every day?" Eat, Drink, and Be Merry (Luke 12:19) – Food and Wine in Byzantium. (2007). Society for the Promotion of Byzantine Studies Publications 13: Papers of the 37th Annual Spring Symposium of Byzantine Studies, p. 63

14. Unknown. (1902). General Mess Manual and Cookbook. Washington, DC: Government Printing Office, p. 16

15. Mortimer, p. 226

16. Pybus, William (1810). A Manual of Useful Knowledge. London., p. 91

17. Roger, N. A. M. (2006). The Command of the Ocean. New York, NY: W. W. Norton & Company, p. 213

18. ibid, p 133

Chapter 5

1. While Henry Stephens' book is period and is an excellent work, most authors will not need the intense detail of it. For an overview, Alex Langlands' abridged addi-

tion of The Book of the Farm is significantly superior and highly recommended for anyone writing a rural Victorian story.

2. Traditional folk song, England

3. Hazlitt, p. 227

4. My version of Rundell's Mushroom Ketchup, p. 183

5. Martinelli, p.182

6. Stephens, Henry. (1852). The Book of the Farm. Edinburgh and London: William Blackwood and Sons.

7. Global Crop Diversity Trust (Unknown). Crops. Retrieved May 6, 2012 from http://www.croptrust.org/content/crops.

8. Faas, p.3

9. Diamond, Jared (2005). Guns, Germs, and Steel. New York, NY: W. W Norton & Company, p. 393

10. Civitello, p. 41

11. Kimball, p. 150-151

12. United Nations Office on Drugs and Crime. (2012). General Assembly President calls for redoubling of efforts to end human trafficking. Retrieved May, 2012, from http://www.unodc.org/unodc/en/frontpage/2012/April/un-general-assembly-president-calls-for-re-doubled-efforts-to-end-human-trafficking.html?ref=fs1.

Chapter 6

1. Radcliffe, M. (1823). A Modern System of Domestic Cookery. London, p. 638

2. This is a jab at Willoughby'sWillougby's rescue of Maryann Dashwood in Jane Austen's Sense and Sensibility.

3. Marshall, p. 90

4. Lee, p.22

5. Acton, Eliza. (1864). Modern Cookery for Private Families. London: Longman, Green, Longman, Roberts, and Green, p. 124

6. Ibid, p. 60

7. Goodman, Ruth, et al. (2010). Victorian Farm: Christmas Edition. Pavilion: Great Britain, p. 94, 95

8. Hazlitt, p. 142

9. Rundell, p. 263

10. Kimball, p. 33-34

11. History Magazine. (2010). The Impact of Refrigeration. Retrieved April 10, 2012, from http://www.history-magazine.com/refrig.html.

Chapter 7

1. Gerwin, Marcin (ed). (2011). Food and Democracy. Poland: Polish Green Network, , Introduction

2. Lee, p. 42-44

3. Faas, p. 19

4. Lee, p. 21

5. Lee, p. 40

6. Dargie, p. 13

7. Jotischky, p. 72

8. Faas, p. 38

9. ibid, p. 16

10. Broomfield, p. 24

11. Hazlitt, p. 112

12. Hinds, Kathryn (2010). Everyday Life in the Roman Empire. New York, NY: Marshall Cavendish Benchmark., p. 134

13. Fass, p. 41

14. Dargie, p. 13

15. Faas, p. 39

16. Jotischky, p. 118-120

17. Since the oven would have ash on its floor, the bread bottoms would be covered in blackened ash. Bread would be cut horizontally, as opposed to vertically, and the top, unburned upper crust would be given to the, well, upper crust.

18. Freedman, Paul. (2009). Out of the East. New Haven, CT: Yale University Press, p. 3

19. Freedman, p. 51

20. Civitello, p. 62

21. Freedmanp. 4

22. Freedman, p. 47

23. Lee, p.22

24. Freedman, p. 61

Chapter 8

1. There are several variations of this saying in period literature from Europe, including in mice, rats, pigeons, and rabbits. I've used this one, as it's my personal favourite.

2. Global Crop Diversity Trust (Unknown). Crops. Retrieved May 6, 2012 from http://www.croptrust.org/content/crops.

3. Roach, John. (2002, June 10). Saving the Potato in its Andean Birthplace. National Geographic News. http://news.nationalgeographic.com/news/2002/06/0610_020610_potato.html

4. Marshall, p. 45

5. Democracy Now. (2009. September 9). The Slave Next Door: Human Trafficking and Slavery in America Today. Interview between Kevin Bales and Amy Goodman (transcript). http://www.democracynow.org/2009/9/9/the_slave_next_door_human_trafficking

Chapter 9

1. Lemery, Louis. (1745). A Treatist of all Sorts of Foods. London., p. 332

2. Civitello, p. 71

3. ibid, p. 72-73

4. Rundell, p. 283

5. Cuvelier, Paule (2008). Chocolate. Paris, FR:Flammarion, p. 17

6. Coe, Sophie D. and Coe, Michael D. (2007). The True History of Chocolate. Great Britain: Thames and Hudson, p. 98-99

7. Lemery, p. 364

8. ibid, p. 364

9. ibid, p. 364

10. Off, Carol. (2007). Bitter Chocolate. Toronto, ON: Vintage Canada., p. 7

11. Coe, p. 245

12. Heiss, Mary Lou, and Heiss, Robert J. (2007). The Story of Tea. Berkeley,. CA: Ten Speed Press, p. 7

13. Faas, p.122

14. Horn, Brad. (2010, July 17). Aged 9,000 Years, Ancient Beer Finally Hits Stores. NPR. Retrieved January 25, 2012, from http://www.npr.org/templates/story/story.php?storyId=128587208.

15. Faas, p.121

16. Hazlitt, p. 152

17. Hazlitt, p. 152

18. McGovern, p. 242, 244, 246-247

19. Civitello, p. 8

20. Southgate, Henry (1876). Things A Lady Would Like to Know Concerning Domestic Management and Expenditure. Edinburgh, p. 376

21. Civitello, p. 30

22. McGovern, p. 141, 142

23. Ibid, p. 64

24. Bloomfield, p. 117

25. Faas, p. 107

26. ibid, p.123

Chapter 10

1. Civitello, p. 62

2. Kershaw, Linda. (2004). Edible and Medicinal Plants of the Rockies. Edmonton, AB: Lone Pine Publishing.

3. Montserrat

4. Markham, Gervase. (1656). The English Hous-wife. London.

5. Montserrat, , p. 31

6. Diamond, p. 89

7. Martinelli, p. 25

8. Medievalists.net (2011). The Sweet Side of War: The Place of Honey in Military Provisioning. Retrieved October 12, 2011, from http://www.medievalists.net/2011/09/28/the-sweet-side-of-war-the-place-of-honey-in-military-provisioning/

9. Roberts, Sheilah. (2010). For Maids Who Brew and Bake. St. John's, NL: Flanker Press, p. 135

10. Based on the work by http://elfshotgallery.blogspot.ca (2009) and M. A. P. Renouf personal interview (2010).

Chapter 11

1. Renouf, M. A. P. (2011). The Cultural Landscapes of Port au Choix. New York, NY: Springer, p. 189

2. Black, p. 17

3. Antarctic Heritage Trust. (unknown). Appendix 5: Stores List of Supplies and Equipment Taken to Cape Royds – British Antarctic Expedition 1907-09.

Retrieved September 1, 2012, from http://www.nzaht.org/content/library/Extract_from_CR_Conservation_Plan_List_of_Supplies1.pdf

4. Northwest Territories Health and Social Services. (2012). Inuit Traditional (fact sheet). Retrieved from http://www.hss.gov.nt.ca/sites/default/files/inuit_traditional.pdf.

Chapter 12

1. Large grain couscous can be precooked, fine grain couscous can be used directly, both should be mixed with some olive oil before cooking to keep the kernels from sticking to each other.(Martinelli, 59)

2. Martinelli, p. 59

3. Faas, p. 83

4. Rundell p. 233

5. Austin, Thomas (ed). (1888). Two Fifteenth-Century Cookery Books. London: Early English Test Society.p. 8

Appendix 1

1. This section pulls information from many different sources, including Goodman (both the books and the documentaries), Henry Stephens (both the original and the abridged edition by Alex Langlands), plus the period cookbooks by Beeton, Acton, and Rundell.

Appendix 2

1. Loosely based on the feast menu for Henry IV, Austen, p. 57-59

2. Hazlitt, p. 227

Select Bibliography

A book of this focus and scope can be a tricky thing to organize, in terms of its bibliography and references. If I were to include every single book, magazine, and text I read during the 18 months I've been working on this book, I'd have an entire book of references alone.

I've opted to go with a selected bibliography, listing references cited in this work and also sources that I feel would be useful for further reading and research. All of these references are excellent starting points and I recommend you picking up a few from your local library.

Acton, Eliza. (1864). *Modern Cookery for Private Families*. London: Longman, Green, Longman, Roberts, and Green.

Al-Baghdadi , Muhammad Ibn Al-Hasan (13th century) and Martinelli, C. (2012). *An Anonymous Andalusian Cookbook from the 13th Century*. (Charles Perry, Trans.) Retrieved from http://italophiles.com/andalusian_cookbook.pdf.

Al-Baghdadi , Muhammad Ibn Al-Hasan (13th century). (2005). *The Baghdad Cookery Book*. (Charles Perry, Trans.). Great Britain: Prospect Books.

Antarctic Heritage Trust. (unknown). *Appendix 5: Stores List of Supplies and Equipment Taken to Cape Royds — British Antarctic Expedition 1907-09*. Retrieved September

1, 2012, from http://www.nzaht.org/content/library/Extract_ from_CR_Conservation_Plan_List_of_Supplies1.pdf

Apicius. (4th or 5th century). (1926) *Cookery and Dining in Imperial Rome.* (Joseph Dommers Vehling, Trans.). Washington: Unknown Publisher.

Angus, Mike. (2009, November 25). Feeding the Homeless. *Vue Weekly [Edmonton]* Issue #736.

Austin, Thomas (ed). (1888). *Two Fifteenth-Century Cookery Books.* London: Early English Test Society.

Beeton, Isabella Mary. (1865). *Mrs. Beeton's Dictionary of Every-Day Cookery.* London.

Black, Maggie, *et al.* (1997) *A Taste of History.* Great Britain: British Museum Press.

Braban, Cassie (Producer). (2010). *Victorian Pharmacy [DVD].* UK: Lion Television.

Broomfield, Andrea (2007). *Food and Cooking in Victorian England.* Westpost, CT: Praeger Publishers.

Cabre, Montserrat (2008). Women or Healers? B*ulletin of the History of Medicine, 82*, 18-21.

Civitello, Linda (2011). *Cuisine and Culture: A History of Food and People.* 3$^{rd.}$ Edition. Hoboken, NJ: John Wiley and Sons.

Cockayne, Emily (2007). *Hubbub: Filth, Noise, and Stench in England.* Great Britain: St. Edmundsbury Press Ltd and Yale University Press.

Coe, Sophie D. and Coe, Michael D. (2007). *The True History of Chocolate.* Great Britain: Thames and Hudson.

Cowley, Robert, and Geoffrey Parker (editors). (1996). *The Reader's Companion to Military History.* New York, NY: Houghton Mifflin Company.

Crombie, Neil. (Director and Producer). (2011) *At Home with the Georgians [TV]*. Episodes 1-3. UK: BBC Four.

Curtis, Rick (2005). *The Backpacker's Field Manual*. New York, NY: Three Rivers Press.

Cuvelier, Paule (2008). *Chocolate*. Paris, FR: Flammarion.

Dargie, Richard. (2005). *Rich and Poor in Ancient Rome*. London, UK: Smart Apple Media.

Davis-Kimball, Jeannine. (2003). *Warrior Women*. New York, NY: Warner Brothers.

Daunton, Martin. (2011, January). 10 Terrible Taxes. *BBC History Magazine*. p. 58

Democracy Now. (2009. September 9). *The Slave Next Door: Human Trafficking and Slavery in America Today*. Interview between Kevin Bales and Amy Goodman (transcript). http://www.democracynow.org/2009/9/9/the_slave_next_door_human_trafficking

Diamond, Jared (2005). *Guns, Germs, and Steel*. New York, NY: W. W Norton & Company.

Donnelly, Jim (2011, February 17). The Irish Famine. *BBC History. http://www.bbc.co.uk/history/british/victorians/famine_01.shtml*

Eggen, Mette. (unknown). The Plants Used in a Viking Garden A.D. 800-1050. *Centro Universitario Europeo per I Beni Culturali*. [Retrieved] 2012, [from] http://www.univeur.org.

Elliot, Stuart. (Director). (2011). *Edwardian Farm [DVD]*. UK: Lion Television.

Elliott, Stuart. (Director). (2009). *Victorian Farm [DVD]*. UK: Lion Television.

Faas, Patrick. (2005). *Around the Roman Table*. Chicago, IL: University of Chicago Press.

Fernandez-Armesto, Felipe (2002). *Near A Thousand Tables: A History of Food*. New York, NY: Free Press.

Freedman, Paul. (2009). *Out of the East*. New Haven, CT: Yale University Press.

Freedman, Paul. (2007) Some Basic Aspects of Medieval Cuisine. *Annales Universitatis Apulensis, Series Historica*, *11*, 44-60. Ecopy accessed 2011 from http://istorie.uab.ro/publicatii/colectia_auash/annales_11/4%20paul_freedman.pdf

Garland, Robert (1998). *Daily Life of the Ancient Greeks*. Westport, CT: Greenwood Press.

Gerwin, Marcin (ed). (2011). *Food and Democracy*. Poland: Polish Green Network.

Global Crop Diversity Trust (Unknown). *Crops*. Retrieved May 6, 2012 from http://www.croptrust.org/content/crops.

Goodman, Ruth, *et al.* (2010). *Victorian Farm: Christmas Edition*. Pavilion: Great Britain.

Goodman, Ruth, *et al.* (2011). *Edwardian Farm*. Pavilion: Great Britain.

Hazlitt, W. Carew. (1902). *Old Cookery Books and Ancient Cuisine*. London.

Heiss, Mary Lou, and Heiss, Robert J. (2007). *The Story of Tea*. Berkeley, CA: Ten Speed Press.

Hinds, Kathryn (2010). *Everyday Life in the Roman Empire*. New York, NY: Marshall Cavendish.

History Magazine. (2010). *The Impact of Refrigeration*. Retrieved April 10, 2012, from http://www.history-magazine.com/refrig.html.

Horn, Brad. (2010, July 17). Aged 9,000 Years, Ancient Beer Finally Hits Stores. *NPR*. Retrieved January 25, 2012, from http://www.npr.org/templates/story/story.php?storyId=128587208.

Isenor, Billy. September 5, 2011. *Hospitality.* Newman Theological College. M.T.S. Dissertation.

Jotischky, Andrew (2011). *Hermit's Cookbook.* New York, NY: Continuum Press.

Kershaw, Linda. (2004). *Edible and Medicinal Plants of the Rockies.* Edmonton, AB: Lone Pine.

Koder, Johannes. (2007). Stew and salted meat —opulent normality in the diet of every day? In Leslie Brubaker and Kallirroe Linardou (eds.) *Eat, Drink, and Be Merry (Luke 12:19) — Food and Wine in Byzantium : Papers of the 37th Annual Spring Symposium of Byzantine Studies, in honour of Professor A.A.M Bryer (56-72).* Aldershot, England ; Burlington, VT : Ashgate.

Kurlansky, Mark (2002). *Salt: A World History.* New York, NY: Thorndike Press.

Langlands, Alex. (2011). *Henry Stephens's Book of the Farm.* Great Britain: Batsford.

Lawton, John (2004). *Silk, Scents, and Spice.* Paris, France: UNESCO.

Lee, Christina. (2007). *Feasting the Dead: Food and Drink in Anglo-Saxon Burial Rituals.* Woodbridge: Boyell and Brewer.

Lemery, Louis. (1745). *A Treatist of all Sorts of Foods.* London.

Lieven, Dominic. (2010). *Russia Against Napoleon.* New York, NY: Viking Penguin.

Luminarium. Anniina Jokinen. 2010. Accessed: 2011-2012. http://www.luminarium.org

Markham, Gervase. (1656). *The English Hous-wife.* London.

Marshall, Ingeborg. (2009). *The Beothuk.* Canada: Breakwater Books Ltd.

Matyszak, Philip (2009). *Legionary: The Roman Soldier's (Unofficial) Manual*. London, UK: Thames and Hudson.

McGovern, Patrick E. (2009). *Uncorking the Past*. Los Angeles, CA: University of California Press.

Medievalists.net (2011). *The Sweet Side of War: The Place of Honey in Military Provisioning*. Retrieved October 12, 2011, from http://www.medievalists.net/2011/09/28/the-sweet-side-of-war-the-place-of-honey-in-military-provisioning/

Mintz, S., & McNeil, S. (2012). The Irish Potato Famine. *Digital History*. Retrieved June 1, 2012 from http://www.digitalhistory.uh.edu/historyonline/irish_potato_famine.cfm.

Mortimer, Ian. (2012). *The Timer Traveller's Guide to Elizabethan England*. Great Britain: Bodley Head.

Mortimer, Ian. (2011). *The Time Traveller's Guide to Medieval England*. Great Britain: Touchstone.

Northwest Territories Health and Social Services. (2012). *Inuit Traditional* (fact sheet). Retrieved from http://www.hss.gov.nt.ca/sites/default/files/inuit_traditional.pdf.

Off, Carol. (2007). *Bitter Chocolate*. Toronto, ON: Vintage Canada.

Pybus, William (1810). *A Manual of Useful Knowledge*. London.

Radcliffe, M. (1823). *A Modern System of Domestic Cookery*. London.

Renouf, M.A.P. (2011, June 20). Personal interview as part of Phillip's Garden Archeological Site Visit.

Renouf, M. A. P. (2011). *The Cultural Landscapes of Port au Choix*. New York, NY: Springer.

Roach, John. (2002, June 10). Saving the Potato in its Andean Birthplace. *National Geographic News*. http://news.nationalgeographic.com/news/2002/06/0610_020610_potato.html

Roberts, Sheilah. (2010). *For Maids Who Brew and Bake*. St. John's, NL: Flanker Press.

Roger, N. A. M. (2006). *The Command of the Ocean*. New York, NY: W. W. Norton & Company.

Rohr, Christian (2002). *Feast and Daily Life in the Middle Ages*. Lecture at Novosibirsk State University. Oct 22-25, 2002. Lecture notes: https://www.sbg.ac.at/ges/people/rohr/nsk11.pdf

RTO Task Group RTG-154 (2010, March). *Nutrition Science and Food Standards for Military Operations (TR-HFM-154) in NATO: Science and Technology Organization Collaboration Support Office*. http:/www.cso.nato.int

Rundell, M. E. (1808). *A New System of Domestic Cookery*. London.

Sommer, Peter. (Director and Producer). *Tales from the Green Valley [DVD]*. UK: Acorn Media UK.

Southgate, Henry (1876). *Things A Lady Would Like to Know Concerning Domestic Management and Expenditure*. Edinburgh.

Stephens, Henry. (1852). *The Book of the Farm*. Edinburgh and London: William Blackwood and Sons.

United Nations Office on Drugs and Crime. (2012). *General Assembly President calls for redoubling of efforts to end human trafficking*. Retrieved May, 2012, from http://www.unodc.org/unodc/en/frontpage/2012/April/un-general-assembly-president-calls-for-re-doubled-efforts-to-end-human-trafficking.html?ref=fs1.

Unknown. (2007) History of the New Forest National Park. *New Forest National Park Authority*. http://www.newforestnpa.gov.uk/__data/assets/pdf_file/0008/26648/history1-forweb.pdf

Unknown. (2011) An Army Marches on its Stomach (Defence Procurement International). *Electrothermal*. http://www.electrothermal.com

Unknown. (1902). *General Mess Manual and Cookbook.* Washington, DC: Government Printing Office.

Unknown.(2009) Elk Island National Park of Canada: Wildlife Watch. *Parks Canada.* http://www.pc.gc.ca/pn-np/ab/elkisland/natcul/natcul1/a/iii.aspx

Vickery, Amanda. (2010). *Radio 4's A History of Private Life [Audio].* UK: AudioGo Ltd.

Worsley, Lucy (2012). *If Walls Could Talk: An Intimate History of the Home.* Great Britain: Walker and Company.

Index

Author Biography

Canadian author Krista D. Ball combines her love of the fantastical, an obsession with pottage, and a history degree from Mount Allison University to bring fantasy writers and food lovers a new and unique reference guide.

Krista was born and raised in Newfoundland, where she learned how to use a chainsaw, chop wood, and make raspberry jam. She lives in Alberta these days. Somehow, she's picked up an engineer, two kids, six cats, and a very understanding corgi off ebay. Her credit card has been since taken away. You can find her causing trouble at http://kristadball.com

CPSIA information can be obtained at www.ICGtesting.com
Printed in the USA
BVOW05s0753311015

424536BV00002B/32/P